Loyal
LAWYER

JEANNINE COLETTE
LAUREN RUNOW

A zodiac-themed romance series that celebrates the unique qualities of men based on their zodiac sign. Each book features a distinctive trope, a kick-ass heroine, and a love written in the stars!

This book's hero is the *Leo*

Charismatic. Outgoing. Faithful. Bossy. Loving. Dominant. Spontaneous. Creative. Intolerant. Extroverted.

CHAPTER ONE

"That rat bastard!"

It *was* a good day. A great day actually.

It'd started with me waking up to a hot shower without having to wait the required fifteen minutes for it to warm up.

Then, I got back to my room without running into any of the sweaty gym rats.

There was no line at the coffee shop, and the customer in front of me paid for my latte, so I was kind and paid it forward to the person after me.

I found a penny, heads up, on the ground.

A woman offered me her blessings for no reason as I walked through Chinatown.

And the sky was a perfect, cloudless day, unseasonably warm for the first week of March.

Yes, it was a good day in Philadelphia.

Then, I got the phone call.

"Damage? You've got to be kidding me!" I yell at my former landlord, Gerry, on the other end of the line.

"Amy, you signed the lease. That makes you liable."

I growl in frustration. "I haven't lived there in three months. Hardin and I broke up, so I moved out. You have to call *him* for the damage."

"Hardin moved out last weekend and stiffed me on last month's rent. Your lease still has one month left, which means you'll owe for that too."

That good-for-nothing jerk. Hardin, not Gerry.

A year ago, I thought Hardin and I were going to get engaged. We moved into a sweet one-bedroom apartment in the Fairmount area of the city. We bought new pots and a blue duvet for the bed. And then he went and screwed the dog walker on it.

"I'm sorry he did that to you, but you have to get the money from him," I state firmly.

"Your name is the only one on the lease," he responds even firmer. "And you moved out without telling me. I've been working on getting him to sign a new lease since I found out you left. I couldn't even evict him, so don't remind me of the situation you put me in."

Damn my philandering ex-boyfriend. He couldn't keep his dick in his pants but knew how to keep his wallet secure. When it came time to sign the lease, he insisted just my name be on it since the leasing agent needed to print our credit reports. I have an 800 credit score—something I'm very proud of—where Hardin's was so poor that he didn't even want it to be run. I didn't mind since, at the time, I was blinded by love and not seeing just how stupid I was being.

"We gave you the last month's rent when we signed the lease. What about the security deposit for the rest of the money owed?"

"You wanna come down here and see what this place looks like?" he argues over the phone. "The hardwood floor is all scratched up; the sink in the bathroom is completely removed from the wall, like it was sat on or something; there's a crater-sized hole behind the bed; and I'm gonna have to get the entire place painted. It smells like my grandmother died in there."

Incense. The dog walker had a love of yoga and incense. You could smell it on her clothes every time you saw her. It's how I knew something was amiss. My boyfriend had started to stink of woody florals and balsam. Now, he's living with Miss Spices and Herbs and making holes in walls. Holes I do not want to imagine how they got there.

"You have two weeks to get me the money, or I'm gonna have to take this to court."

"Court?" I practically jump. Actually, I do. I'm standing on the corner of Third Street, yelling into my phone and swaying my arm so fast that my latte spills on my coat. "Oh, no, no, no, no! You can't do that. I have a business and am waiting on a loan application approval from the bank. This can't be on my record, or I'll lose everything."

"Forty-five hundred dollars, or I'm at the courthouse."

"Gerry, I—"

He hangs up.

Of all the terrible, horrible things that could happen, this is the very worst! So much for my perfect day. I should have known Hardin was going to destroy my life yet again. That's what I get for falling for the fun guy. The one who is always buying the next round, is up

3

for the next adventure, and tells the best damn stories. I used to love listening to him talk about his day. Too bad they were all tall tales. Jerk probably never helped that old woman move into her apartment. I bet he was banging her too!

I pick up my phone to text the son of a bitch, but his number is no longer in my contacts. I erased it when I moved out in some sort of metaphoric cleaning of the slate.

Now, I can't quickly message him like I want.

Instead, I have to open a new message and enter his number before my thumbs start moving, typing out a message with the same fury that's racing through me.

I hope you had fun, putting holes in the wall with the bed!

The text bubbles instantly appear, and I stand, absolutely fuming, as I wait for his response.

I feel like this is a euphemism for something.

Although I have been known to be a bit of a wallbanger.

This is a joke to you? Typical.

First, you screwed around behind my back.

Then, you damaged and skipped out on paying rent on the place that was in my name!

I believe you have some misplaced anger here.

Don't be so coy. I want Lady Featherington too!

She has delicate feet, and I know you're not tending to her hair needs.

She definitely sounds like she belongs in your care.

I have a great doctor and stylist recommendations.

And I want my Loui Jover back.

You have excellent taste in art.

What is wrong with you?

Let me explain …

Explain? I haven't heard from the man in a hundred and eighty days, and now, he wants to talk it out?

My phone rings, and Hardin's number appears. I pick it up immediately.

"Oh, you have some explaining to do all right. And by explaining, I mean, forty-five hundred dollars, a piece of contemporary art, and a Pomeranian!"

A deep, sultry chuckle sounds from the other end of the line. "Ah, Lady Featherington is a dog. That makes more sense now."

I freeze, confused by who the person I'm speaking with could be because that deep baritone voice is most definitely not my ex-boyfriend.

"You're not Hardin."

"Thankfully, I'm not. You seem pretty pissed at him."

I look around like I'm being pranked or something but then realize I'm the one who texted him. "Listen, I don't know what kind of joke you're playing, but just put my ex on the phone."

"I can't," he says so nonchalantly that I want to reach in the phone and smack him.

"Why not?"

"Because he's not here."

"Where the hell is he?" I yell, holding up my arm to the side and leaning into the call like he can see how mad I am through the line. I must look like a madwoman, standing on this city street, acting a fool, waving my coffee around, but I'm so angry that I don't even care right now.

"You have the wrong number," he states matter-of-factly.

I pause, pulling my phone away from my face to check the number and then bringing it back to my ear. "Excuse me. No, I don't."

"The number you texted was not your ex-boyfriend. Believe me, I've never had a dog named Lady Featherington, but I have had this exact number for over ten years."

"Of course this is the right number. I dialed it myself."

"Are you positive?" I can hear the condescending tone in his voice, albeit with a little teasing added.

I hold the phone away from my face again, staring at the numbers. They seem perfectly correct at first. And then I go one by one again and realize in my haste to text, I inverted the last two digits. I bring the phone back to my ear.

"Oh my God. This is so embarrassing." I drop my hand to my side and tilt my head up to the sky in frustration.

That smooth laugh sounds again. "Happens to the best of us. I'm sorry to hear you're having trouble. You said this is with an ex-boyfriend?"

I sigh. "Yes. I'm sorry to bother you. Have a nice day."

"Wait, please. I'm dying to know how you came across the name Lady Featherington for a dog."

I let out a breath and laugh about the entire situation. I mean, right now, that's all I can do. "It's from a book I read, and then Netflix made it into a series called *Bridgerton*. She's this quick-witted and outspoken anonymous gossip columnist. I felt the name fit our tiny Pomeranian, who was quick to bark at anyone who walked by."

"So, I take it, he kept the dog in the breakup?"

"Yes, that asshole," I say without thinking twice. I mean, I am talking to a complete stranger. "I'm sorry. I'm not usually so foul-mouthed. And I surely don't need to bore you with my drama-filled life."

"Quite the contrary actually. Your text was the only exciting thing to happen all day. So, now that we've cleared the name issue, please, tell me about the hole in the wall you referred to."

I glance around to see a bench and sit down, needing to take a break from life for the moment. Leaning forward, I put my head on my hand while I hold the phone up to my ear.

"I'll give you the *Reader's Digest* version. I was with a guy who said and did all of the perfect things. That was, until he slept with the dog walker."

"No. Not the dog walker!" he says breathlessly but obviously kidding.

A slight chuckle escapes my lips, and I inhale a deep breath, thankful for the action to help calm me down.

"I moved out because the jerk was moving her in—with me still living there."

"Wait. What?" Now, he's not kidding around, and his tone is all serious.

"Yep. He said he wanted to move on and couldn't afford to live anywhere else. So, as he stated, I was 'just going to have to get used to it.' Oh, because did I tell you that he had shit for credit and the entire apartment was in my name?"

"Damn. That's one shady dude. What did you do?"

"I did the only thing any sane person would do. I moved out. There was no way I could stay there with the two of them. Plus, I couldn't kick him out and swing the rent myself. I already pay an astronomical fee for the lease on my business space. So, I packed up and took off."

"But you left without the dog?"

"Don't even get me started on the dog. He took her when he knew I was moving out. I tried to get her back, but the sneaky bastard changed the locks, so I couldn't even break in to take what was rightfully mine."

"Now, you're homeless, dog-less, and calling him because he's leaving holes in walls?"

"Yes. Our landlord just called, saying he skipped on the last month's rent and left an insane amount of damage in the place that I'm on the hook for." I let out a frustrated groan. "And I'm not totally homeless. I'm staying at my—" I pause and sit up straight. "Wait, why am I even telling you this? I'm sorry. You don't need to hear all of my woes. Plus, you're a stranger." I stand up, heading in the direction I was going in the first place before my day took a complete dump.

"Listen, I'm not trying to be some creeper and get all up in your business, but I am an attorney, and you seem like you have some legal issues you need to work through. I can help."

"Thanks. I appreciate the offer—I truly do—but I have, like, zero money to hire an attorney."

He laughs into the phone. "Please don't think I'm some ambulance chaser who tries at any chance he gets to land cases. That's not what I'm doing here."

"Then, what *are* you doing?" I ask skeptically.

"Well, for one, I'm responding to a text that you sent me. And two, I'm intrigued now, and I feel like the universe is telling me I should help you with your dilemma."

I tap my foot on the pavement and contemplate his offer. *What are the odds that the total stranger I dialed is an attorney who happens to be able to help me with my current predicament? A bazillion to one, I'd guess.*

No. There is no way I can work with this guy. He's probably a serial killer or a rapist. Or has some weird Pomeranian fetish. Those guys do exist.

"Thanks, but I can handle it." I try to be polite in my refusal.

"If the determination in your voice is like the rest of you, I have no doubt you will."

I smile, though I know he can't see me. "Thanks. It was … actually nice, talking to you. Thank you for brightening my day, if only for a little bit."

"You're welcome. Can I at least get your name?"

I open the door to the bank, where I was heading, to work on the loan that I'll probably never get now. "I'm Amy."

"Well, Amy, my name's Sebastian Blake. If you do decide you want to take this guy to court, you have my number."

I laugh out loud. "Yes, that I do. Thank you."

We both hang up on what was possibly the strangest phone call I'd ever had. There's still a slight grin on my face as I take a seat across from the banker who is helping me with my small-business loan.

Correction: the banker who *was* helping me.

An hour after my meeting, I'm sitting in my office, which has become my bedroom since I left Hardin, staring at the screen of my laptop and the funds in my account. I have a decent savings, but if I want to grow Amy Morgana Chocolatier, I'm gonna need money to invest in a multitude of things.

In order to get all that, I need more capital.

The banker said the loan process would take a few weeks. When I asked what would happen if a judgment was placed against me by a former landlord, she informed me that my application was already on the verge of being denied due to a lack of assets. Having anything against my credit would put the entire thing in jeopardy.

I extra-hate my ex-boyfriend right now.

When I left the bank, I called Hardin on his correct number and gave him a piece of my mind. It was no use. He's moved on, and the fact that he's held our dog hostage for three months gives me little faith that he'll do the right thing and fork over the money to Gerry, like I demanded.

This is a matter I'll have to fix on my own.

Needing some Zen, I put my Spotify on to a contemporary jazz playlist and make myself a cup of tea. I wrap myself in my favorite afghan, blow on the hot mug, and listen to Cécile McLorin Salvant. Sometimes, when I get stressed, smooth jazz, my grandma's blanket, and Earl Grey help calm me.

Sadly, it's helping only a little. I need to come up

with forty-five hundred dollars—fast. I can't make any large withdrawals from my account because the bank wants every dollar accounted for while my application is in review, so dipping into my savings isn't an option.

I could ask my friends, but they don't have that kind of cash lying around.

My parents would help me. Of course, that would come with my perfect siblings chiming in about the lack of proper direction I have in my life, how I'm not running my business correctly, or how they all told me Hardin was trouble. I didn't listen to them then, and I certainly won't go running to my parents for help unless it's my absolute last resort. Nothing in my family is ever secret, and I'd never, ever … ever hear the end of it.

No, I have to get myself out of this pickle on my own.

I would seek a lawyer's opinion, but that means money.

Unless …

I put my cup down and start typing on my phone.

Sebastian Blake. Lawyer. Philadelphia.

The first search entry shows me Blake, Fields, and Moore—a leading Philadelphia law firm with nine attorneys promoted as *super lawyers. Over two hundred million dollars recovered for clients. Counsel who cares. Research that matters.*

I click on the link and am brought to a sophisticated website for personal injury and civil rights attorneys.

Virtual badges of the multimillion-dollar verdicts that were won are on display. They represent people in everything from personal injury to car wrecks, workplace accidents, and discrimination. The site is certainly impressive, as are the cases they've taken on and won.

There's a link to meet the members of the firm. I scroll over, and the first face I see is one Sebastian Blake.

Well, he certainly is handsome.

A charismatic smile, strong jaw, and kind-looking eyes. His hair is combed back, and he looks very polished in the black-and-white photo.

If I were in the market for a man, I might even deem him attractive.

But I'm not. I'm in need of an attorney's opinion and one who offered his services—for free.

"What do I have to lose?" I ask myself.

Famous last words.

I open the text exchange I had earlier with Sebastian and hope this isn't a colossal mistake.

You still interested in helping me out?

Lady Featherington would appreciative it.

Absolutely. Name the place.

Pick somewhere busy with lots of people around.

A man has to protect himself from strange women who cold-call him. ;-)

I roll my eyes as I find that smile I had on earlier back on my face.

And so it begins …

CHAPTER TWO

I'm sitting at Love and Lavender, a boutique coffee shop in Center City that has great lattes and is always busy yet never so packed that you can't get a seat.

I know what Sebastian looks like, yet every time the door opens, I do a double take to see if the person walking in is him. It's nerve-racking to meet a stranger like this, but that didn't stop me from changing three times today before deciding on a sweater dress and knee-high boots.

I fidget with the manila folder I prepared with my leasing documents and set it on the table. Then, I cross and uncross my legs while adjusting my pendant around my neck.

Since I've already come off like a lunatic to this man, I want to come off as professional as possible now that we're gonna be face-to-face.

A man in a gray suit appears outside, walking briskly and talking on a cell phone. I sit up as I recognize the man immediately.

Sebastian Blake.

He holds the door open for a man who is exiting the shop with two drinks in his hands and then stays there as he lets a woman who is pushing a stroller inside. He saunters in, switching the phone to the other ear as he looks around the shop, still talking.

When he spots me staring, he mouths the word, *Amy?*

I nod with a wave and point to the seat beside me that I saved for him.

He smiles, and my breath hitches.

Damn, this man is hot.

The black-and-white photo of him on the company website did nothing to showcase how attractive he really is. Sandy-colored hair that's browner than blond, tanned skin, a chiseled jaw, and a Romanesque nose. His photo made him seem studious and neat. In the flesh, with his unbuttoned jacket, lack of a tie, and the top button of his shirt undone, he is roguish and disarming.

He walks over to me, pointing to the phone, letting me know that he'll need another minute.

I nod as he turns away, and I'm happy for the reprieve because Mr. Blake has made my heart speed up and my palms clammy. I really need to stop acting like I haven't seen a decent-looking man before. It has to be because of the unfamiliar situation of meeting a stranger for coffee.

Sebastian turns back to me with his hand over the mouthpiece and asks me in a whispered tone, "Have you ordered already?"

I shake my head and start to rise, but he motions for me to stay seated.

"I'll get it. What do you want?" he asks.

"Um … caramel latte, please."

He walks to the counter and stands in the short line before it's his turn. I watch as the barista blushes as he makes a joke of some sort while she rings him up, and I'm glad I'm not the only one affected by him.

With two white saucers in his hands, he walks the mugs over to our table and places them down between us.

"Sorry about that. I had a conference call that ran long. Thanks for saving us a table." He takes a seat.

"No problem. Thank you for the coffee. How much do I owe you?"

"Don't worry about it." He takes a sip of his drink and places it down, looking around at the café's decor. "This place is cool. You come here regularly?"

"I try to. When possible, I prefer to support local proprietors as opposed to big chains."

"That's admirable." His mouth rises on one side in a look of appreciation.

"Plus, they make a great latte. This is my favorite. It's caramelly with a hint of roasted almonds and maple syrup. When I'm feeling extra indulgent, I get the cocoa espresso. It's chocolaty with notes of vanilla-like Swiss," I muse and then catch myself from rambling. "Sorry, I'm really into flavors."

"Please, carry on. I got the Kona black coffee, so it must seem pretty boring to you."

"Not at all. It has a sweet and fruity taste with hints of spice. Very bold."

He takes another sip and grins. "You're right. That's an impressive talent you have. You should work for the

15

coffee industry and help them make write-ups for their labels."

"I'm actually a chocolatier."

A smooth, velvety chuckle escapes his lips.

"You find that amusing?" I quip.

"I find it very surprising. When you said you had a lease on a business, I honestly had no idea what to expect. It's not every day you meet a woman who makes her own candy."

My mouth drops as I uncross my legs and lean in. "Chocolate is the new fine wine. It is every bit as sophisticated and complex. Not to mention, it takes precision to make the perfect truffle. You can purchase a fifty-dollar box of chocolate that's just as good as a hundred-dollar bottle of wine."

"Your chocolate is better than a 2016 Napa Valley cabernet?"

"It's better than sex," I state proudly.

A slow, wide smile builds on his face as he sits back and nods. "I'll have to come by your shop someday."

"It's not a storefront. I lease a kitchen in Chinatown, where I make my products. Right now, I mostly work with corporate clients in the Philadelphia area but also get orders for special events. If things go well, hopefully, I'll be able to get a loan from the bank to open a real shop and be more competitive with prices on my website, so I can produce more and ship nationally."

"Which is why you need help with your landlord."

I've been chatting away so much that I nearly forgot why Sebastian and I were having this meeting. "Right! Here is a copy of my lease."

He takes the folder I offered him and opens it,

looking through it quickly. "Has your landlord given you an eviction notice?"

"No."

"A certified letter stating that you are late on rent and that he plans on filing an eviction notice?"

"Not that I know of. Yesterday was the first time he mentioned any of this."

"Is anyone living in the apartment?"

"Nope. The landlord is keeping the first and last month's rent that we gave as a deposit to cover the back rent. He's asking for forty-five hundred in damages."

He whistles through his teeth. "What the hell kind of damage costs that much?"

"Apparently, the sink is off the wall, the floor is ruined, the place smells like a house of sacrificial offering, and there's a hole in the wall behind the bed. Not one of those things was done by me. I left that place looking pristine."

"Damn, what kind of animal is your ex?"

"I'm assuming one who had some wild times with his new girlfriend." I shiver at the thought of them together in that way.

Sebastian closes the file and leans forward. "I'm sorry. This must be uncomfortable for you. Breakups suck."

I wave him off. "Actually, this one wasn't so bad, I guess. I mean, I loved Hardin—that's his name, by the way—but when he cheated, it was like these rose-colored glasses fell off my face, and I saw him for what he really was ... this lowlife of a guy who used me," I say almost to myself. Then, I slap my hand over my face and shake it in embarrassment. "Wow. I don't know what's gotten into me. I just can't stop oversharing with you."

He smiles. "That's good. It helps me understand the situation, so I can help you."

"If you want to help, you can get the landlord to waive the damages and get my dog back from Hardin."

"Lady Featherington," he states. "Did you adopt or purchase her?"

"Hardin bought her from a breeder." I take a sip of my coffee, hoping it will stop me from babbling more.

"That makes it difficult. Was she a gift?"

I nod while I swallow. "For my birthday."

"That makes it easier." His comfort with this conversation makes me smile.

"Thank you for helping me, but full disclosure: I don't have a lot of money to pay you."

"I already knew that. Being that you don't have cash lying around to pay your ex-landlord, you painted the picture that money is tight for you. I charge seven hundred dollars an hour."

I nearly spit out my drink. "Seven! You said seven, didn't you?"

He laughs. "I'm not charging you though. I want to help."

This is the moment where the seemingly perfect scenario starts to get morphed in my brain to something more sinister. *If this high-profile attorney doesn't want my money, then what the hell does he want?*

"I'm not paying you in sexual favors," I state firmly, making sure he knows this is an absolute no-go for me.

His mouth opens and closes in surprise as he blinks rapidly and raises his hands. "I was not expecting that at all. Let me explain. At the risk of sounding pompous or cocky, if you will, I am very successful."

"The seven hundred bucks an hour kind of gave that away. As did the Rolex and the Ferragamo shoes."

"What I mean is, I believe in Karma. For every large verdict I win, I pay it forward by helping someone else pro bono."

"I'm the pro bono?"

"Unless you want to pay." He grins, raising his eyebrows as he brings his mug up to his lips. His very sexy, very luscious lips.

"No. I'm just not used to handouts. I'm actually horrible with receiving them. You're talking to the girl who worked two jobs, so she could save enough money to launch a business on her own. I have no personal debt, and I own one hundred percent of my business."

"Do you not like owing favors?"

"I don't like taking from others."

He sits back again and lifts his coffee off the table, drinking it in long sips. "Yet you're here." He grins, and I purse my lips in response. "You knew who I was when I walked in here today," he says as he crosses his leg, resting his foot on his knee. "You looked me up."

I roll my eyes. "I wasn't going to ask a stranger for help unless I knew who he was."

"You must have been impressed enough."

"I was moderately taken aback by how accomplished you are."

"You need me."

It totally sucks that he's right. I can't explain why, but I have a feeling Sebastian will be able to get me out of my situation quickly. Plus, not being charged is a huge bonus.

"Tell me about yourself," I ask, not quite ready to answer him.

He raises a brow. "What would you like to know?"

"Name three things about you that are more important than what's on your résumé."

His eyes light up, showing he's intrigued. "I'm an only child. My father is an orthopedic surgeon, and my mother is an English professor at Yale. When I was in elementary school, I had one buck tooth that was sideways. My friends used to give me tin cans to open with my teeth. God bless the orthodontist who gave me braces. I'm a black belt in Brazilian jiu-jitsu, and I've run four marathons, all for charity. My favorite book is George Orwell's *Nineteen Eighty-Four*, I'm a huge Coldplay fan, and Lake Como, Italy, is the most beautiful place I've ever traveled to."

"That's more than three."

"There's a hell of a lot of things more important about me than what it says on my résumé. I'm an attorney and a good one. I'm also a man who happens to like doing the right thing."

"Why make me the offer? The way we met was wildly unconventional. I could have been an insane person."

"You still could be," he jokes. "Just so happens, I won a seventy-million-dollar verdict yesterday, right before you called, so it very much feels like fate."

"Fate. Right," I say rather sarcastically. I don't particularly believe in fate.

"Plus, I was curious to meet the woman behind the text messages."

"And?"

"You've surprised me immensely. Though I have a confession to make. I also wanted to see if you were half as pretty as you were entertaining on the phone."

I look down, not wanting to know the answer to that. Well, actually, I do. I look up and stare into his eyes and take a deep inhale.

A slow smile builds on his face. It reaches his eyes, which crinkle as he stares at me with a Cheshire grin. "I'm gonna save that opinion for a rainy day. So, what do you say?" He reaches out a hand in offering to make a deal. "You need a lawyer?"

I bite my lip. This could be a terrible idea. The worst. And yet I find myself extending my hand and shaking his.

"You're hired, Mr. Blake."

"Oh. So, we're formal now. I could get used to that."

Leo

CHAPTER THREE

Whenever I go to my office, I feel like I'm going on a covert mission. There's a nondescript door in a dark back alley that leads directly into my kitchen, or you can access it through Ben Franklin Gym, *Where Real Men Go to Work Out*—their slogan, not mine.

Ben Franklin Gym and Amy Morgana Chocolatier are cotenants in an old brick building that used to house a restaurant that closed down. The building's owner now rents the front half of the building to the gym while I get the back half, which is where the actual kitchen used to be.

The space I rent is not ideal. Some might even call it a shithole. Doesn't matter to me. It has a commercial-grade kitchen and decent-sized office, and it's all mine.

When I started this business, I was on a less than shoestring budget, and it was all I could afford. If and when my loan gets approved, I'll be able to move into a large space that doesn't smell like moldy, sweaty socks.

During gym hours, I use the main entrance because

it's way easier to access than the alley. As I make my way through the weights section, I head toward the dumbbell rack, where there's a door covered in mirrors. The gym owner purposely put the mirrors up, so people wouldn't know there was a door here. I constantly get guys staring at me, wondering why I'm walking to the wall until they see I can indeed pull on the side of it and slide it open. That, of course, opens up all kinds of different questions about what's behind there and what kind of secret lair I have uncovered.

I don't bother telling them it's the entrance to my dream, the business I created from the ground up. Most of the time, I just smile and act like I didn't hear them as I walk by.

When I enter my portion of the building, I hear blaring rap music coming from the kitchen. I walk down the hallway to see Shawn, my one and only employee, putting together gift boxes and bobbing his head to the beat.

"I'm back!" I shout.

He doesn't hear me, so I walk up to the speaker sitting off to the side and lower the volume. His voice continues rapping the song even though it isn't playing anymore, and I have to stifle a laugh.

"What the—" He doesn't finish his sentence when he sees me standing here with my eyebrows raised in question, making him change his tone. "You came back fast."

"There was no line at the post office," I say as I turn the radio back up but keep it down a few—or ten—notches. "Loud much?"

"I had to drown out the gym rats." He points to the

wall. "Some dude kept grunting. That is not a sound I need to hear."

Shawn is a no-bullshit kind of guy. He says it like it is and doesn't beat around the bush for anything. He's still in school at the Institute of Culinary Arts, and he works for me part-time, which is why I can afford him. When this loan comes through, I'm going to snatch him up full-time before someone else does.

Shawn is a chocolate dream. He's always on time, he's incredibly neat, and he follows each recipe to the utmost precision. He says working with chocolate gives him peace in his messed up head that's always thinking a mile a minute. All I know is, he brings Zen to my world by getting his work done without having to be told twice.

"You know how the afternoon crowd gets. All testosterone, all the time. They're here to get shredded."

"Like the guy who screams out like a crow when he squats." Shawn rolls his head back and mimics, "Cawww!"

"I was getting my mail the other day when I heard these two guys talking, saying, 'Bro, you're looking good,' followed by, 'Nah, man, you're the best-looking guy in the gym.' I turned around, and they were identical twins!"

Shawn laughs. "I'd ask what the hell you were thinking, renting a kitchen at this place, but I know your situation. Soon though, you'll be out of here and soaring."

"Your lips to God's ears, my friend." I walk into my office. "Have you seen a UPS box anywhere? I'm expecting a new roll of stickers."

I glance over and see I left my bra hanging on the side of the futon from when I took it off last night. It's lacy and black and definitely not something you want your employee to see. I quickly pick it up and tuck it in my suitcase, which doubles as a closet.

"Yep, it came while you were out. I placed it on your desk," Shawn calls. "It's across from that sexy-ass bra you have lying around in there."

Damn it, of course he saw it.

I lean out my door to eye him, and he holds his hands up in defense.

"I'm a hot-blooded American male. I saw lingerie, so of course, I was going to look. Sue me."

The words *sue me* ring in my ears. Hearing him mentioning a legal action puts unease in my stomach.

I turn around and head toward my desk and start up my laptop, trying not to think about this debacle I'm in. Spreadsheet and invoices will certainly do the trick. Every day, we fulfill anywhere between twenty to thirty orders, and seeing our numbers standing steady always fills me with pride.

A loud bang on the alleyway door gets my attention.

As Shawn walks over to open it, he calls out, "Your girl is here."

I laugh at how he knows without having to look at the security camera. Only my best friend, Charity, bangs on the door with her fist like she's making a drug bust. She says it's the sketchy path you have to walk to get to the alleyway door that makes it feel like she's here on illegal business.

"What's up, Charity?" Shawn says, letting her in. "Did you have a hot date last night?"

Charity pulls up a stool that we have dubbed Charity's Spot because she stops by so often. The kitchen is on her way to the Garden Room, a lounge where she works as a server a few days a week. "Nah, had to work, and no cute prospects came in. You?"

The two of them are constantly comparing dating notes. I find it hilarious because Charity is searching for a guy who has a great work ethic, doesn't take himself too seriously, and loves to dance, which is Shawn to a T. Shawn always finds the kind of girls who are exactly like Charity—beautiful, smart, spontaneous, and wants more out of a relationship than a few dates.

I keep pointing out the irony of it all, but they blow me off.

I stand from my desk, grab the order list from the printer, and walk out to the main kitchen area, where Shawn is finishing the last of the boxes so we can package an order that's going out tomorrow morning.

"Met this hot chick named Ryanne online and took her out last night."

"Rain, like the weather?" Charity asks.

"I think he meant Rae Anne," I explain.

"No. I said Ryanne," he dictates with emphasis before annunciating out the entire name. "Like rye bread. Rye-Anne."

"Ohh," Charity elongates the O sound. "Figures she has a *Y* in her name."

"Shawn, what is it with you and girls who spell their names in the unconventional way?" I ponder.

"It's like you look for it on those swiping dating apps," she adds.

"No, I don't."

27

"Yeah, you do," we say in unison.

His mouth twists as he leans back and crosses his arms, daring us to explain.

I start, "Alyson, Londyn, Caryn," counting them off on my fingers.

"Don't forget about Jasmyn. That girl was cray. Actually, all the women you've dated with a *Y* in their name have been nothing but trouble."

Shawn looks at us, bemused. "How do you know so much about the women I date?"

"You overshare," she deadpans.

"It's your best and worst quality." I pat him on the shoulder as I place the order form on the counter in front of him.

His brows rise, and his head nods. "Huh. Never realized that before. What can I say? I have a type. When their name is unique, so are they."

"You just watch out for Ryanne. If your track record is any indication, she'll be going through your cell or combing your carpet for other women's hair." Charity sits up on her stool with a raised finger and excited expression. "Remember the girl who was always convinced you were cheating?"

He nods as he recalls. "Mylie. Shit. She had a *Y* in her name too. I do have a type." The look of revelation on his face is comical. "I'm gonna do some research on this. You might say they're crazy, but someone named Donna or Samantha is not going to be a freak in the sheets. I'll have to put this to the test—in the name of science, of course."

"Good luck with that. I swear, it's a carousel of dud after dud in this city. Go to work, drinks at the bar, watch sports. That's all guys in Philadelphia want to do because there is always a game on." Charity rolls her eyes as she pops a chocolate morsel in her mouth.

He nods. "We do live in the best city for sports fans. Phillies, 76ers, Flyers, Eagles—"

"I can't stand that fight song—'Fly, Eagles Fly,' " she drones on. "I blame the sports. Men here think everything is a game."

He leans over the counter. "Don't hate the player—"

She throws a piece of chocolate at his nose, cutting him off. "Ugh. Why can't men be smooth and sophisticated, like they are in the movies?"

The two continue their diatribe while my mind instantly roams to thoughts of a man who seems smooth and sophisticated. There was something about his hands and the way he touched his face as he spoke. It brought attention to his features as he moved them about, like a conductor eliciting a melody from an orchestra— fluid and soulful. An unexpected smile crosses my lips as I think about Sebastian. That handsome stranger certainly came into my world at the right time. It's been days since we met for coffee, and I've thought about him more than once. His chivalry, the way he listened, his smile …

"What are you thinking about? You have this dreamy-schoolgirl stare," Charity observes.

I clear my throat and grab a pen. "I was just thinking about a new recipe I want to try, using unsweetened Dutch-processed cocoa powder and espresso beans," I say nonchalantly as I scroll down the printout of today's web orders.

When I glance up at her from the paper, she's eyeing

me to see if I'm telling the truth. Thankfully, she knows new recipes to me are like sexy men to her, so I know I'll get away with this one.

Yes, most would jump all over the chance to tell their best friend that the attorney who is assisting them is quite handsome, but I have to be careful with Charity. She's a true romantic, always looking for the one, and any mention of meeting someone new instantly turns into a million questions, like: *Is he single? Does he have children? Where does he live?*

Questions I have zero answers for since he's a stranger I met in the most peculiar way. Most importantly, he's my lawyer. I shouldn't be thinking of him and smiling like a goof. It's unprofessional. Unethical.

I set my cup and my phone on the counter and grab an apron. The three of us chat about our weekend plans. Shawn cracks the funniest jokes, and Charity tells the best stories. I hum along as I listen to my friends.

I'm lifting a pot to heat heavy cream when my cell phone ringer goes off.

Charity picks it up, looking at the screen, and hands it to me as she questions, "Who's Sebastian Blake?"

"My lawyer." I feel my face flush as she pulls the phone back into her, keeping it from me.

"You're blushing."

"I'm not blushing."

She holds my phone up and away. "You totally are. Did you see that, Shawn?"

My employee does nothing to help me dodge Charity's inquisition.

I lean forward and grab it from her hand rather viciously. "He's the attorney I told you about. The man who's going to get my stuff back from Hardin." My voice is a little bit of a huff when I swipe the call to answer. "Hello? This is Amy."

"This is Amy," they both singsong my words back, taunting me.

I hold my hand up to the mouthpiece to block them out as I jolt away from the counter, getting away from the two of them.

"Miss Morgana, it's Sebastian. I hope this isn't a bad time."

Charity rushes over to my side. "Is he cute?" she whispers rather loudly.

I shush her away and scurry toward my office, closing my office door in her face and resting my back against it. "Yeah. Now's great. What's up?"

"I'm looking over the file you gave me, and I'm going to do some digging. I have a cancellation tomorrow and want to set up a meeting with you before I book it up with something else."

"You want to meet in person again?" I raise my hand to my heart and wonder why the heck it's beating so fast. It must be his voice. It's warm and inviting, spoken from his chest.

"We could do it over the phone if you can't—"

"No. In person is fine. What time?"

"Well, I have to do all of my pro bono stuff after work hours. But we can still meet at my office." He's quick to say, which makes me smile. "Can you meet me at six? Here, at my office? I can text you the address."

"Tomorrow at six is perfect. Thank you."

"No problem. See you then."

He hangs up, and I let out a huge puff. When I

open the door, Shawn and Charity are as close to the threshold as possible, obviously eavesdropping, and they stare at me with smirks on their faces.

"What?" I ask.

"Oh, nothing. You don't have to say anything. Your complexion says it all." Charity points at my face, circling her finger as if it proves her point. "You said a lawyer was helping you. You didn't say you had the hots for him."

"I don't!" I declare. "I just want to come off as professional as possible, and having my friends ask if he's cute is not putting my best foot forward. Now, can we get back to work?" I point at Shawn with a stern expression.

He grins as he walks back to the workstation.

"And don't you have a shift that starts soon?" I ask Charity, moving my eyes to the clock and back to her.

"Is it that time already?" She pouts as she grabs her bag. "This isn't the end of this conversation. Shawn, see what you can find out from this one. Remember, she says nothing, but those cheeks of hers reveal everything. If anything with this attorney turns romantic, I want to be the first to know." She blows air kisses to the two of us as she closes the door behind her, shouting, "Happy chocolatiering!"

I'm filling the pot with cream as Shawn changes the music to play jazz. Not only does it relax me, but it's also the only music I'll cook to. The fact that it's the best way to get my mind steady before I meet with Mr. Blake tomorrow is a plus as well.

CHAPTER FOUR

As I enter the high-rise where the law offices of Blake, Fields, and Moore are located, I get this overwhelming sensation of wealth and power. In a city that is mostly historic buildings, the tiered skyscraper that's distinctly hued in red granite stands out like a modern marvel.

I step inside and immediately look up and around. Large glass windows let the rays of the setting sun into the lobby of sandstone porcelain and gold accents. There's a glass elevator that overlooks the vast lobby.

I'm staring in awe of the mosaic design on the far wall when a woman behind the front desk asks, "Who are you delivering to?"

Walking up to the desk, I smile. "I'm here to see Sebastian Blake."

"You can leave the food here." She nods to the bag of Chinese food in my hand that I picked up on the spur of the moment.

I glance down at my clothes. I wore jeans with a silk top and blazer. The outfit is moderately casual, but I didn't think I looked like a messenger. Between the impressiveness of the building and this woman's assumption, I'm feeling way out of my league.

"I have an appointment with him. I'm Amy Morgana."

Her eyes widen as she flips her hands up to the keyboard and starts typing. Then, she picks up the phone. "My apologies, Ms. Morgana. I saw the bag and thought you were the delivery driver. One moment. I'll ring Miles."

"I'm here to see Sebastian," I correct.

"Miles is his assistant," she answers before speaking into the phone after someone appears to have picked up the other end. As she hangs up, she says, "He'll be right down."

I smile to myself at how different Sebastian's office and mine are. Where he has a rotunda, I have a back alley and a sweaty gym. There are security guards here while I have a Ring doorbell. Sebastian's assistant comes down to escort guests. I'm lucky if Shawn, who is the closest thing I have to an assistant, answers the back door when Charity knocks.

"You must be Amy." A gentleman, who I assume is Miles, walks up to me. He has on khakis, a white button-down, and black-framed glasses. "If you'll follow me, I'll bring you up to Mr. Blake."

I adjust the tote bag on my shoulder and grip the plastic takeout handles with both hands in front of me as I follow him to the glass elevator.

We step in, and he hits the third floor before standing to the side and waiting patiently. I fidget with the bag, hating the awkwardness of being enclosed with a stranger in an elevator.

"You're Sebastian's assistant," I muse.

He nods in a professional manner. "I've worked for Mr. Blake for five years."

Glancing at my watch, I take in the time. "You must put in some late hours."

"When there's a big case, Mr. Blake has been known to pull all-nighters. The man is incredibly dedicated, and I've learned so much from him. He's one of the best attorneys in Philadelphia," Miles boasts with a raised chin.

I smash my lips together and giggle. "It's okay, dude. I'm not a personal friend or anything. I'm not even a paying client. You don't have to show off for your boss for me."

Miles swivels his head toward me and stares like I have three eyes. "No, I'm serious. The man is the nicest and most generous guy I've ever met."

My brows furrow. Not because I'm disappointed in that news. I'm actually surprised. Everyone has something negative to say about their boss. Not that I necessarily expected this man to word-vomit about his boss to me, but he didn't have to go above and beyond to say nice things. His response was natural.

The glass walls of the elevator take us up, and the doors open to a waiting room with the law firm's name emblazoned on the wall. All of the awards the firm has won line the back wall like they're gold albums sitting in a record label's office.

"Give me a second. I'll let him know you're here." Miles picks up a phone at the front desk while I take the opportunity to look at the photos on an adjacent wall.

Sebastian is in many of them, all with various charities around the city. Each photo is labeled with the organization's name and the amount the firm has donated to them.

Miles hangs up the phone and comes around the desk. "He said I can bring you back."

I follow him down a long walkway that overlooks the main lobby of the building. It's funny how it feels so different from this angle. Downstairs, this space felt out of reach, like only the elite belonged up here. And now that I'm here, it still feels as elegant and opulent, but I don't feel like such an outsider.

"He's meeting you in conference room number two." Miles points to a set of double doors and then opens them to escort me inside.

"Thank you," I say, and he nods with a smile before walking away.

I enter the room and see Sebastian standing by the long mahogany conference table. He's in suit pants and a button-down that's rolled up to his elbows.

His face ignites in a huge grin as he splays his hands out to his sides. "You're going to love me," he says.

I stop in my tracks, his enthusiasm catching me off guard, as is the way his impressive physique is on display under the thin white shirt. Sinewy muscle makes him look larger than his over six-foot frame.

"I do." I pause and then correct myself. "I will." I try not to smack myself in my head for sounding so dumb. "I mean, I am?"

"Yes. Here, come in." He motions for me to join him where he has a few different papers laid out on the table.

I place my bags on the table, dying to know why I'm going to love him.

"Do I smell Chinese?" he asks, pointing to the takeout bag.

"Oh. I thought you'd be hungry since it is practically dinnertime. I wanted to thank you for helping me with dinner. I figured you can't go wrong with General Tso's chicken, lemon chicken, and chow mein. I hope that's okay."

His face morphs from confusion to surprise to wonderment. "Wow, yes. What a great offering. Thank you."

I open the bag and empty the contents, including paper plates and chopsticks.

"Do you want me to get you real plates, Mr. Blake?" Miles asks from the doorway.

I look up at Sebastian. "These plates are just fine for me unless you want something nicer. Don't go all formal on my account."

Sebastian grins. "This is just fine." He looks up to his assistant. "Miles, I'm all set for tonight. Once Amy and I are finished, I'll be heading off. You can go home early tonight."

"Are you sure?" Miles asks.

Sebastian nods. "Take the time now. We have a few long days ahead of us next week. Call your girlfriend and take her out to dinner at Buddakan. Use the company account."

"Thank you. That's our favorite restaurant." His face grows with excitement.

"I know." He tosses Miles his cell phone. "Place that

on my desk, please. I don't want to be disrupted for the next hour."

"Will do, sir. Good night. And pleasure meeting you, Amy."

I smile at Miles. "Likewise."

Miles walks out and closes the doors behind him. It's now just Sebastian and me in the room. The outside windows show a night sky, as the sun has now set fully. Out the window is a view of the Ben Franklin Bridge and the lights of Philly.

I grab the plates and hand him one as we both take our seats.

"So, why exactly am I going to love you?" I ask as I pick up my chopsticks.

I offer him either the chopsticks or a fork. He grabs the chopsticks. Good choice.

"My investigator went to your apartment today to see about the damage." He scoops rice onto his plate.

I hand him one container as I dish from the other. Then, I put chow mein on my plate. "Please tell me it's not really trashed and this was all just a scam," I say, ever so hopeful.

He makes himself a plate of lemon chicken and chow mein. "No, it's certainly damaged. When I first looked up your address online, I saw it was in a multifamily house and not a building, and I had a hunch. So, I needed the investigator to check on it for me, and I had him go there, posing as a contractor." He slides a piece of paper in front of me and then picks up his chopsticks.

"What's this?" I motion toward the paper.

"That's the letter we're sending to him, stating your lease is null and void because the unit isn't a legal rental."

"It's not?" I ask, so shocked that I almost choke on my food.

He waits for me to stop coughing before he explains, "Your unit was semi-underground with long, narrow windows high on your wall, correct?"

"Yeah. They let in a lot of light without taking up wall space."

"You entered through a side door instead of the main entrance?"

I nod.

"If there were a fire near the entrance of the unit, how would you get out? I bet those windows were pretty small. Could you have fit through them?" he asks.

My eyes open wide. "I never even thought about what would happen if there were a fire."

He points his chopsticks at me. "Bingo. Not many people do. Not until it's too late anyway."

When I left that apartment, I hated leaving my cozy, little place, but all I can think of now is that it was a death trap waiting to happen.

"I don't understand how this will help me." I put the paper down and take a bite.

"Many properties in that area have garages that were converted to apartments years ago, using them as rentals. Unless they were upgraded to meet standard code, which says every unit needs two forms of egress in the event of an emergency, then they can't legally be rented."

"How do you know it wasn't upgraded?"

"I looked up the building permits on the property, and there were none, but it was possible he made them without paying for permits and filing with the city. So, when my investigator went to the property, he confirmed no such safety upgrades had been made."

"Wait. Do you think he'll drop all money owed for the unpaid rent and damage?"

"I don't think. I know. This letter says that we know it's not being leased right now, so if he starts the renovations needed to make the space safe, we won't bring legal charges against him for putting you, the tenant, in harm's way."

"Is it really going to be that easy?" I ask with a tilt to my head.

"It also helps that the letter is printed on our fancy stationery with the company letterhead. It's amazing how threatening this piece of paper can be."

"Must be the letterhead." I smirk.

"I think it's the paper. Rumor has it, the heavier it is, the more intimidating," he jokes with a wink.

I let out a snort-laugh, sitting back in my chair with my hand over my mouth, feeling embarrassed in front of this extremely smart, very handsome man.

"Are you disappointed it wasn't more dramatic and drawn out? Expecting your day in court?" he asks before taking another bite.

"Gosh, no. I'm beyond relieved. It's a shame that ordinary people like myself fall for such unsafe living conditions."

"You just need to know the right questions to ask. That's why people need an attorney's advice. Knowledge is power."

"Any knowledge on how I can get my dog back?" I sigh as I think of my Pomeranian.

"You really love her, huh?"

"I do. I only had her for a few months before Hardin took her, but she's my pup. She would curl up on my lap whenever I sat down, and if I had my laptop, trying to work late at night, forget about it. She would literally put her head on my hands and her paw on the trackpad while I was trying to type."

His eyes crinkle as he listens to me speak. And he's not just sitting here, staring at me while I talk. His shoulders lean in, and he nods sincerely.

"It's like she was trying to make sure you weren't working too hard."

"You're making her seem sweeter than she is. Lady Featherington is the center of attention at all times. She is very playful, but have no doubt, she is a diva. Honestly, I love that about her. She melts my heart, you know?"

He grins, and my heart picks up a little.

"I get that," he states as he sticks his hand into his pocket and pulls out his wallet. He opens it and shows me a picture of a dog, gray in color with one ear up and the other flopped. He's scruffy yet handsome. "I have a rescue mutt of my own. Duke. He's a Wowauzer. A Welsh terrier schnauzer mix. He's very friendly and playful. Got him seven years ago, and he's my best friend. I understand why you want your dog back. Their lifespan is only so long; you don't want to lose any time."

"Exactly."

He closes his wallet and then slides it to his pocket. "I can help you get her back."

"Thank you, but this is something I need to do on my own. Hardin has been a huge prick to me. Walking away from the apartment like this was the final straw for my silence. I'm going to get my dog back myself."

"Good for you," he states with a firm nod, like he's proud of me.

"Thanks." I pause and go back to picking at my food. "I guess this means, you're not my attorney anymore."

"No. I guess I'm not."

I get the feeling I should leave now, but I honestly don't want to. "Can I ask you a question?"

"You can, but I can't guarantee I won't plead the Fifth." He smirks, making me do the same.

"If you won the lottery today, would you continue to work?"

"That's a random question. Any particular reason?"

"Just something that came to mind. It's silly. Forget I even asked. You can plead the Fifth."

Leaning back in the leather conference chair, he steeples his hands and holds them up to his mouth. He eyes me with a quizzical look, which makes me feel uneasy. As his mouth quirks up on the side, I see a dimple on his cheek, which surprises me with how sexy I find it.

"This," he states easily. "I can honestly say, there is nothing I'd rather do than be an attorney." He drops his hands to the armrests and swivels toward me. "The work challenges me, and being in charge is a good place to be." That cavalier smile of his is enchanting. "Plus, I really enjoy helping people. I got into law to further public good and change the way the world is run. My cases haven't all been easy, but I've never taken a case I didn't believe in."

Of all the answers he could have given, his is the very best.

"What about you?" He leans in, his tone deep and

hushed. "What would Amy Morgana do if she never had to work?"

I raise a shoulder. "Funny you ask since I've never worked a day in my life. Making chocolate is my passion. How can I claim it's work when I'm having so much fun, doing it?"

Those eyes. The caramel hue of his sinful gaze is looking at me like I just gave him the answer to the most interesting question. His tongue darts out and licks his lips as he smiles slowly.

With a swallow, I divert my attention to the table and remember the gift I brought him in my bag. I reach in my tote and grab a narrow box. "Before I forget, this is for you."

He accepts the mauve-and-white box, adjusting it so he can read the words engraved in navy script on the top.

"*Amy Morgana Chocolatier*. You brought me dinner and dessert?"

"Again, it's part of my thank-you."

"I'll savor these."

I lift my chopsticks and go back to eating, trying to hide my blush from the way he glances over at me every few seconds and grins.

We finish our meals, and there's this looming feeling of our night coming to an end, no matter how much I don't want it to. Our conversation has flowed so easily, and the hour has flown by.

I start to clean up our mess and throw our trash in the bag that I brought it in when he stands.

"Here, let me help you."

"Oh, don't worry about it. I got it." I reach for the

last container and tie the bag, tossing it in a nearby trashcan. Next, I grab my tote, looking toward the door, and hope I remember the way back to the lobby.

Sebastian must sense my unease because he offers, "I'll walk out with you. Just let me get my things from my office."

He leads me out of the conference room and into an office with Sebastian's name on a gold placard. When I enter, I instantly feel like I'm in a no-bullshit zone.

Bookshelves filled with legal books line the far wall with his dark cherry wood desk in front of it. Everything on the desk has its place, all angled toward a leather chair like little soldiers, and there doesn't seem to be a speck of dust anywhere. The plant in the corner doesn't have one leaf that's turning color, and the view out the window of the city is to die for.

While it's impressive and regal, none of it compares to the personal touches that make the office warm and welcoming. His law degree from University of Pennsylvania that sits in the corner is framed, but an old hat with a *P* on the front of it hangs off the side.

A photo of who I assume are his parents sits in a frame next to it with him in the middle. His father, a man with tan skin and a wide smile, stands beside Sebastian, who has his arm around a woman with blonde hair and eyes the same as his. They're clutching to him with pride as they pose on a dock overlooking the ocean.

I glance to the other side of the room and have to hold in my laughter at a photo of Sebastian with the Phillies mascot, Phillie Phanatic, on the wall.

"Baseball fan?" I ask.

"Absolutely. One of the charities I volunteer for got honored at a game last year, and they let us go on the field." The way he says it with so much excitement makes me smile.

"Pretty fun day then, I guess." I try to downplay.

"Just another day at the office." He grins.

"I suppose you get a lot of perks, working as a high-profile attorney. Are you living out all of your twelve-year-old boy dreams?" I tease.

"Twelve-year-old, nineteen-year-old … hell, even thirty-year-old dreams."

I laugh as he grabs his stuff, and we head out the door.

We walk down the hallway and make our way to the elevator. Inside the glass enclosure, I feel this searing energy in the air, a prickling that something amazing is about to happen.

It doesn't though. Instead, the doors open rather quickly, and we are in the main lobby of the building. There's someone different at the front desk and a security officer by the front doors. We walk toward them and onto the street.

"Well"—I pull my bag up high onto my shoulder— "thank you again for your help. I never would have even considered it not being a legal apartment."

"I'm glad we could solve the problem easily."

If I'm not mistaken, I see a hint of indecisiveness with his body language.

I pause, staring into his eyes, seeing if he'll say anything else. When he doesn't, I take a deep breath and turn to leave.

I walk away when I hear him say, "Amy?"

My feet spin around so fast that my hair whips in my face.

Sebastian takes a step forward. "Do you have any plans for tonight?" His voice is almost hesitant. "I was going to go out for a drink and would love if you could join me. Totally platonic, of course. I'm not your attorney anymore, but I don't want you thinking I'm trying to take advantage of a job well done, like you owe me or something."

I feel my heart instantly pound harder with both nerves and happy sensations flowing through me. "You've been nothing but chivalrous, Mr. Blake. And, well, I'd be more than pleased to have a drink with you."

The cheesy smile that spreads over his face makes him cuter than ever. "Great. I think you'll love this place."

Leo

CHAPTER FIVE

It's a brisk evening as we walk to the bar. With the beginning of spring, warm days are here, but the nights can still bear a winter chill. Like a true gentleman, Sebastian offers me his coat, and I accept with a shy smile, knowing he has his suit jacket underneath.

Though our conversation flows easily, I start to wonder where we're going after about fifteen minutes of walking, and I'm surprised when we stop outside McGillin's Olde Ale House. Beer has been pouring in this tavern since 1860, shortly after the Liberty Bell was cracked.

"I can't tell if you're impressed or disappointed," Sebastian comments as he holds the door open for me to enter.

"Pleasantly surprised," I chide as I walk by. "I love this place. It has so much charm."

The brick walls are adorned with paraphernalia of the bar's history from liquor licenses to old photographs and a sign from the old Wanamaker's Department Store that used to be nearby.

The place is packed, so the waitress waves us through the crowd to a small table near the back. We order craft beers and settle in after Sebastian removes his suit coat. I stand to do the same when I realize I'm still wearing his jacket.

"Thank you for letting me borrow this." I hand it back to him.

"Are you sure you don't still need it?"

"It's okay. I'm sure I'll warm up real quick in here." *Both with how many people are here and getting to stare at you for the next hour or so.*

We sit, and he instantly rolls his sleeves back up. Seeing those forearms bare with his muscular flesh on display definitely heats me right up.

A gentleman's arms aren't given nearly enough attention. You can tell a lot about a man with one quick glance. Smooth skin shows outer care while corded forearms declare he treats his inside equally well. He has home-gym arms, curled and toned but not bulky. He has no creases in his shirt, except at the elbows, as would someone who has his shirts professionally cared for. The rolled-up sleeves show a laid-back confidence, but it's how they're folded in an even, precise manner, as if he needs to be able to roll them down to pristine perfection with ease. He appears ambitious and dedicated to his work. And the thought of those arms wrapped around you on a cold March night is just damn sexy.

Our beers arrive quickly, so I take a sip and try to

rid my mind of all thoughts of cuddling and forearms and flesh.

"Did you know McGillin's is the most romantic place in Philadelphia?" I muse.

He looks around with a grin as he leans forward. "I thought you'd get a kick out of the history, but I didn't think of it as romantic."

"Oh, but it is. More couples have met, become engaged, and even gotten married here than any other place in Philadelphia."

He leans closer in a flirtatious way. "Given how old it is, the odds work in its favor."

"True. I can only imagine the amount of booze that has been drunk within these walls. I suppose, too, that most people find their soul mates over a couple of drinks."

He laughs. It's thick and rich, like dark chocolate mousse. "You're a true romantic, aren't you, Amy Morgana?"

I blush a little. "You're not incorrect. I do love a good romantic comedy, and I'd never refuse a walk on the beach."

"Don't forget chocolate," he muses.

"Yes, chocolate. Eating a small morsel is a voluptuous experience. Even if you didn't know it had aphrodisiac qualities, the flavor alone would make you feel romantic."

He takes a sip of his beer and licks his lips. "Do you really believe chocolate makes you horny?"

"When the Spanish conquistadors arrived in modern-day Mexico City, they say Montezuma drank fifty cups of chocolate a day and he had a harem of fifty women. They assumed the chocolate must have increased his stamina."

He raises his brows in amusement. "Meaning … it was the original Viagra."

I laugh and almost spit out my drink. "It must have been—or so the conquistadors thought. They returned to Europe with cacao, where it immediately caught on as an aphrodisiac and a luxury that was tightly controlled. I mean, they couldn't have lust-filled peasants running amok."

"That would have been a travesty," he jokes, acting very serious. "So, I take it, it was reserved for the aristocracy?"

"Bingo. Rumor has it, Marie Antoinette wouldn't start her day without a cup of chocolate." I take a long swallow and grin. "That chocolate was made with chile though, which was too spicy for Europeans or Americans. So, they replaced the chile with sugar to create what we know now as chocolate today."

"Do you think the chile was the trick to it being an aphrodisiac?"

"If you ever want to try it, I can make a special batch in my kitchen." My words come out far flirtier than I intended.

Based on Sebastian's grin and the heat in his gaze, I'd say, my unintended comment just got a rather welcome reaction.

"Why chocolate?" he asks as his hand wraps around his pint glass. "Why did you choose it as your career?"

I blow out a breath and cross my legs, leaning into the table. "I guess it started when I was a kid on

Valentine's Day. My dad would buy each of us those heart-shaped boxes. You know, the red fabric kind. They were so pretty, and I loved having my special piece of heaven. The diagram was key. There's nothing worse than biting into a disappointing flavor."

He laughs. "I was the kid who took a bite out of every piece and only ate about five in the box."

"Exactly!" I say rather excitedly. "As I got older, I found myself testing different brands, finding the flavors I enjoyed, and I learned fast that not all chocolate makers are alike."

"Any favorites?"

"Godiva and Lindt. Prestat and Montezuma. Pierre Marcolini. Milène Jardine."

"But you knew you could do better." There's a gleam in his eye that makes me smile.

"I hope I can. It's the only thing I've ever wanted to do. I've always admired the miniature artistic masterpieces that emerge from a box."

He nods like he appreciates and understands my words. "Did you go to culinary school?"

"College wasn't for me, so I decided to go learn from the ground up. I've worked in Paris and Belgium, New York and here, in Philadelphia."

"Do you speak French?"

"*Oui.*"

"*Azez-vous un café préféré à Paris?*"

I bite my lip as I try to think of my favorite café in Paris, which is what he just asked. There was one, an impressive pastry cart with rich hot chocolate that was so thick that the spoon slowed with every stir.

"Les Deux Magots. *Les déserts étaient magnifiques,*"

I reply and then add, "You speak French beautifully, by the way."

"You're kind, but I know it's rusty. I'm better at Spanish. I learned French in high school and took *Español* in college. It comes in handy in my line of work more than French does."

"What do you do when you're not saving the world one wrong at a time? *Impressionnant*," I say in French.

"I'm not the impressive one. You're the one who has followed her dreams by traveling the world and running your own business. I'm captivated."

"Do you mean, you're more like shocked that the woman who texted you on accident, telling you off, isn't a mental patient?"

"I told you, I wanted to see if you were as charming as I hoped."

"You mean, crazy."

"I mean, enrapturing. You, Amy, have surpassed everything I could have ever imagined you'd be. More than anything, I'm glad I offered to meet you for coffee the next day."

His charm is impossible to shy away from. Sebastian Blake is easy on the eyes and easier to talk to.

"I know you run marathons and have Duke. What else makes you tick?"

"That's like opening Pandora's box." He raises his eyebrows as he takes a sip of his beer.

"I still have half a drink, and I'm open to getting a second. I'm here for the box. Open the box, Sebastian." I use my most jovial yet tempting voice.

"Okay. Well, I love documentaries and am an avid History Channel buff. If it's a film, I'm a sucker for anything where someone has to overcome an obstacle. *Rocky* and *Rudy* being two of my favorites."

"*Rocky* is a town legend. Even if he is fictional."

"Don't knock it. That movie is a classic. Plus, I might have taken a picture in front of the Rocky statue outside the museum."

"That is the most charming thing about you." I grin as I lean in a little closer.

"Okay, so that's what you're looking for? Anecdotes that aren't so flattering?"

"Your buck-tooth story is the reason I hired you as my attorney," I say with a shrug, not afraid to admit it.

"The can-opener story impressed you?"

"What can I say? I, too, am a sucker for someone who has to overcome an obstacle," I use his words and mean every single one of them.

"More embarrassing things about me then ..."

He grins, and it's the cutest thing ever. If I wasn't sure if this was a date or not, I definitely am now. His flirting is apparent and almost unnerving. I don't think I've ever had someone be so obvious with their feelings toward me. I like it.

He continues, "I sprained my ankle last year, so my mother sent me one of those adult coloring books. It has profanity words engraved in lotus flowers and rainbows. I've definitely finished more pages than any man would care to admit. Is that charming?"

"Forget charming. That is the sexiest thing I've ever heard," I say with a chuckle.

"Then, this is going to drive you wild. I know how to sew."

I place my hand on my chest and fake a sexual pant.

"Do go on."

"As an only child, my mother made me do everything with her. Sewing the holes in my socks was one of my chores. I happen to have a perfect stitch." He shakes his head from side to side, acting hoity-toity.

I laugh but not at him. I'm laughing because I enjoy him. Sebastian is fun and sweet. His stories are cute, as is the way he smiles more on one side of his mouth than the other, showing off that dimple.

He calls the waitress over and gets us another round. We continue our talks and jokes. When I'm halfway through my second drink, I get the liquid courage to ask the question I've secretly been wanting to ask.

"How is a man as handsome, successful, and captivating as you single?"

"You think I'm captivating?"

I like that he called out that adjective instead of the others. He clearly knows how he looks in the mirror, and his reputation precedes him. But his personality … that is what makes him feel good.

"Devilishly charming. And swoonworthy. You have a way about you. Sorry if that comes off strong. I merely meant to pay you a compliment."

"Don't apologize. I love how authentic you are. You say what you feel."

"Too much so sometimes, unfortunately."

"Only because you asked, I'm recently single. I was seeing a woman, but we called it quits about three months ago. Our split was amicable though. It just didn't work out. No love lost. I wish her the best, as I know she does me."

"Couldn't have been a long relationship."

"About six months. But it wasn't like what you had with Hardin. We dated and had fun, but the relationship ran its course. She said she wanted to see other people, and I was okay with letting her go."

"That sounds so simple."

"It is when you're not in love."

"Have you ever been in love before?"

"Yes. At least, I thought I was. We all do when we're young. As you get older, you stop looking for the insta-love—lust that comes with an incredible high. I don't want the kind of love that comes with conditions. Places we need to go and people we need to be with in order to be a couple. I work too hard in the office to have to work for my relationship image. I just want to meet someone I can sit at a table with, alone, have some drinks and great conversation, and even share a few laughs."

"That sounds wonderful. But that sounds more like a friend."

He shrugs. "Maybe that's what I'm looking for. A woman who is my best friend, who lets me take her home when the sun goes down and ravage her in the bedroom until the sun comes up."

My cheeks heat, and my belly tightens just as the waitress brings us the bill, breaking our little trance.

I look at my watch, suddenly more nervous than I should be. "It's getting late. I have to get up early and put a favor order together. A hundred boxes for a wedding at the library."

"I'll get you a car," he says as he pulls out his card, slides it in the billfold, and hands it to the waitress.

"No, it's okay. I can walk."

"It's cold, and you're alone. I'll call you a car," he

insists as he pulls out his phone and taps something on it.

After the waitress brings him back his card and he signs the slip, we walk out to the curb, where a black town car is waiting. He opens the back door, and the scent of leather rolls out of the luxury mobile.

"Thank you for the drinks. This was a great idea." I smile as I fidget with my purse.

"Thank you for dinner. You made my day."

I step into the car, but he says my name, halting my movement.

"Amy, can I call you? I mean, not as your attorney?"

"You're not on the clock anymore, so yes, I would like that."

The smile that crosses his face is like a kid on Christmas morning.

"Good night, Amy."

"Stay well, Mr. Blake."

CHAPTER SIX

When Sebastian said he'd call, I didn't expect my phone to ding the next day, so I'm pretty surprised when I get a text message from him while packing up my wedding order.

I'm sitting here with a gorgeous box of chocolate and wondering if ten a.m. is too early to indulge. Thought I'd ask the expert.

I pick up my phone, my heart beating faster all of a sudden. I can't help the grin on my face as I turn around, lean on the counter, and text back.

It is never too early for decadence.

You have my permission. ;-)

I'm officially spoiled.

You've ruined chocolate for me for eternity.

I'm happy to support your habit.

Just don't tell anyone who your dealer is.

My lips are sealed.

I had a great time last night.

Me too.

LOYAL LAWYER

I believe there's man code that states I should wait three days before asking you out, but I'm not one to follow such rules. Have dinner with me.

Are you asking or telling?

Eagerly awaiting …

It's refreshing to text with a man who is confident enough not to play games or be coy. He sees what he likes and goes for it. He texts again before I can respond.

I'm working late this week on a big case and want to make plans with you before I get too busy to ask. Are you available next Friday?

You're sweet. Next Friday sounds great.

Then, it's a date.

I set down my phone and look up, only to see Shawn staring at me with a raised eyebrow.

"What?" I ask and then turn around to get back to work, not really wanting him to answer.

"Hot date?" He walks over to me and leans against the counter, so he's facing me.

I normally don't discuss my personal life with Shawn even though I know his entire life, but Charity was at work last night, and I'm dying to tell someone about my date.

"Yes, actually." I blush, and I feel it all the way to my toes.

"Lawyer?"

"Yes. We went out after he helped me get out of my lease, and he just asked me out again."

"Damn, girl. Look at you. Getting the attention of some high-class attorney. When's the date?"

"Next Friday." I turn to head into my office to grab the address I'm supposed to mail these to even though

I don't need it right this second. I just don't want to hear—

"As in next week?" He follows me into the office.

I try to act nonchalant. "Yes, he has a busy schedule, and he said he wanted to—"

"Pencil you in?"

"Oh, stop. I think it's considerate and cute. He wanted to make sure he had something to look forward to since he's working on a big case."

"Interesting plan. He keeps the girls waiting and wanting more. Do you think I could get away with that? Maybe say I have a huge order we need to get out?"

I laugh. "Sorry, Shawn. No one will believe chocolate is that busy of a job, no matter how much I want it to be."

Shawn was right when he said having the date planned that far out would keep me waiting and wanting more. Every day, I looked at the calendar, counting down the nights until I got to see him again. I swear it was the longest week of my life.

Now that it's Friday, I can't wait until tonight. I haven't been this excited for a day to come since I was a little girl, waiting on Christmas to arrive.

Sebastian texted late last night, saying he was at work but wanted to make sure we were still on. When I responded, I got so giddy that I had to make myself a drink to calm down my excitement.

Then, he called this morning, saying to be ready by six and he'd pick me up to go to Ocean Prime—the fanciest steak house in the city.

LOYAL LAWYER

I'm wearing my sexiest red dress with black pumps and a necklace that draws attention to my décolletage—one of my favorite parts of my body.

Not wanting to explain having to go through the gym or have him walk through the alley, I decide to wait out front for him to arrive.

An exotic black car pulls up. The purr of the engine is so low that it's almost silent. I glance in to see Sebastian putting it in park and unbuckling his seat belt before hopping out. Since he's not expecting me to be standing here, he's caught off guard, and he stops in his tracks when he sees me.

The expression on his face is one I've only seen in movies. Those chocolate eyes move down my body like silk coating my skin. From my shoulders, down the curve of my waist, and over my hips, lowering from one leg to the other, all with pure appreciation of the person standing in front of him.

And that person is me.

"You look amazing," he says breathlessly.

A grin spreads across my face. "You don't look too bad yourself."

I reach out my hand and lightly tug on the blue designer button-up that fits his body like a glove. Sebastian has always presented himself well, but in this shirt, I can see the definition of his broad chest, fit torso, and the curve of his biceps.

He escorts me to the passenger side and opens the door like a true gentleman.

"What kind of car is this?" I ask as I slide in. "I've never seen it before."

"A BMW i8. It's fully electric and a blast to drive."

He shuts the door and heads over to the driver's side as I take in the high-tech interior.

As he buckles his seat belt, he grins in my direction. "So glad we set this up early. Seeing you again is the one thing that helped get me through the trial this week."

I instantly blush again. He has a way of making me do that. He's so sweet and honest. Those are rare traits, and I like it.

"I hope this doesn't ruin the night, but did you win?"

He glances at me out the side of his eye. A devilish smirk crosses his face. "At the risk of sounding like an egomaniac … abso-fucking-lutely."

I laugh out loud. "Good for you. Now, we have something to celebrate."

He lifts my hand and kisses my knuckle. His warm mouth presses firmly to my skin, sending a wave of excited chills up my arm and straight down the front of my body. I might let out a tiny quiver that I can't hide.

"I'd like that," he says, releasing my hand and putting the car in drive.

A few minutes later, we pull up to the corner restaurant made of brick, and my mouth salivates. I've only heard of this place but never treated myself to a meal here.

I open my door, and Sebastian walks around the car to join me, instantly intertwining his fingers with mine as we head toward the entrance. I try to hide the way it affects me, but inside, I'm a twelve-year-old girl, holding hands with her crush.

The place is bustling with people at tables and lining the bar. Elegance drips from every corner, and I'm glad I chose this dress, as I feel like I fit in here perfectly even though I'm currently sleeping on a futon and living out of my office, which has been making me feel like a vagabond lately.

"Two for Blake," Sebastian says as we approach the hostess station.

"Yes, Mr. Blake. We have your table ready. Right this way," the hostess responds as she grabs two menus.

He motions for me to go first, and I follow her through the restaurant to a private table near the window.

I take my seat as Sebastian takes his, and the waitress hands us our menus. After we order some drinks, our conversation continues with ease. This time, I get to learn some more about him.

"Since my father was a surgeon, as a kid, I used to sit in his office after school and shadow him. He wanted me to follow in his footsteps badly."

"Didn't have the stomach for slicing and dicing?"

"Actually, I wanted to be an actor." He takes a sip of his drink.

"Really? Are we talking Shakespearean plays, toothpaste commercials, or full-on Timothée Chalamet?"

"More like Michael B. Jordan action kind of stuff. That guy is an amazing actor and has the kind of career I would have wanted. He was the new Rocky after all."

"Agreed. He's also really hot." I cheers and take a sip of my drink. "What made you give up on the acting dream?"

"I joined the debate team in high school for extra credit and found I was just as good with arguing in public as I was with reciting lines. In college, my mother encouraged me to take prelaw classes to see how I'd do. I figured they'd help me in the days when I starred on *Law & Order*."

"Because every actor starts out with a role on *Law & Order*."

"Exactly. I quickly learned that I really liked studying casework. I found it was easy to understand and challenging enough to make me want to get better. Conducting a deposition or giving an opening argument is very much like acting. You read from a script and put in the right amount of emotion to get your point across and be convincing. When you're onstage, you should know how to improvise in case something goes wrong. Same with the courtroom. You have to have enough legal research in your brain to be able to spew it off the cuff to counter an argument. It's challenging and fun, if you're doing it right."

"That's an incredible way to compare the two."

"Both crafts take late nights, rehearsals, and research. They're just different disciplines."

"And the pro bono work?"

"That's a bonus. My mother taught me to be generous. To be a good man, you should help someone else in need even if that means having less for yourself."

My teeth skim my lower lip as I take him in. Illegally handsome face, easy smile, and a personality that's flawless. I like what I'm seeing and what I'm hearing. A lot.

"Now that you won your big case, who will you help next?"

"I don't know. Maybe I'll get a text message that inspires me."

That makes me laugh.

Instead of entrées, we select five appetizers to share as our conversation continues.

He's slicing into the goat cheese ravioli while I tell him about my friends Charity and Shawn.

I nibble on a crab cake as he fills me in on the firm, his partners, and the office, making me laugh as he tells stories of his staff pranking him by sending him singing telegrams, which he happens to find incredibly embarrassing.

He chews on calamari as he listens to me go on about this time Charity and I went skiing, only to be stuck at the top of the mountain because she was too scared to come down.

We laugh about our common love of the show *Impractical Jokers* while enjoying our oysters. We happen to have the same favorite episode and a deep love for the comics.

Over a shrimp tempura roll, he reminds me of being an only child, and I tell him about growing up as the youngest of five children.

"My sisters are both married to their college sweethearts. My brothers have gorgeous and equally successful wives."

"Nieces and nephews?" he asks.

"Six," I say, and his eyes widen. "They're awesome and my absolute pride and joy. You'd think that would keep everyone happy enough to not worry about my single status, but it only makes things worse."

"Ah, so you're the spinster of the group."

I raise a fork in agreement. "Yep. My parents aren't my biggest problem though. It's the siblings. They're all professionals—a doctor, day trader, vice principal, and an ad executive—so my entrepreneurial whims are a little too adventurous for them to grasp. Plus, they never approve of anyone I bring home. Heather analyzes his job. Fiona, his looks. Henry thinks he's smarter than everyone—and possibly is—while Matthew is ready to bench anyone just to show he's more masculine. No man stands a chance against the Morgana crew."

"Then, you're not bringing the right man over to see them," he says with a cocky smile.

"Have anyone in mind?" I tease.

"I bet I could come up with someone." He winks.

Everything about dinner is going great. The food is amazing, the service is prompt and friendly, and my date is … well … a dream. As someone who just came out of a one-sided relationship, I can instantly feel the difference. Sebastian is a proud man but not in a negative way. In fact, I feel as if he looks at me, a woman he has welcomed into his world, as something he finds pride in as well.

He wants to know about me, and in return, I'm enamored by him. When you look up the word *swoonworthy* on the internet, I bet there's a picture of Sebastian Blake next to the definition.

Our dishes are cleared, and the waitress comes to ask if we'd like anything else. Sebastian declines and asks for the check. He must sense my confusion as he leans in.

"You seem disappointed in no dessert."

"Surprised actually. I hope you don't think I'm a confection snob."

"Not at all. I happen to have something special planned."

"How special?"

"A jazz club."

"Jazz, huh? What makes you think I'd like that?"

"It's more of a jazz fusion club. When I called last night to tell you what time to be ready, I heard the music in the background."

He has a good ear. I was listening to the *Lady Lady* album by Masego. The artist incorporates the saxophone into his music creation, making a sexy, sultry blend.

"Jazz for dessert it is."

He moves his hand across the table until it's lying on top of mine. His palm is large and hot as it encloses my tiny one. "I also heard they serve the most amazing chocolate martinis."

A slow, sexy smile graces my face as I look at him from under my lashes. "Well, Mr. Blake, it seems you have figured out a way into this woman's heart," I say as I roll my palm over, exposing it to his.

He takes my hand and raises it to his lips. "Then, let's get out of here."

We drive to the other side of town, where a neon sign with the word *Jazz* is lit up in blue outside the building. After we exit the car, Sebastian holds the door for me as I step inside, and I feel like I've been transported to another time.

Red brick walls are on two sides of the room with large windows in the front, and drapes hang tall and long behind a stage. A four-piece band plays up front with someone else on a black grand piano.

The hostess walks us to a table with a placard that says *Reserved*. As soon as we sit down, a waitress, who smiles at Sebastian in a familiar way, places chocolate martinis in front of us.

"I take it, she knew we were coming then?" I run my finger along the rim of the glass.

"I might or might not have sent her a text, saying we were on our way. She dates a friend of mine."

We cheers, and I sip the most decadent martini I've had in a while.

Unlike at the restaurant, Sebastian and I are seated side by side as we watch the band and listen to the music. His arm wraps around the booth behind us, making it easy for me to slide into his side without seeming forward. Our hips touch, and there's something about the contact of our bodies, as simple as it is, that ignites a fire in my belly.

He talks to me throughout the set, speaking directly into my ear so I can hear him over the trumpet. His breath tickles my skin, and the citrusy scent of his cologne is invigorating.

I turn my head to respond, and our faces are close. So close that my chest rises with the deep inhale as I look up into his steely gaze and lick my lips, having to bite down so I don't do something foolish, like attack this man and kiss him senseless.

Because I want to.

From the top of my head to the bottom of my toes, electricity courses through my body, and I'm dying to latch on to this man and taste his lips and touch his body. I could blame it on the martini I've drank or the oysters, which are said to be an aphrodisiac. That would all be a lie, of course. No food or drink could make me want this man more than his mere presence does.

Sebastian Blake is a walking, talking aphrodisiac.

"Dance with me," he croons, and I nod with a swallow.

He rises and takes my hand, walking me over to a small dance floor, where a few people are gliding to the music.

His arm snakes around my waist, pulling me flush to him. His hard body is like a magnet for my soft one. His other hand skims my hip as I raise my arms around his neck and move with him.

We sway to the beat of the saxophone.

My heart pounds with the bass.

As he lowers his forehead to mine, my entire soul gives in completely. It's silly really. A man I met barely two weeks ago has barreled his way into my world, and I'm beyond smitten. I should hate men after what Hardin did to me.

I can't though. Not when this one is holding me close and staring at me from under hooded eyes, like I'm the only woman in the room. No, he's looking at me like I'm the last living being in the entire world.

I move my hand down to his chest and lay it over the space where his heart beats hard and fast. His hand clenches my side, and I know he's just as affected as I am.

"I want to kiss you, Amy," he whispers in the space between us.

"Why don't you?"

"I'm afraid if I start, I won't want to stop, and we're not in the most private of places."

"Good thing you have restraint," I say.

His brows curve in concern. "Why's that?"

"Because I have none."

My cheeks are flush, my body is aching, and my heels rise as I lean up and kiss him. In a jazz club with the rhythmic beats of a sultry ballad, on a dance floor, in front of people who are probably too consumed by their own lives to notice, I kiss him.

His mouth parts instantly and welcomes me in, sliding his tongue against mine, eliciting a moan from deep in my throat. My hands grip his neck as I pull him closer, savoring his delicious mouth. His hands hold me tighter as my fingers grip at his shirt.

Chests press up against each other, and groins roll. It's a good thing we're already dancing because the movement must look lethal. Our kiss is heady and delicious—the kind you can get lost in for days.

Thankfully, Sebastian pulls away before we get too carried away.

Our foreheads find one another again. Our breaths are pants as we gaze into each other's eyes and smile.

"This is happening?" he asks, and I nod happily. "We are happening."

"I like *we*."

"I like you. A lot." He kisses my forehead and takes my hand as he walks us back to the table.

I snuggle into his side and enjoy the rest of the evening, drinking, listening, stealing kisses, and loving every moment of being by Sebastian's side.

When the night is over, we walk to the car and head back to my place. I have Sebastian pull up into the alley this time. It might not be glamorous, but it's my home, and it's late.

He looks out the window, seeming uncomfortable. "This is the only way inside?"

"It's the direct way. You can also access it from the gym but only during business hours."

"This is your business and your home?"

"Yep. My own piece of heaven," I joke.

His face still looks disturbed, so I grab his chin, lean over, and kiss him—a surefire way to get that expression off his face. Now, he is drinking in my kisses, gripping my waist, and pulling me over to him. I kick off my shoes and crawl over the center console to straddle his waist.

My dress rides up my hips, and my lace thong and his pants are the only fabric between us. His thick, granite-like erection springs forward, and I still for a second, surprised by the mass between my thighs before moving on instinct, finding it a welcoming friction.

His hands are in my hair as he groans. I take the opportunity to run my fingertips down his torso, exploring his gorgeous physique over his clothes.

Our simple kiss turns hot and heavy quickly. His hands move to my waist, holding me steady as his hips lift up and push into me, making me gasp at the feel of his cock hitting the most absolute perfect spot to cause shivers all over my body.

We're completely clothed, and yet every move is tangibly erotic. My breasts are heavy, nipples tingling with electricity that rushes down my spine and straight to my core.

We kiss and paw at each other like teenagers until I'm about to combust.

"Do you want to come inside?" I ask, almost coy.

"I do," he says in earnest. "But I won't." He leans his head back against the seat and closes his eyes, frustration evident in the bite of his jaw. His expression says it all. "I'm going to hate myself in a few minutes for doing this, but I should call it a night."

My shoulders fall, as does my face, I'm sure, because the rejection stings.

"Hey." He grips my chin and kisses me again. "I'm putting the brakes on this because I like you, Amy. More than I'm ready to explain. I think this thing between us can go somewhere, and I'm not in a rush. In fact, I want to do everything correctly. If that means going home with an insane case of blue balls, then so be it. I hope I'm explaining this clearly because telling you to go inside without me is the last thing I want to do. But it's the right thing to do."

Well, how can a girl be upset after a declaration like that?

I smile and kiss him again. We don't stop for a while, making out like teenagers who just can't get enough of each other. Because that's how I feel. Like I will never get enough of Sebastian Blake.

It pains me to slide off of him, but I do. He helps me fix my dress and then gets out of the car to open my door.

He walks me to my stoop and kisses my cheek. It's so chaste that it's adorable.

I unlock the door and walk inside when he grabs

me and pulls me back for yet another long, deep kiss after pushing me up against the wall.

"Sweet dreams, Amy."

"Good night."

"Get inside quick because I'm rethinking this decision."

"I'm more than happy to help you rethink it," I tease, but he swats me on the butt, and I yelp in laughter as I rush inside and close the door.

As I stand in my dark, empty kitchen, I can honestly say I've never felt more alive.

It's going to be very easy to fall in love with Sebastian Blake.

Leo

CHAPTER SEVEN

"Someone is smitten." Charity shimmies her hips as we walk down the street.

There's a vendor on the corner, selling flowers. I stop and smell a bouquet of roses. They have a fruity and spicy scent with a bit of moss. So fresh and invigorating, like a certain man.

"What makes you think that?" I ask as I check out the sign to see how much they are.

"You're practically skipping, and you're buying yourself flowers."

I hand cash to the gentleman at the booth and grab a pink bouquet. The smile on my face is huge as I look over at my best friend. "Let's just say, I'm enamored. Punch-drunk," I say and then add, "Hooked!"

Charity stops walking. It takes a second for me to realize she's not by my side. When I turn around, I see her jaw has dropped, and her brows are raised.

"I was wrong. You're not smitten," she says. "You're love-struck."

I roll my eyes. "I'm not there … yet."

"Hell yes, you are. When was the last time you spoke to me about a guy? I'll tell you. It was Hardin, and you were so in love that you moved in with him. You, my friend, are not a kiss-and-tell kind of lady, but I'm going to demand you tell. Because with that goofy expression on your face, you most certainly kissed him."

I smash my lips together and grab her by the arm, bringing my nose close to her face and declaring, "We kissed. Oh my God, did we kiss. It was … amazing."

I'm practically dancing at the memory of just how heated our make-out session became last night. My toes curled, my thighs tingled, and my senses came alive. Today, I feel like the sun is hotter, the sky is brighter, and everything smells extraordinary.

"Does he have a brother? Because I'm ready to drink from whatever fountain you're tasting."

"Sorry. Only child."

"Of course he is." She stops again, holding her arms out to her sides and looking up at the sky when she yells, "What does a girl have to do to meet a good man in this city with a steady job and a semi-decent face, who doesn't want to dip and ditch?!"

I grab her forcefully and pull her to walk again, away from the woman with her dog, staring at us like Charity is a mental patient. "Maybe you need to *ditch* the dating apps."

"And what, start randomly texting guys to see if they're single?"

I shrug. "Worked for me."

She lowers her chin and stares up through curved

brows, as if to say, *Fuck you, Amy, and the white knight you humped last night.*

"Teasing. Kind of. Swiping left and right isn't getting you anywhere. Maybe you need to hit the clubs like Shawn. He always has a girlfriend."

"That's because he's hot."

Now, it's my turn to freeze and face her with a wild expression. "You think Shawn's hot?"

She points a finger at my face. "If you ever tell him that, I'll kill you." With a sway of her hair, she starts to walk again. "That man's ego is already huge."

"I knew you felt something for him."

She waves a hand in dismissal. "No. I was just making a point, and you can't deny that he's not a catch."

"I suppose you're right. He does make a steady paycheck, has more than a semi-decent face, and probably won't ... what was it? Dip and ditch?"

"Mock away, my friend. My standards are starting to become lower and lower. Did you know that in Philly, there's point-seven-six-nine men to every woman? I can't even get a whole man! I have to share a piece of him with some other broad who's also looking for her true love!"

A car drives by and honks at us, the driver screaming obscenities about our butts. We both turn and give him the finger as he rolls on by.

"Where is my Romeo? When am I going to find someone to snuggle and watch movies with? To take me dancing and laugh with?"

Poor Charity. She might come off needy to some, but she's just vulnerable to love. She wants it badly. It breaks my heart for someone so beautiful, successful, and fun to still be on the lookout for her guy.

I snake my arm around her shoulders and pull her in as we stroll. "Tell you what. I'll ask Sebastian if he has any friends. There's a whole law firm of men. I bet he can find someone who has Romeo potential."

She grips my hand that's resting on her shoulder and perks up. "A lawyer, huh? I can definitely go for some courtroom role-play in the bedroom."

I laugh loudly. "That's my girl." I give her the flowers in my hand, which makes her smile in thanks.

Charity takes off for her apartment while I head back to my place. The gym is bustling today, but I sneak into my secret door without a strange look, making sure to lock it behind me since Shawn isn't coming in.

I put on some music and tie my apron on, getting to work on making extra-dark truffles. I grab a cutting board, metal bowl, and Santoku knife. The chocolate bars are in a box on the counter, so I unload the bricks of semisweet chocolate and start chopping it up. The trick to successful truffles is to get the chocolate into very small pieces. The finer the chocolate chunks, the quicker they are to melt.

I'm getting things ready while singing along to the music when there's a ring at the back door. I look at my phone to see a man on my Ring app, holding a bouquet of flowers toward the camera. After I wipe my hands on the side of my apron, I head toward the door to see who it is.

"Delivery for Amy Morgana." He hands a large vase to me with an impressive assortment of sunflowers, and I falter a little, not prepared for how heavy it is.

"Wait one second," I command. I put the vase down on a table and then rush over to my purse to grab money for a tip. I hand it over, and then I close the door behind me and look at the arrangement.

It's covered in cellophane and tissue paper, so I peel away the decoration and remove the card that's stapled onto it.

A little something to brighten your day.
—Sebastian

A giggle escapes my lips. It's so ridiculous since I'm alone, but this guy has totally gotten under my skin in the best way. I place the flowers closer to the window and throw out the excess paper. Then, I snap a picture to send to him.

A beautiful display of flowers just arrived.

Looks like you have an admirer.

Shame for him because I met this very handsome, very loyal lawyer who has whisked me off my feet.

Sounds like a catch.

If not a little cocky. ;-)

I've heard cocky can be very good …

My teeth are gripping my lower lip as I let out a frustrated growl. Sebastian put the brakes on us fooling around, and it's all I can think about. I'm usually not the one who is desperate to jump into bed with a man, but this wild and crazy energy has taken over me lately, and I'm dying to move things to the next level with him.

I'd love to see you tonight.

I'm making truffles … are you interested in trying them?

Death by chocolate and a beautiful woman.

How can I say no?

You can't.

I'll even whip you up my famous lobster bisque.

I'll bring wine.

Make it a champagne blanc.

And I'll come to you. My place isn't the best for company.

Lucky for you, my place is.

See you at eight.

There's a knock at the back door as I slide my phone into my back pocket. I lean over and open it, only to try to close it immediately when I see Hardin on the other side.

"What the hell, Amy?!" Hardin pushes his palm against the door, halting me from closing it fully. "Are you trying to take my hand off?"

I let out a deep, exasperated breath and reluctantly open it up. "You're lucky I haven't tried to cut something else off. What do you want?"

He's standing in the alley, looking devilishly rugged, wearing a black leather jacket over a blue T-shirt, and his dark hair is styled back, which is kinda cute.

"I'm here because Gerry won't return the security deposit."

I balk at the audacity of him coming here with this gripe. He's flustered, too, like he can't imagine why the landlord would hold on to our funds.

"You skipped out on two months' rent."

"So?"

"And you trashed the place!"

"It wasn't trashed. That sink was old as fuck. I called

him and told him it fell off the wall. He's the landlord. He should deal with it."

I place a hand on my hip while the other runs up and down my face, flabbergasted by his reaction. I try to hold back, but I can't.

"You rat bastard!" I've been dying to yell at him. I suppose now is as good a time as any. "Get it through your thick skull that you can't bail out on rent, especially when the lease is in my name. You haven't a clue what I've been through to save my credit from getting destroyed because of your carelessness."

He places his arm on the door and tries to taunt me. "You didn't do a good job. He kept the money."

My hands spread wide, my fingers outstretched, as I shake with how dense he is acting. "Go home, Hardin."

"Not until you give me my half of the security deposit back."

"Why would I pay you?"

"You lived there too."

There's a skillet hanging on the wall. I grab it and lift it, ready to hit him over the head with the steel pan. I'm not really going to hit him—at least, I don't think so. I'm just so angry that I need a physical show of how much I want him to get the hell out.

"You are such an asshole! You cheated on me with the dog walker!" I cock the skillet back like it's a bat ready to crush a ball.

He holds his hands up. "Calm down. You're acting like a lunatic." His dark eyes widen as he backs up a little.

"In my own bed!" I step closer and pull the pan back a few more inches.

"We have a connection. These things just happen."

I move closer and force him back into the alley. "I want my dog back."

"No. Mindy is really attached to her."

I swing the skillet in the air, missing him. It was on purpose, but if I accidentally hit him, I wouldn't be too upset. Mindy, the dog walker, is attached to my dog—that was the straw that broke everything.

"I want Lady Featherington back—now," I demand.

"Not gonna happen."

"Fine. What do you want for her?" I ask, and his hands drop to his sides.

He narrows his eyes and shrugs. "Ten grand."

Of course he'd put a price on her. He doesn't love her nearly as much as I do. She's just a pawn in his game of taking whatever he wants.

"Jerk! You damn well know I don't have that kind of cash."

"Five."

"Are you fucking serious, Hardin?"

"If she means that much to you, you'll figure out a way." He saunters over to his car like a peacock, looking proud of his accomplishment.

The man came here for money. He didn't get it, but he sure seems to think he's gonna get it one way or another.

I can't believe I once loved him. He strolled into my life with a bad joke and a devilish smirk that I fell for like a fool. Our first date was tacos from a food truck, followed by a wild night on the lower east side. We drank and laughed, and I was foolishly led into a life that I thought was filled with love.

He nursed me when I was sick and was there for me

when my grandmother died. My dreams were big, and he never shot them down. Hardin believed in me, and yet … he never helped.

When he needed money to pay off medical bills, I gave him my savings, which had been for a new stove. He bought himself a car instead. He never worked, and yet every time I asked for help on a delivery, he was busy. His friends, his car … the dog walker. Everyone was more important than me. I didn't see it then, but I do now.

He just used me.

I'd rather burn my car to the ground than give him a dime.

Maybe I can kidnap her, I ponder. *I bet Charity would help me.*

No. I shake my head, realizing I'm just not that kind of girl. I should be though. I should go and take what is rightfully mine. Instead, I'm the one who has to do everything the right way. *Damn my parents for raising me right.*

Hardin starts his car and drives away.

I slam the door shut, dead-bolt it, and then hang the skillet back on the wall. While that visit from Hardin was shitty, the sight of Sebastian's flowers sitting in the sunlight, cheerful and happy, brightens my mood.

My shoulders fall, and I breathe a little deeper.

It's good to know there are decent men in the world. At least I know Sebastian Blake won't break my heart.

At least, I hope he won't.

Don't let me down, Sebastian.

CHAPTER EIGHT

Knowing how Sebastian dresses and after seeing his office, I assumed his apartment would be in a luxury high-rise. I'm a little surprised to see he lives in a brownstone in Rittenhouse Square.

I walk up the stone steps and look for his name on the directory for the proper bell to ring. Only there is no directory. Just a lone doorbell. I ring it and wait.

He appears at the door, looking as dapper as ever. His dress pants are still on from a day at the office, and his shirt is buttoned up with his tie tight. Those chocolate eyes are molten, serious, taking my breath away.

"Am I dressed appropriately?" I motion to my jeans and beige sweater with a suede-and-metal buckle on the collar.

He stares at me for a beat before giving a closed-mouth smile. "Yes, of course. You look great. I just got home. Much later than I had hoped. Something came up, so I had to meet a friend, and the time got away from me."

I follow him into the vestibule, which leads right into a living room with beautiful, intricate woodwork. There's a staircase to the left and a kitchen in the far back.

"This is your place?" I surmise. Obviously, it's his place. He invited me over. I'm just shocked because everyone else I know who lives in a brownstone rents a floor. "I've never known anyone who lived in a full brownstone before."

"Yeah. It's a lot of home, but I like the space."

"It's extraordinary. The ceiling moldings are gorgeous."

"Thanks." He hands me a glass of white wine that he grabbed from the kitchen and brought back to me quickly. "I had a company come in and renovate the space back to its original architecture. The last owner had wallpaper everywhere. Pastel pink and golds. It was … interesting."

I giggle as I brush my hair behind my ear. "I'm sure it was a sight to see."

He's staring at me, smiling, yet there's almost a hint of sullenness behind his eyes. "I'm going to get changed. Make yourself at home."

A gray dog about twice the size as Lady Featherington comes running up to me and places his paws on my knees.

"Duke, down," Sebastian commands in his deep vibrato, but I wave him off.

"That's okay. I love dogs." I rub Duke's head and say hello to him. "You are a very handsome gentleman, Duke. Hopefully soon, I'll have a friend for you to play with."

I grin up at Sebastian, who is staring at me with a blank expression. I raise a brow and tilt my head. He gives me a small smile in return and then jogs up the stairs.

I rise, Duke at my heels, and take a moment to familiarize myself with Sebastian's home. The walls are cream with walnut moldings and millwork throughout. His couches are leather, but there's softness to the space from added throw blankets, pillows, and a wingback recliner in the corner, next to a built-in bookcase.

The fireplace is in the center of the room with a mantel full of photos—Sebastian with his father at a football game in one frame, he and his mother on a beach in another. There are various family and friends in other pictures. From the smiles on their faces to the way their arms are around each other, the laughter, and even the one of him dancing with a group of people, it's easy to see he's a family man. Someone who loves and is very much loved.

I bring my tote bag into the kitchen and place my wineglass on the granite. I brought the soup in a giant Tupperware, so I search through the cabinets for a pot to warm it up in. In minutes, I have the bisque heating, and I'm taking the makings for a Caesar salad out of my bag.

It's nice, being in Sebastian's house. He has a candle burning and music playing low. I take a sip of my wine while I add all of the ingredients into a porcelain bowl I found.

Once everything is in place, I lean back on the counter and start to wonder where Sebastian ran off to, as I assume men can change out of work clothes pretty fast. I take a second to see if I hear a shower running, but there's nothing.

Just when I'm about to start heading his way, I hear footsteps coming down the stairs, so I pick up the spoon to make it look like I was busy and not sitting here, thinking I should go search for him.

"Sorry that took so long. I, um …" He clears his throat. "You seem to have made yourself at home."

"I know my way around a kitchen, so I was able to find all I needed."

His eyes crinkle as he steps toward me, placing one hand on my hip and pulling me into him with his other splayed on my back.

"I'm really glad you're here," he breathes as he leans down to briefly kiss me.

His lips are warm, his hands firm, yet there's a pause in his purpose. There's something different about this kiss. Our last was pure lust and passion. This isn't an invitation, like I felt before from him. It almost feels like a question.

If he has to wonder how I feel, then I'm not showing him enough. How we ended our date had nothing to do with alcohol or horniness. It was all him, and I want every inch of what he has to give me, as I plan to give him every inch of me.

I wrap my arms around his neck, bringing him closer to me. My chest is pressed up against his firm one. My fingers dance in his hair and work their way down the side of his neck and glide onto his pecs. I bounce on my toes, lightly lining my groin up with his, moving up and down ever so gracefully, so he knows exactly what I want from him tonight.

He kisses me long and hard, the kind of kiss that leaves me breathless.

Until, suddenly, he pulls away.

"We're going to burn the soup," he says.

I pause in question and then turn back to the stove, where my bisque is still on a low simmer. "Oh. Yeah. It's okay. I don't have it too high. But it's probably ready. Can you grab some bowls?"

He walks over to a cabinet on the other side of the kitchen. His side profile is on display as he grabs the bowls. I look for that dimple, the one I've come to adore, but I haven't seen it since I got here tonight.

"How was the rest of your day?" I ask, seeing if I can get a glimpse into his mood.

He said he got home late tonight. Maybe a horrible client has his mind distracted.

He fumbles with the bowls, nearly dropping one of them. "Almost had a chance to show off my juggling skills for you," he jokes awkwardly.

I let out a heavy breath, feeling like something's up. He smiles lightly, and it relaxes me a little.

"You know how to juggle?"

"I have a few party tricks up my sleeve."

I smile and stir the soup, talking loudly as he walks into the dining room with the bowls, "Perhaps after dinner, you can show off a bit. I've never met a man who could juggle, aside from the performers near the carousel in the summer. Shawn loves to walk over and is just dying for the day they drop something. I keep saying he's wasting his time, but I think the guy is just a giant kid who wants to watch the performers without admitting he likes them."

I laugh at my own remark, and it trails off into silence. My long tirade goes without a response.

I set the spoon I'm stirring with down and walk into the dining room. Sebastian is standing near the table with his hands on the back of a chair. I watch as he takes a deep breath. His back is arched as his head faces down.

"Everything okay?" I ask, placing my hand on his arm.

He looks up, seeming surprised that I'm standing here. His face is drawn, and his eyes have lost a little of that sparkle. He stands up tall at the sight of me and gives a sad smile.

"Sorry. I have a lot on my mind," he says, not in the sure tone he normally has.

I take a step away and stand near another chair. "If you had a shit day at the office, I don't want to pry, but I hope you know I'm here if you need to vent."

A small smile graces his lips as he takes a large breath in and then exhales deeply. I wait as he stares over into my eyes. He's not just looking; he's searching, seeking something from this connection we share, yet I'm not sure what he needs from me.

"Do you …" I point toward the front door. "Do you want me to go? It's okay if—"

"I don't want you to go." He takes a step toward me and grabs my hand.

"Okay. Then, what's going on?" I tilt my head to the side and place my hand on his cheek.

His jaw has a light stubble that is coarse under the pad of my thumb. I lean into him, making sure he knows I'm here if he needs to talk.

His chest rises and falls.

He drops his head.

He grips my hand tighter while his other weaves into my hair as he caresses my face.

"It's been a long time since I've felt the kind of connection we have, especially this soon into a relationship. Last night, at dinner and then at the club"—he closes his eyes, tilting his head to the side, smiling before opening them back up and looking at me—"that was the best date I'd had in years."

I return his grip, pulling him into me. "I feel the same way. In fact, I wanted to jump your bones last night. You're the one who stopped it." I try to lighten the mood.

He lets out a soft chuckle and stands up straight, glancing down at me so I can see his face. "I kicked myself the entire way home for doing that."

"Is that what this sudden mood change is about? Do you think we're moving too fast? Are you not used to these kinds of feelings?"

He closes his eyes and takes a deep inhale before opening them again. "Opposite really. This is what— *you* are what—I've always wanted in my life."

There's a pause, and I lean back, realizing I'm about to get a *but* thrown in my face. Every second that passes, my stomach knots even more, like it's wringing out a towel and every last drop is being expelled with nothing else left to give.

"I got a call today," he finally says as he drops my hands, making the words he just said sting even though I have no idea what they mean.

I step back, realizing there's no reason for me to still be this close to him. "Is everything all right?"

He raises his eyebrows in a wishy-washy way as he takes an inhale. "Yes. No." He shrugs. "It all depends."

I place my hands on the table behind me, needing to do something with them. This feels like a very intense conversation, yet I barely know this guy. "Depends on what?"

"I got a call from my ex-girlfriend."

My breath hitches. There's only one reason why a man would let a woman know he got a call from an ex-girlfriend. At dinner, he made it seem like his last relationship had fizzled out. From the look on his face, there's clearly unfinished business. She wants to get back together, and he's willing.

As a woman who has already been cheated on, I'm not ready to hear the words he's about to say.

He hesitates for a second before standing tall, lifting his chin, and declaring, "She's pregnant."

Okay. Maybe there are two reasons he'd get a call from an ex. I did not see that coming.

I purse my lips as I take a slow inhale through my nose, letting those two words wash over me.

"I take it, the baby is yours?"

He nods. "I would never question a woman who says the baby she's carrying is mine."

"Oh no, I didn't mean it like that. I just … I don't know. I guess it's just the normal question people ask." I let out a nervous laugh and run my hand along my head, feeling like an insensitive jerk. "How far along is she?"

"Fifteen weeks."

"And she's just telling you now?" My tone is anything but coy or non-accusatory. Fifteen weeks is a hell of a long time to hang on to a bomb of information like that.

He nods with a grimace. If he's upset at her for keeping the news from him for this long, he's not letting on. "She wasn't sure if she wanted to keep it."

"I hope, at this point, she's keeping it."

He nods again, and my stomach drops.

I finally meet the man of my dreams, and he's having a baby with another woman.

There's a rapid uptick in my heart, and my hands get clammy. I'm nervous, and I'm not sure why. I think it's because I'm unsure of my own feelings in this very moment, and I don't know how to process them.

A baby.

With his ex-girlfriend.

Sebastian is going to be a father.

I twist my lips to the side, biting on the inside as I will myself not to show how upset, albeit confused, I feel.

He backs up to the wall and lets his weight crash against it. His head rolls back as he looks up at the ceiling.

"She's scared," he says. "Anxious. She didn't know if she wanted to be a mom on her own. She's a career woman. Bright, intelligent, and climbing the corporate ladder. She's also the type who has a plan. Marriage was part of it. She called this afternoon and asked me to come by. She wanted to know what I thought she should do." He lowers his head and grins. "I told her I want the baby. I can't let her terminate my child or raise it without my full support. I promised that I would be there for her every step of the way. Monetarily, physically, emotionally. I'm all in."

All in.

I swallow hard, trying not to let the tears that are building behind my eyes fall. "Does this mean …" I start to ask but am unsure exactly what I'm asking.

He steps closer to me and holds out his hands, and then he drops them in surrender. "It means, I spent the entire day walking around Philadelphia, feeling a mixture of anger, excitement, confusion, and elation. And I came to the realization that I'm happy. It might not be what I expected, but life doesn't go as planned."

"That's good." I give him a shaky smile. I feel like a fool for wanting to ask, but I do it anyway. "Do you want to be with her?"

He sighs. "No, I don't, and I feel like an asshole, saying that."

"You're not an asshole for being honest. Is she the girl you told me about at the bar? Who you dated for six months but she wanted to see other people?"

"She is. We went our separate ways. It wasn't like some big blowup or anything. There just wasn't that spark."

I look into his eyes, and I see that spark he's talking about. That's what we have. It's bright and powerful. Magnetic even. But sparks fade if there's nothing there to burn.

"So, what are you going to do?" I ask.

"I'm gonna be there for Lauren," he says without skipping a beat.

I have to respect him for that. No matter how much I wish this weren't the case, it is.

"She's having my baby, and I'm going to be there for my child."

Lauren. The ex has a name. It's a pretty name. A pretty name for a girl who is having who I hoped was my boyfriend's baby.

A baby.

Wow, I can say the word in my head over and over, and it just feels surreal. If Lauren waited this long to tell him, she must have been distraught over the decision. I'm sure it didn't come lightly and that she had many sleepless nights filled with anxiety. I don't envy her for the decision she had to make, but I respect her for the willingness to be a single mother. She's going to need all the support she can get. And the best support would be from the father of her child.

"What does this mean for us?" I ask, not sure if I want to hear the answer.

He sighs. "That's up to you. Amy, I want you to know a huge part of my day included thinking about you. What we have and where it's going. I'm trying to figure out how to make sense of it all. How I can explore this thing between us and be a father." He pauses and blinks a few times as he straightens his back and smiles a full-dimpled grin. "Holy shit, I'm going to be a father."

This tiny burst of energy comes out of him with that revelation. It's sweet even though it makes my heart sink a little.

That smile softens as he looks at me in earnest. "I don't want to lose you. I really want to see where this goes, but I understand that this is a lot of baggage. When we met, I didn't realize I'd be a package deal."

I almost want to laugh. His honesty is so forthcoming. My dear, wonderful, loyal Sebastian is laying his cards out on the table. He's going to be a father with another woman, and if I want to keep this relationship going with him, then I have to accept it.

I haven't even slept with the man. I don't know his favorite color or how he likes his eggs in the morning, but I have to make a decision right now if I want to be part of his new little family.

It's endearing and crazy, all at the same time. He's doing the right thing, and damn if that isn't sexy. But there's a woman who needs him right now. A woman who is carrying his child. If I didn't text him that day, he'd probably still be with her tonight, consoling her, helping her … maybe even seeing if he could love her at some point.

I search around the room, wondering how my night went from so high to so low in a matter of seconds.

"This is a lot to take in," I finally say. My mouth feels like cotton.

"I completely understand." He holds up his hands, like he's not trying to push.

I walk back to the kitchen and glance at the soup that I was so looking forward to, but I've totally lost my appetite now.

"Maybe I should go," I say as I grab my bag that I brought everything in.

"You don't have to."

He reaches for me, but I step back. Not because I don't want Sebastian to touch me—I do—but if I let him, I'll just lose myself in him, his scent, his kisses.

"No. I should." My words are abrupt.

His eyes widen in surprise by my dismissal. My intention was not to come off that way.

I lower my shoulders and take a deep breath, staring

up into his soulful eyes. "Sebastian, I'm happy for you. You're going to be a father, and that is probably the coolest thing in the world. This is just a shock to me, and that's a problem because this isn't my story. It's yours and Lauren's, and you don't need me to crowd up the emotional pool I'm sure you're swimming in right now."

I lick my lips and continue, "And the truth is, I'm crazy about you. Like, wildly insane about you. Earlier, you said you've never felt this connection. Neither have I, and it's amazing, but, you see, I just had a broken heart, and I'm still mending myself over that."

"I don't want to hurt you." He takes a timid step toward me.

"I know you don't. And I don't believe you would—intentionally. This news of yours is big and exciting, and you need to focus on that. I want you to take the time to figure out what you want without thinking about me. If there is any chance you and Lauren want to be a family, I don't want to get in the way of that."

"I don't want to be with her. Our relationship is over."

"You say that now, but just give it a minute and make sure that being with her isn't what you want in the end. It's better to put the brakes on this thing between us while it's still fresh instead of possibly ending it later with someone getting hurt."

His brow furrows, and there's hesitation in his breath. I watch as his hands slide in his pockets.

His head bows down, and he nods with a heavy exhale. "If that's what you think is best."

I purse my lips and nod. "Okay, well … thank you

again for helping me with my old landlord. I really appreciate it."

"You're welcome." His tone is laced with formality. "Here, I'll walk you out."

"No. Um, don't worry about it. I'll let myself out if that's okay with you."

He steps back. His smile is turned down, and for a moment, I want to run over to him, but I don't.

I meant what I said. A heart will surely be broken, and I'm afraid it will be mine.

"Congratulations," I say when I get to the door. "The baby is lucky to have such a wonderful man as his or her father."

He smiles lightly.

I'm gonna miss that dimple. God, I'm gonna miss this man.

"Thanks."

I close the door behind me and rush down the stairs. If I thought breaking things off with Sebastian was going to save me from getting hurt, I was mistaken. It's only been a moment, and my entire soul feels like it's been shattered.

Leo

CHAPTER NINE

One of the positive aspects—or drawbacks, depending on how you look at it—of being a chocolatier is, there are definitely busier times than others. With Easter approaching, our orders were through the roof. Shawn and I were working harder than we had over the past few weeks. Now that the day is here, I kind of wish I had more orders to fill to get me out of going to spend Easter with my family.

Or at least, a good excuse to be late.

Don't get me wrong; I absolutely love my family, but being the only one without a significant other leaves a certain spotlight shone on a stage I didn't plan on performing on. If it's not my career they're harping on, my love life never fails to come up in conversation, and I get to hear everyone's opinion whether or not I want it.

I pull up to my parents' house, grab the chocolates I brought as gifts for everyone, and head up to the door.

"Auntie!" my gorgeous niece Kelsey says as she runs

up to me, her pigtails swaying as she wraps her arms around my legs.

I place my bag of chocolates and my purse on the floor to pick her up. "Look at how big you've gotten!" I hug her tightly and then lean back to see her more clearly. Big blue eyes like mine, platinum-blonde hair like Heather's, and a silly grin that matches most of the Morgana clan.

"I've grown! Mommy measured me, and I was a whole inch bigger than last time."

"A whole inch?!" I say dramatically.

"Yep. She even had to get me new pants because mine were all too short."

My sister Heather appears in the hallway, looking beautiful with her growing baby bump. "Yeah, she still had pants with tags on them. Thank goodness I kept the receipt, so I was able to take them back to get the bigger size," she says, lifting my tote from the floor, rifling through the boxes. "Which one is mine?"

Grabbing the bag by the handle, I pull it toward me. "Straight to the good stuff, huh?" I tease as I put Kelsey down. I find her box of four perfect truffles and hand it to her.

"Yes! This is the ultimate benefit of having a sister who makes chocolate. Especially when pregnancy cravings are through the roof." She rubs her belly.

Instantly, I think of Sebastian.

It's been weeks since I walked out of his place. That was the hardest thing I'd ever done, and a day hasn't gone by that I don't wonder what would have happened if I'd stayed. I keep telling myself that I did the right thing. He needs to make a decision about his new family without thinking about me.

I place my hand on my sister's belly, hoping to feel my nephew kick. "Is he active today?"

"When is he not active? This kid is going to be up all night the first few months, I can tell. I'm lucky my maternity leave will roll right into summer break because there's no way I'd be able to stay up all night and then get to the school by six in the morning."

I kneel down, eye-level with her belly, and talk to the baby, "Are you already giving your mommy a hard time?"

He kicks me, and a huge smile spreads across my face.

"He's a kicker!"

"Told you. And I still have another month to go."

I grab my purse from the floor and rise. "Maybe Dad will finally get that soccer player he's been dreaming of. The other four grandsons don't look so promising."

She giggles as she pops a truffle in her mouth. "You said it, not me."

I hand Kelsey a chocolate bar I designed with her name on it. She squeals as she runs off, and Heather wobbles into the kitchen with me right behind her.

"Look who finally made it!" my other sister, Fiona, says. "How is it the only one who has no one else to get ready is the one who arrives last?"

"I've been busy. People were still calling for last-minute orders this morning," I defend myself as I shrug off my coat and place it on the back of a chair at the kitchen table.

"Leave my baby alone. She's working hard during

this holiday," my mom says as she pulls me toward her for a hug.

I might hate being the youngest on most days, but being Mom's "baby" still has its perks in the form of love and affection.

"Thanks, Mama. At least someone around here stands up for me." I stick my tongue out at Fiona and then place my bag on the table, looking for the biggest box of them all. It's a mix of ganache and pralines—Mom's favorite. "Hide these before Heather sees them. I think she's already inhaled her truffles."

Mom laughs with a wave in the air. "I'll put a few on the side for her. She's probably the only one who deserves to eat them with that basketball she's carrying around."

I toss Fiona her box, but she doesn't act as excited as Heather did. "I got you a house plant," she states with a hand on her hip. "I'd have gotten you an Easter lily, like everyone else, but you don't have a yard, like the rest of us."

I take a deep breath while smiling. "Where's the rest of the family? It's so quiet."

"Henry and Dad set up an Easter egg hunt for the kids. I swear they forgot just how young everyone is because they hid those things like they were hiding them from adults. The kids are still searching," Fiona says.

"Or"—Mom points her knife at Fiona—"they're super smart, and they knew it would keep the kids occupied while I finished up the food."

I nod, raising my eyebrows. "She's got a point."

Matthew walks in through the back door and

barrels into the kitchen, already talking. "They've only found half the eggs. It's a good thing Dad counted how many they hid."

Mom puts down her knife that she was cutting some onions with. "They'd better not leave any in my yard. Those hard plastic shells will ruin my lawn mower. You know Daddy doesn't pay attention when he's doing yard work."

"Don't worry. Henry has a diagram with every place he hid an egg. The guy is anal retentive, even when it comes to a damn egg hunt," he says, and we all laugh. Matthew walks over and gives me a hug. "Hey, little sis. How's life?"

"Busy. Hopefully, the pace keeps up past the holiday. I'm trying to drum up Mother's Day orders already."

"Don't overwhelm yourself just because you're trying to get over that jerk off, Hardin," Fiona drones.

"That guy was such a tool. Weak-ass arms too," Matthew adds.

"He had a cute face, but the whole emo thing was lame," Fiona says.

Mom interjects while stirring the caramelized onions, "Amy went on a great date with a lawyer."

I don't miss the way her tone inflects to a higher pitch at the end or how Matthew and Fiona stop and gape at me in surprise.

I pick up a grape from the plate sitting out with cheese and crackers and chew. When I don't answer, my mom looks back to me, like she, too, is waiting for a reply. Mom sighs like she's sad for me while Matthew and Fiona practically roll their eyes.

"He was great. It was going really well with the few

dates we had. Until his ex-girlfriend called and told him she was pregnant," I say matter-of-factly.

"That is so your luck," Fiona says as she slaps her hand on the counter in amusement.

"Yep." I pop another grape, not amused.

"Did he go back to her?" Mom asks.

"I don't know. He said he wanted to be a dad and would support her—"

"As he should," Matthew chimes in.

I nod in agreement. "They broke up a few months before because they didn't really have that spark, and it was a mutual breakup, so I'm not sure what they'll do."

"You haven't spoken to him since, right?" Matthew asks.

"I told him I wanted him to make up his mind about trying to be a family without having to worry about me."

"Figures." Matthew leans against the counter and crosses his arms. I look at him in challenge. He accepts and finishes his thought. "You always pick losers."

"Do not!"

Fiona shrugs. "And you always want to run back to them, even when they screw up."

"He didn't really screw up. He got her pregnant before we met and is doing the right thing by her."

"Ditch the dude, Amy." Matthew kicks off the counter and holds his hands out in explanation. "Unless you want to be the next chick pregnant with some guy as your baby daddy. That's how these guys operate. They just spread their seed all over Philly."

I raise a hand for him to stop. "First, that's disgusting, and second, he isn't like that at all. He's a decent man with a good heart."

"Just calling it like I see it. You deserve better than these douchebags," he states.

I drop my shoulders and then take his box of truffles from my bag and throw it at him, which he catches with one hand.

"Those are for you and your wife to share. Although I should just give them to her since she doesn't give me a hard time about my love life."

He walks over and kisses me on my cheek. "This is what big brothers are for. How are you not used to it by now?"

He walks through the back door, and I blow a vibrating breath through my lips.

"Maybe if you just let us set you up, you'd meet some nice guys," Fiona says as she leans on the center island.

I can't imagine the grief I'd get if a date of mine ran to my siblings and dished about all the reasons the date didn't go well for them. And Lord knows, I'd never hear the end of it if it did go well and I just wasn't interested.

"Thanks, but I'm good. And busy. I have a business to run. When my loan comes through, things are going to explode for me. You just watch," I say with an upbeat smile because Amy Morgana Chocolatier is the love of my life right now. As sad as that might be.

"Suit yourself. Just remember, when you're old and gray, those chocolates won't love you back." Fiona walks out of the kitchen and toward the bathroom.

I close my eyes and place my fingers along my temple.

Mom walks up and rubs my back. "I'm sorry, sweetheart. You'll find a good guy one of these days."

I smile even though it physically hurts to do so.

Sebastian is a good guy, and now, he's going to have a family with another woman and not me. I know it's petty of me to be upset, but I'm still bitter.

"Maybe I'm just destined to be alone," I say out loud and instantly regret it as I see the frown on my mom's face.

The back door swings open and slams into the wall, causing us to look as Luke, Fiona's son, comes bustling in. "Look what I got!" He holds up the basket that's almost bigger than him.

"Let me see." I rush around the counter and kneel down to his level. "Wow, good job, buddy. Which one's your favorite?" I ask, checking them all out.

He places the basket down and grabs the bright blue one. "This one. It's my favorite color."

"Ooh," I singsong. "I do like that one. What about this pink one? Can I have the pink one?"

He sighs, and his shoulders sag, so I pinch his little tummy.

"What's that expression all about?"

"Mom keeps saying I have to learn to share. So"—he sighs overdramatically—"I guess you can have it."

Mom and I laugh out loud.

"It's okay, little man. You can keep it." I kiss his tiny cheek, and he grins from ear to ear. "Here, I have something for your very admirable attempt at sharing." I hand him his chocolate bar, and his eyes widen.

Fiona walks back into the kitchen, and Luke holds up his chocolate to show her and then his basket of eggs.

"You did good, Luke. What about your brother? Did you help him find any?"

"Yeah. He has a few in his basket."

"Just a few?" Fiona asks with her hands on her hips.

He shrugs. "I don't know. I was too focused on my stuff. I'll go look." He turns and races to the backyard with his basket in hand.

Fiona sighs as she stands. "I'd better go check to make sure. God forbid one gets more than the other."

Mom and I are alone again in the kitchen. She's still giving me that concerned look, so I plaster a huge smile on my face.

"I'll be back. I have some very special deliveries to make."

I walk outside and see all of my nieces and nephews in their Easter outfits, running through the yard. There's nothing like the joy on a child's face to make you forget about all of life's troubles.

My nieces and nephews have been the brightest parts of my life since each of them was born. I'm lucky we all live in or around Philadelphia. Being able to see them hit their milestones and to be an important part of their life are all that matters to me … even if they only love me because I spoil them rotten with chocolate. I'm okay with being cool Aunt Amy who fills their bellies with high-end chocolate.

While I'd like to have a family of my own someday, I'm thankful I have these little monsters in my life to fill the gaps. My family isn't half-bad either. Except at times like these when I walk outside and see my four siblings and their spouses staring at me like I'm covered in head-to-toe glitter.

I give them a wave. "Hey, guys. Happy Easter."

Henry is the first to speak. "Hey, Amy. Matt told us your boyfriend got some other girl pregnant."

LOYAL LAWYER

Yeah, they're not half-bad.
Half being the operative word.

CHAPTER TEN

I'm just about to exit my office when I hear my phone ringing. Seeing Hardin's number on my screen is not the way I like to start my morning. I consider sending it to voice mail but know that he'll just hang up and dial right back. It was my biggest pet peeve when we were together. If I didn't answer his first phone call, he would dial me again and again until I did. Why would anything be different now?

I swipe the call to answer. "Yes?"

"Why do I have a lawyer calling me?" he spits out.

I shake my head while staring up at the ceiling, wondering why I ever loved this man.

"I don't know. Maybe the landlord is suing you personally. Maybe you finally did something dumb enough to get caught. Who knows? Why would you call me?"

"Because they said it has to do with you."

My mind wanders to Sebastian, but I have no idea why. It's been a month since I walked out of his

107

apartment, and we've had zero contact since that night.

"Are we being sued?" I ask in concern.

"No. I am!"

I sigh in relief that it's not our old landlord. Then, I remember that him getting hit up in a lawsuit serves him right. Bastard. "Maybe Karma has finally caught up with you."

"You had to have done something, Amy, because I'm supposed to go for a deposition or some shit."

"Then, get a lawyer and stop bothering me, Hardin. Ask your girlfriend for help."

"She doesn't know about this. She'll be devastated."

My mouth tilts up a little at the thought of Mindy being up and disappointed because of Hardin. "Surprised she's not used to it already."

"Amy, you have to—"

"I don't have to do anything for you, Hardin. I mean it when I say, I have absolutely no idea what you're talking about. Get a fucking lawyer and stop bothering me!"

I hang up, and for once, it feels amazing. I think that's the first time I've hung up on him. I only wish it were like the old days that you see in '80s movies, where they get to actually slam down the phone and then leave it off the hook for hours so the busy tone rings in the person's ear. Hitting the End button doesn't have anywhere near as much physical satisfaction as I hoped, but emotionally, I feel pretty powerful.

I let out a huff and open my office door, only to see both Shawn and Charity sitting on the other side of it, staring at me, waiting for me to say something.

"What?" I ask as I walk by, acting like nothing was just going on.

"She asks *what*," Charity says in disbelief to Shawn and then turns to me. "We heard you talking to somebody about a lawyer. Who was that?"

I ignore them as I tie an apron on. "It was Hardin."

"Ew. Why is he calling?" she asks.

"He said a lawyer called him and thought I had something to do with it. He's such a jerk. You know, I've tried calling him at least fifty times this month about my dog. He won't answer my calls, and I don't even know where he lives. If I did, I'd be there every night, demanding he give me my dog back."

"Like you did after you first broke up? That dude pretended he wasn't home just to avoid answering his door," Shawn says.

"Exactly. And now, he calls, acting like I owe him a favor."

Charity takes a seat on her stool. "We were hoping you were talking to Sebastian."

Shawn spoons melted chocolate into molding trays. "Correction: Charity was hoping you were talking to Sebastian. I was just trying to ask what color you wanted these chocolate squares accented with when Miss Thing here stopped me, so she could be nosy."

Charity shrugs like what he said is true and she isn't afraid to admit it.

I look down at the order form that says the squares should be accented in pink chocolate, but we have about seven shades of pink. I walk to a supply cabinet and grab the red food coloring. "Hot pink looks the best. I'll start melting the white chocolate to dye for the design."

Shawn and I continue working while Charity sits there, drumming her fingers along the steel counter.

"Sorry to burst your bubble, but that definitely wasn't Sebastian," I finally admit.

She leans her arms down. "Still no word from him, huh?"

I take a breath and stir. I think this is the tenth time she's asked me this. It almost feels like she's more heartbroken than I am. I mean, yes, I'm still sad over him because I really felt like we had a connection, but Charity is legit crushed over the fact that we broke it off. I get the feeling he was her last hope of finding a good guy. Like, if I found one as great as Sebastian, then she would too. I hate that I broke that last glimmer she had left.

"If he hasn't called, then it must mean he's happy, and that's all that matters, right?"

"That's bullshit. You were on cloud nine when you were with him."

"We went on a few dates." I laugh to myself. Crazy to think that's all it was. It felt like a hundred.

"And it was fucking awesome!" she declares. "You should have stayed at his place. Giving him the out to be with his ex was a foolish move. I bet he would have chosen you."

I shake my head. "That's something I would never feel right about. Doesn't mean it doesn't suck though."

She pouts because she knows I'm right. "What about you, Shawn? Anyone new in your life to make both of us jealous over?"

I take my time to look at Charity while she's turned to Shawn, waiting for his answer. I've seen the way she's been checking him out more and more, and if I'm not mistaken, I think she has a little something for him. And the way she said *jealous*, I think that means more than she's implying.

Shawn gets a shit-eating grin on his face, which means he got laid last night.

"You didn't!" we both yell in unison.

"Where'd you meet this one?" Charity asks, and I sense that jealousy even more.

"Her name is Victory," he says, and we both look up. "I shit you not. And believe me, it was one hell of a victory for me."

"Oh God," I say as Charity rolls her eyes.

"Kind of disappointed. There's no way to misspell Victory but you still got the Y in," she says with an eye roll.

Shawn laughs. "Wanna bet? V-I-C-T-O-R-I-E."

Charity and I laugh hard at that. Leave it to Shawn to find the girls with the odd-spelled names.

"Her parents' names were Victor and Torie or some shit like that, so they did one of those mash-ups. And I don't want to hear it. The girl was on fire, and I just might be in love with this one."

My phone rings, so I wipe my hands on my apron. "Shawn, can you watch that chocolate for me?"

My phone is still on my office desk, so I look at it and the 215 area code on the screen. I answer the unknown call. "This is Amy."

"Miss Morgana, it's Miles, Mr. Blake's assistant."

My breath hitches as my eyes shoot up to meet with Charity's as she sits in the kitchen, looking at me in my office.

"Um, hi. Yes. How can I help you?"

"Mr. Blake would like to set up a time to meet with you, Mr. Hardin Reynolds, and his attorney, if he brings one. I have a few openings the last week of the month, but if you want something sooner, there is limited availability next week."

"I don't understand."

Miles pauses for a beat. "I'm here to assist you. What do you need help understanding?"

How do I explain to this guy who worships the ground his boss walks on that I broke it off with him because he's having a baby with another lady?

"Sebastian and I aren't working together anymore."

"That's surprising. He told me today to set up this meeting. It's concerning a dog and some artwork that are your possessions that he's been working on getting back."

Charity heads toward me and moves her hands, as if to say, *Please tell me what's going on.*

I turn around to try to focus on my conversation instead of her. While placing my hand over my eyes, I let out a sigh. I don't know what to think about this. It's been a month of not one word from Sebastian, and then I get this phone call. I didn't even know he could legally do something to help me get my dog back. My sweet dog.

"Miss Morgana? Are you still there?" Miles asks.

"Yeah, sorry. I guess I'm just surprised, is all. Please tell Sebastian thank you, but no, thank you. I don't want to take up any more of his time."

"Are you sure? He said it's all pro bono, no charge involved."

Am I sure? No. I want Lady Featherington back like crazy. It's been months since I last saw her, and having her picture on my screen saver isn't enough to stop me from missing my girl.

While I want her, I just don't think taking more from Sebastian is right. He already helped me with my financial trouble.

"Yeah, I'm sure. Please tell him I appreciate the offer."

"Well, okay then. I guess I can call Mr. Reynolds back and—"

"Don't do that. Just let him sit on it for a while. Hardin can afford to sweat it out."

I hear a slight chuckle on the other end of the line.

"As you wish. Have a great rest of your day."

We hang up, and I feel just a little bit better about hearing how they are the ones who called him earlier. I like the idea of having Hardin thinking he's in legal trouble. Let him stew on that fact for a little while.

I turn around to see Charity staring at me, wide-eyed.

"I'm definitely not making it up this time. Was that who I think it was?"

"No. Not exactly. It was Sebastian's assistant, calling to set up a meeting. He wants to sue Hardin for my dog and the painting."

"And you turned him down?" she asks, exasperated.

I drop my head back and stare up at the ceiling. "What's the point? Lady Featherington probably wouldn't even remember me—it's been so long since I've seen her. And really, what am I supposed to do with a dog in here? I'm sure it would break all kinds of health

113

code rules. Where would I keep her until I have a real place to live?"

"I don't know. We would figure it out because he does not deserve to keep her—that's for damn sure. Stop acting like such a defeatist. This is not my best friend, Amy, speaking. This is some other chick who's throwing in the towel!"

"I'm being practical."

"This is about Sebastian because my best friend wouldn't let her ex walk away with anything that is hers without a fight."

I sag my shoulders. "Fine. I admit, I don't want to see Sebastian again. He's probably back together with his ex, and it would hurt to see that."

"Girl, you need to get your dog, get your art, and get your man."

"No!" I demand. "I'm not going to tell you anything if you keep throwing my feelings back in my face."

My phone dings with an incoming text, so I flip it over in my hand to see Sebastian's text.

Please don't let what happen between us stop you from getting what is rightfully yours.

I turn my screen, so Charity can see.

"Oh my God! See, let him help you!" she squeals. "He obviously wants to see you again, or he wouldn't be giving you or this case the time of day."

Ignoring her, I text him back.

I really appreciate the offer, but I don't want to take up more of your time.

Charity reads what I'm typing as I type it and lets out a breath as she chastises me, "Put your pride aside and get back what's yours."

I told you, I want to help you.

That hasn't changed.

Don't let this asshole get away with this.

Charity reads what he texted and then says, "Exactly! I agree one hundred percent."

As I mull over the idea in my head some more, my phone rings with Hardin calling—yet again.

I swipe the call with a scowl on my face. "I thought I asked you to stop bothering me," I say as my greeting.

"Yeah, well, I spoke to the law firm, and now, I know you're lying to me. What the hell, Amy? Are you really suing me for our dog? How fucking petty are you?"

"Excuse me?"

"You heard me. It's been a few months. Get over it and move on. There's no need to obsess over me and our relationship this way. I know you loved me, but this is a pitiful way to get my attention. I'm sorry, but I'm not coming back to you."

My jaw drops open, and I gasp. *The nerve of this asshole.* "No, you listen to me. This has nothing to do with you. I want my dog and my painting back, and if you don't give in to my demands, well then, I'll see your ass in court!" *Damn, I've always wanted to say that.*

I hang up on him for the second time today, but this one feels one thousand percent better. *Screw him.* If he wants to act like that, then I will do everything in my power to fight his ass for what is mine.

I text Sebastian back.

Never mind.

He's an asshole, and you're right.

Let's do this.

CHAPTER ELEVEN

Miles is waiting to greet me as I arrive at the building where Blake, Fields, and Moore is located. My heels clank in the vast rotunda as I saunter in, wearing my smartest black pencil skirt and blazer. It's my armor to show Hardin I mean business.

"Miss Morgana, nice to see you again. Please, follow me."

We head up the see-through elevator and into a small conference room with glass on two sides. Through one side of glass is the hallway we walked down. On the other is another conference room, larger in size. It's the one Sebastian and I had Chinese food in all those weeks ago.

"Can I get you anything to drink while you wait?" Miles asks as he stands by the doorway.

"No, I'm okay, thank you," I say, taking a seat in one of the guest chairs.

"Mr. Blake will be right with you."

It's quiet in here. So quiet that I can hear my heart

117

pulsing in my eardrums. I might not have wanted Sebastian's help, but now that there's a real possibility I can get Lady Featherington back, I'm a wreck. Before, it felt like she wasn't with me only because Hardin was a douche. If I lose her today and she becomes his permanently, I'll be devastated.

As I sit by myself, something catches my attention. In the adjacent conference room, Hardin is standing by a high-backed leather chair. As he faces me, I sit up straight. The way he seems to look right through me makes my blood boil. I glare at him, shooting beams of hatred at him, yet he appears to not even notice I'm here. Of all the low-life, rude, and conniving—

"He can't see you," I hear Sebastian say.

I gasp both at the sound of his voice and at the *Sound. Of. His. Voice.* It's been too long since I've heard that deep baritone, and it still has the same tingling effect as it washes over my body.

I turn to see him, hoping maybe he's gotten a cold sore or really bad acne since I saw him last, but no such luck. He's still absolutely gorgeous, and my chest tightens at the sight.

I bite my lip, not sure what to say.

Thankfully, he speaks up first. "Hi."

I take a deep inhale and stand. "Hi."

"I'm glad you decided to take me up on my offer to help." He takes a timid step forward.

I force a smile through my nerves that feel like they're playing racquetball inside my body, bouncing back and forth. "I appreciate it."

I glance at Hardin and then back to Sebastian. The difference between the two men is almost laughable.

Where Hardin is dark and mysterious, the artsy type, Sebastian is ruggedly handsome and manly with a glow about him that's radiant. Hardin is a good six inches shorter than Sebastian, who also makes this large room feel ever so small. He commands it, dictates its energy, and oozes sexual intensity with every breath he takes.

I point to the glass wall. "Can he really not see me?"

"No." He holds up a remote. "There's a setting on the glass that makes it viewable one way. All he sees is fogged glass. We can turn it off and on with this."

I walk over to the wall and stare at it like it's the most complex thing in the world when, in actuality, it looks just like a normal piece of glass.

Sebastian steps up to me. My chest rises, and my stomach flutters. My palms feel sweaty, so I play with them. Even though he's not touching me, just having him close sends chills up my spine.

"Do you do a lot of interrogating here? Feels like an episode of *Law & Order*," I joke—poorly.

He laughs anyway. "We use it sparingly, and we never record anything that happens inside these walls. Hardin brought an attorney. Can't imagine he's a very good one though. His business card also stated that he's a realtor and part-time electrician. Still, it could get ugly. Can you handle it?"

My heart says no, but my mind is telling me to put on my big-girl panties and get this over with. I lift my chin, square my shoulders, and declare, "Let's do this."

My eyes meet his, and my face feels flush. His lips tilt to the side as he steps toward the door that leads to the other conference room, stopping just before walking through.

"Just sit back and enjoy the show." He winks, and I swear my heart flutters at the sight.

I try to gather my emotions as I walk in and take my seat opposite Hardin at the large conference table.

Sebastian remains standing. His demeanor changes into one of a hardened man who is ready to get down to business. "Let's get started with the matter of Lady Featherington, Miss Morgana's Pomeranian."

Hardin's attorney speaks next, pulling a slip from inside a folder and placing it on the table. "The dog is a clear possession of Mr. Reynolds. This receipt shows the animal was purchased by him, and the license is assigned to Hardin J. Reynolds."

The lawyer's smug face is so shrewd. It matches the cocky one plastered on Hardin's. If it was appropriate to bitch-slap him, I would.

Sebastian looks at the document, and my heart drops. I didn't know Hardin was getting me a puppy at the time, or I would have been there when he got her and put her in our names jointly. Not that it would have helped. She'd still be half his.

Sebastian drops the paper and places his own folder in front of him, opening it and looking at the pile.

"In Pennsylvania, a pet is a personal possession. Seems ridiculous when they're really a member of the family, but that's the law," Sebastian starts.

Hardin's attorney takes out a receipt. "My client's name is on this receipt. He purchased the animal; therefore, it is his possession."

Sebastian doesn't flinch. "That receipt makes Mr. Reynolds the purchaser. These documents, including"— he lifts up a piece of paper—"veterinary bills, signed by

Miss Morgana"—one by one, he piles the papers up—"grooming bills, also signed by Miss Morgana; and a prescription for heartworm medication as well as tick and flea, which is charged to Miss Morgana's Amazon account monthly, all show she was the intended owner."

"That means nothing. Mr. Reynolds's girlfriend walks the dog three times a day. Does that mean she owns the animal?"

Sebastian lowers his gaze to him. "Thirty-two letters of reference. That's what we have from people in your own former neighborhood who can vouch that Miss Morgana is the one who walked, owned, and loved Lady Featherington. Of course, except when she was at work and Mr. Reynolds's new girlfriend was hired—by Miss Morgana—to walk the dog. Not one of these letters states your client has ever been seen with the animal."

I look up at Sebastian in complete and utter shock. I had no idea he was doing research into my ownership, nonetheless soliciting references on my behalf. I lift one and see it's from a woman who says she lived in our building.

"This is a joke," Hardin says. "She ran errands. Doesn't mean the dog's hers."

My jaw drops, but Sebastian keeps calm as he makes his case as to why Lady Featherington belongs to me.

"Well, actually, it does. Because she was a gift from Mr. Reynolds to Miss Morgana, and here is proof of the gift, posted to *both* of their social media accounts, stating, in fact, that she was a birthday present. Which means she is indeed Miss Morgana's property." Sebastian lays multiple photos from Facebook and Instagram along with the captions that say just that.

Seeing him command the attention of Hardin and, even better, putting him in his place is the sexiest thing I've ever seen. The attorney skims through the vet records, grooming bills, pictures, and letters. He looks to Hardin like he's disappointed he didn't know all of this beforehand.

Without putting that matter to bed, Sebastian moves on to the artwork. His tone is impressive while his body speaks in a language that I'm dying to learn the dialect for.

Before I know it, we're talking about furniture, pots and pans, and who paid rent on which month. Hardin's attorney gets in some good lines, but Sebastian's are better, smarter, poised in a condescending way, and the men on the other side of the table appear to be caught like deer in headlights.

Sebastian pushes away from the table and places a hand on my elbow to rise. "We'll give you a few moments to digest this while I discuss something with my client."

I follow him calmly through the fogged-out door and into the other conference room. As soon as it's closed behind us, I start laughing and squealing, totally in shock at what just transpired.

"You're amazing. I didn't know you had all of those documents," I state as my hands shake a little from all the nerves that have built up inside me, trying to make their way out.

His smile is big as he slides his hands in his pockets. "It's called discovery. We have to make a case, even in the smallest of personal suits. I don't like to walk into a room unprepared."

"You definitely took charge of this. So, now what?"

"We're just making him sweat." He leans against the wall, cool and collected.

I glance over to Hardin. He's definitely flustered. When he runs his hands down his face in frustration, I turn back to Sebastian. "Is this a normal tactic?"

He laughs. "This isn't a normal case for me, so no. But I think they need a moment to realize that they have a weak case. Then, I'll go in for the kill and close this baby up."

"Do you think I'll get my dog back?"

"I don't lose."

"Let's hope not. Should we go back in?"

He lifts a finger and sways his head. "I'm on the fence about that. Something tells me Hardin will have an easier time, admitting defeat, if you're not around. He doesn't seem like the kind of guy who loses easily."

I shake my head. "Most definitely not. So, I just stay here?"

"If that's okay with you?"

Rubbing my hands together, I try to think of a reason why I should go back into that room. Sebastian has been nothing but wise in this whole endeavor. I'd be a fool to not take his advice. "I'll wait here."

He exits the room and heads back to Hardin and the attorney.

Sebastian's stance obviously shows he means business. Seeing them talk without hearing the words is frustrating, yet there's so much you can learn from watching someone's actions. You can see their motivations.

Sebastian maintains balance, keeps his posture steady and his eyes locked. He looks like a warrior. A protector. And at best, someone who wants to do right.

Hardin cowers, throws his arms up in defiance, and curses under his breath while staring at the floor. He doesn't want to give in, but I don't think he has a choice, and he knows it.

Sebastian keeps talking, and Hardin's hard exterior melts right before my eyes. A minute later, I see him close his eyes and nod. A blue-and-white paper document is slid in front of Hardin, who slams the top of the table with his fist.

Sebastian presses a button on a phone in the conference room. A woman walks in with a stamp. Everyone signs papers, the woman stamps them, and the next thing I see is Hardin standing, kicking his chair back, and heading toward the door.

Sebastian stops him by pointing his finger out to him in a stern manner. Whatever he asks, Hardin nods his head and then leaves with a huff.

Once he's out of the room, Sebastian turns toward the glass wall with a grin covering his face. When he winks my way, my entire body melts even though he's in a completely different room from me.

He exits through the same door, but to my surprise, he doesn't head toward me. Instead, I watch as he leaves in a completely opposite direction. For a second, I wonder if I should follow him when Miles appears.

"Miss Morgana," he says, getting my attention. "Please follow me."

I grab my things with much more happiness to my step than when I got here and head to where he's standing in the hallway. He grins before turning to lead me to my next destination.

I recognize the office we're heading toward, and my stomach flutters with each step we take.

Miles stops just outside the door and holds out his hand, motioning for me to pass by him. "Mr. Blake is ready for you in here."

"Thank you, Miles." I smile politely as I walk by and stand just a few feet inside of Sebastian's office.

When our eyes meet, he stares at me, not saying anything, but his eyes speak a book's worth of material. They're telling me he's in his element. What he just did is what he loves and what he's good at. But they're also showing me just how much he's missed me and, if I'm not mistaken, how much he wants to kiss me right now too.

Okay, maybe that's just wishful thinking.

After a few seconds more of him not saying anything, I finally break the silence. "Well?"

He cracks his stoic expression with the biggest smile I've seen on him yet. "How much do you love me?"

I feel like I just tripped over a proverbial curb on a street. "Excuse me?"

"I got you everything." He stands and heads to the other side of his desk, leaning back on it with his legs and arms crossed. The stance is so sexy because he seems so relaxed and pleased with himself.

Confidence is intoxicating on a man.

I playfully eye him. "What do you mean by *everything*?"

He raises his eyebrows with a slight tilt to his head.

"What did you want?" he asks.

"You got Lady Featherington?" I jump slightly with excitement toward him.

"And …"

"My painting?" I ask, cautious of getting my hopes up as I step closer.

"And …"

I tilt my head. "I didn't ask for anything more."

"He owed you money."

Now, my eyes bug out as I move right next to him. "You got Hardin to repay me?"

"A man needs to pay his fair share in this world. He's the reason you didn't get your security deposit back, and he risked your credit being tarnished. He was a joint occupant with his mail being sent there for a year. You are entitled to reimbursement."

"You're my hero."

"It took everything in me to waive the rights to any of the furnishings in the apartment, but I assumed the money was better. You can buy new and start over."

I throw my arms around him with so much happiness. I'm beyond thrilled to be getting my dog and artwork, and the money is the absolute cherry on top. I'm squeezing him so intensely that the intoxicating scent of him invades my senses. Warm citrus and an earthy musk pour off of his neck, which is so close to my mouth that it's dangerously inappropriate.

I shouldn't be touching my lawyer this way, so I pull back slightly. His arms, which weren't around me a second ago, grip my waist and pull me in.

I lower my palms to the lapels of his suit jacket and stare at them as I speak, "No one other than family has ever gone above and beyond for me the way you did today. It must have taken so much time and money to get all of those documents."

"You were worth the investment."

I glance down. "Sometimes, I don't feel that way."

"Amy." He brings my attention back to him. "You are bold and courageous. A spitfire with unquestionable passion. You give yourself fully to your dreams, friendships, family, and love. I've yet to meet someone as independent and smart, who lacks self-pity and only takes what she can return. That is why you are worth every moment of my time."

Our eyes meet.

Flames seem to ignite all around us. His brown orbs darken, and a visceral molten lava of heat shines from them.

My chest tightens, and my breasts rise. I lick my lips, and his eyes lower at the sight.

He swallows and moves closer.

I whimper and part my mouth.

It takes point-two seconds until our lips collide in a crash of desire and passion bursting at the seams. His tongue glides against mine as my lips caress his. We've kissed before, but this one is different. It's desperate and maddening. So damn needy that my head is in a foggy haze.

His fingers grip my blazer, bringing me flush against him as he deepens our kiss. I roam mine up to his shoulders and into his hair. When his mouth moves to my neck, nipping and sucking, sending tingles down to my core, I yank his hair and pull.

A deep growl escapes his throat as his mouth comes back to mine, and we kiss again, backing up until my butt hits the top of his desk.

He lifts me, and I move willingly. I shift back

and accidentally knock his phone onto the floor in the process. He pushes his suit jacket off, and I start loosening his tie. The sound of a dial tone fills the room. We laugh, as it must have also hit the speakerphone button when it fell.

As he leans down to pick it up, I roll my head to the side, and that's when I see it.

On his desk, in a silver Tiffany frame, is a sonogram—a black-and-white image that looks like nothing and everything, all at once—sitting next to his computer screen. A prime space for a photo of something you cherish and want to look at often.

Sebastian sets the phone back in its place and comes right back to me, but my head is now turned toward the photo. He must sense how my mood has changed because a sigh escapes his lips.

With a deep breath, I adjust my blazer. Sebastian does the same with his tie. He holds out his hand to lift me up back to my feet, and I take it. Once I'm planted firmly on the ground, he reaches for the picture. He holds it, running his thumb over the glass and the promise that grainy photo presents.

"Did you find out the sex?" I ask, leaning in to see it.

His smile is soft, proud. "We did. It's a boy."

I place my hand on his arm. "I'm really happy for you, Sebastian."

His eyes meet mine, and they pause, almost in conflict. His lips part to say something, but nothing comes out.

I save him the trouble of finding the words. "Hey, don't worry about it. We got lost in the moment. I should get going."

"I don't want you to go."

I take in a breath. "I have to. Thank you again. Truly. I can't tell you how much I appreciate everything you've done for me."

If I could wish for Sebastian to be anything but who he is, it would be a travesty. He's too damn good. Charming to a fault. Ambitious and inspiring. Loyal. Beautiful.

Not mine.

I look at the sonogram one more time and smile. "Make sure you spoil the hell out of that kid."

As I turn to leave, my heart hurts when he doesn't stop me. Not that I really thought he would. I've watched enough movies to want the call back, but that doesn't happen in real life, not when one person is having a family with another woman and the other doesn't have the balls to admit what she wants.

So, I leave without a word.

I had no idea what I was expecting when I walked into Sebastian's law firm today, but I can say that I definitely wasn't expecting anything that happened.

CHAPTER TWELVE

"There you go, my sweet girl," I say to Lady Featherington as I get her settled in her new bed in my office.

Hardin didn't even knock when he dropped her off the other day. He tied her to the doorknob of the alleyway door and then sent a text to let me know she was there.

Since he didn't bring anything but her, I spent the afternoon installing a gate, so she'd stay in my office for now. Then, I got her a new bed, toys, kibble, and a fancy collar with pink rhinestones because she's regal and she deserves the very best.

"I believe you would like a treat, Your Highness." I hand her a pooch cookie I made myself, using dog-safe ingredients.

She gobbles it up before lying down in her bed, resting her head on her new pillow.

I give her a rub on her belly and then close the door behind me. I stop at the bathroom and wash my hands twice to make sure I don't have any dander on my skin.

In my kitchen, I turn on my music. I don't have an order, but for some reason, I feel like making some brittle. I get the peanuts, toss them with salt and olive oil, and pop them in the oven to roast.

Norah Jones sings to me as I dance around the kitchen and gather my ingredients to bake. After I spray my baking sheet, I pour myself a glass of wine.

There's a knock at the door, so I check my phone to see who it is. When the handsome man I haven't been able to get out of my mind appears, my heart pounds, and I nearly spit out my wine at the sight of Sebastian standing in my doorway.

"Shoot." I look down at my T-shirt and jeans, feeling like a scrub. "One minute," I say into the speaker and then run into the bathroom.

My hair is in a messy bun. I stare into the mirror, pushing back a few loose tendrils, checking my makeup, and pinching my cheeks.

Before opening the back door, I shake my head, ridding myself of all the jitters rushing through my body because I'm acting like a silly teenager. Squaring my shoulders and lifting my chin, I open the door with a cavalier attitude.

"This is a surprise. What brings you to this neck of the woods?"

He holds up an envelope. "Special delivery. I didn't want to make you come down to the office again, so I thought I'd do the honor of delivering it to you personally."

He hands me the manila envelope, and I unclasp the metal at the top. Inside is a document with a check paper-clipped to the side. It's a check from Blake, Fields, and Moore, made out to me in the amount of three thousand dollars.

"Wow. This is amazing. I still can't believe you got anything out of him."

"In my opinion, you're entitled way more, but that's the amount we settled on. I hope you're pleased."

"Beyond. Thank you. I just wanted my dog back, so this is gravy." I'm stunned as I run my fingers over the amount. "This isn't from you, right? Your name is on the check." I turn to show him like he doesn't know.

He holds up his hands in defense. "Standard procedure. After a case is settled, attorneys receive settlement funds, and then we cut the check to our clients. This ensures your money is guaranteed not to bounce."

"Pays to have a high-priced Philadelphia attorney." I'm smiling big and staring at him.

It's awkward—him in the alley and me standing inside. I'm not sure what the protocol is for something like this.

"Thank you for coming all this way." I grin and shrug my shoulders.

"Not a problem." He nods. It's seems he, too, doesn't know what else to say.

My oven timer goes off, and I remember my peanuts are inside it.

"Smells good in there. What are you making?" he asks, checking out what's in front of us.

"Sea-salted chocolate peanut brittle."

He tilts his head in question. "I don't recall seeing that on your website."

I'm flattered he paid enough attention to my website

to know what is on it. "I'm pleasure-baking tonight. Had a craving."

"I love peanut brittle. I haven't had it since I was a kid. My grandmother used to make it."

"Mine too," I answer quickly and way too enthusiastically. "I'm using her recipe."

"I never had the chance to make it with her. I wish I had, but she passed when I was just a kid." His eyes crinkle with his words as he looks down.

It's sweet, the way he thinks of his grandmother. If his was like mine, she must have left a grand impression on his heart.

I'm not sure entirely what convinces me that this is a good idea, but I find myself asking, "Do you want to come in? I can show you how to make it."

"I'd like that." He walks inside, past me, before I have a chance to process the fact that he agreed.

I close and lock the door and turn to see him in my space.

The kitchen is large, having originally been used to serve enough people for an eighty-seat restaurant. With its all-white walls and stainless steel tables, it looks almost like a sterile environment—until you look down and see the dark red tile squares with grout so old that it's black instead of the tan that you can see in the corners and under the tables. There's a large island in the center with massive appliances around the U-shape setting, making it possible to cook multiple items at once without having to move much.

It's a clean workspace, esthetically speaking. I added mahogany shelves to a blank wall to bring in a homier feel, and the stools where Charity likes to sit are matching dark wood. Adding my Loui Jover painting, which Hardin left sitting outside too, on the other blank wall really brings life and color to the space.

Just when I thought my room was complete, I realize no amount of wood could provide the amount of warmth to this space as one Sebastian Blake in his dark jeans, cashmere sweater, and leather loafers. His presence alone is warm and inviting and everything this cold room needs.

"This is where the magic happens," he muses, taking in the counter space where I have three apothecary vases filled with herbs, growing near the window.

"Where dreams come true." I walk over to the oven, take out the peanuts, and set them on the counter to cool.

That's when I hear Lady Featherington whimpering on the other side of my office door with her tiny nails clawing on the hollow wood. I would let her out, but with Sebastian here, I don't know if that's a good idea.

"Is that your dog?" he asks, pointing to my office.

"Yes. I know I'm not supposed to have an animal in a commercial kitchen, but since Hardin gave her back, I haven't found a place to keep her. Charity is allergic, and Shawn refuses to walk a dog. I'd ask my siblings who live outside the city, and I know one would say yes, but to be honest, I just got her back, and I don't want her to go far. Plus, she's been shuffled from my custody, to Hardin and Mindy's, and back to me, and I'm afraid she'll get custodial whiplash."

Sebastian grins that gorgeous half-smile that rises on one side as he walks over to my office door, opening it and then picking up Lady Featherington from behind the gate.

"Aren't you a precious little thing?" he says, kneeling to the ground and allowing her to jump on his knee, sniff his shirt, and lick his face.

Her hair is a big poof with the little bow at the top of her head falling slightly to the side.

"I can see why you named her what you did. This dog is dainty. She can definitely rock the bling though." He points to her collar as she laps up his neck.

I've never been so jealous of a dog before.

"Lady Featherington, no," I command, and she follows my order.

"Nice. Glad to see she's well trained."

"The only perk to my ex's new girlfriend being a dog walker was, she kept up the good habits."

He scratches her head and then rises. "You know, when we were compiling those letters from the people in the building, I was surprised how many saw you out and about with the dog, given you had a dog walker."

"Mindy was only around to take her out while we worked. The shitty part of this whole thing is, she was a really good dog walker. Reliable, helped train her, and I never worried about her stealing anything from the apartment while we were gone."

"What will you do now that you have her back?"

"I've taken her for seven walks today because I feel horrible that she can only stay behind closed doors, for fear she'll contaminate my kitchen. My loan from the bank should come through in the next week or two. I'll look for something small around here, so I can run home on my break and walk her."

I take Lady Featherington and head back to my office, putting her in her bed. When I turn, Sebastian is in the doorway behind me, his broad shoulders taking up the entire space and making him seem almost larger than life.

"You sleep in here?" His brow furrows.

"Yep. The futon is surprisingly comfortable, and all my clothes fit in that suitcase. I have a closet in the front, and the bathroom is a decent size. The windows are all fogged glass, so I can dance in my underwear without anyone watching."

"Habit of yours?" he asks with a crooked grin.

"It's a mood booster," I state easily. "The gym next door opens at five, so I shower there in exchange for chocolate. Don't worry; there's a secret door, so it's not like I'm walking outside in a towel. I bring my clothes with me and get fully ready there."

His mouth twists. "Seems dangerous. How many men see you walk through that door?"

"Are you getting all protective of me, Mr. Blake?"

"Fiercely." He steps back and walks over to the other side of the room. "Through here?" He points before heading down the hallway that leads to the gym. After inspecting the locks and then unlatching them, he opens the door and looks into the weight area.

I stand and watch him close the door and then relock it.

"Does it meet your approval?" I tilt my head to the side.

"No." He clenches his jaw as he searches around my space again.

"You know, my dad didn't even give me this hard of a time about it." I place my hands on my hips.

He raises a brow. "Does he know you shower in there while juiced-up guys are working out?"

A laugh escapes my lips. "Do you think I shower in the middle of the room for all men to see? It's called a women's locker room. Every gym has one."

His surprised expression makes me grin. I get the feeling he's not used to being called out.

"Anything else, Mr. Territorial?" I tease.

"Doesn't seem to bother you."

"The fact that I shower in a gym? Of course it does, but it's only temporary. I didn't choose this living situation—"

"I mean, you're not bothered by me being territorial of you?"

Oh. I blanch and think about that for a moment. "No. Not really."

A wide smile graces his face, making his dimple appear. "Good. Now, let's make some brittle." He motions for me to walk ahead of him.

He heads to the sink and washes his hands, and then I do the same and meet him at the counter, where I have my ingredients laid out.

I lift the heavy four-quart saucepan and place it on the stove over medium heat.

Sebastian rolls up his sleeves and starts grabbing the ingredients I dictate to him.

"One and a half cups of sugar," I say and watch him measure out the precise amount.

Next, he adds the water and corn syrup as I direct

him, "Stir until the sugar dissolves, and then we'll raise the heat."

He pays close attention to the job at hand to make sure he's got the hang of it before he turns to me. "What was your grandmother like?" he asks as he stirs.

"Funny. Glamorous. Loved to tell stories of her days in Manhattan when she danced at the Copa."

"She was a New Yorker?"

"Born and raised. My mom too. My grandparents relocated to Pennsylvania when Mom met Dad in college and they decided to marry and settle here."

"Family that stays together is important."

I sense a tiny bit of remorse in his words. "Do you see your parents often?"

"Not as often as I'd like, but I do. They live in Connecticut, and it's only a few hours' drive. I try to see them once a month, plus the holidays, and they usually come down this way for my birthday."

"When's that?"

"The last week of July."

"Ahh. So, that makes you a Leo?" I say as I get the nuts ready.

"I hope that's a good thing." He grins, unsure of the question, which is adorable on him.

"Very actually. It means you're dedicated with high ideals and inspired views on life." I laugh at how high and mighty I make him sound. "About a year ago, I was toying with the idea of making zodiac-themed chocolate boxes. Thought they'd be fun birthday gifts."

"That's a great idea. What did you envision for the Leo?"

"At the time, I was thinking something tried and

true, like a chocolate mousse truffle." I glance at him out of the corner of my eye. "Now, I'm thinking it has to be sophisticated, like a luxurious, soft caramel, blended with gourmet sea salt, nestled inside a dark chocolate shell." With a deep exhale, I look up at him and see the quirk of his mouth as he looks back at me with a raised brow. I clear my throat and get back to work. "So, what do you and your parents do on this annual birthday trip?"

He laughs lightly and looks down at the pot, continuing to stir. "They spend the week here before Mom has to be back on campus for freshman orientation. They love the museums, and Dad always visits colleagues over at the Children's Hospital of Philadelphia. Dad and I catch a ball game, and then Mom has us wait in line at Geno's for cheesesteaks because she says they're the best. I think that's the only time all year I eat a cheesesteak."

"Same. Not for any real reason though. But I must disagree with your mother. I'd go with Pat's cheesesteaks all the way."

"I have a very important question to ask, and this could be a deal-breaker for our friendship."

I lean back and feign seriousness. "A question that could call the whole thing off. Well, Mr. Blake, I'd best be careful with my response."

He stands tall and asks as seriously as possible, "How do you take your cheesesteak?"

"Oh, man. I already know this is not gonna go well. A Connecticut boy is not gonna order it right. I'm a *without onions, wit' Whiz* girl."

He slaps his chest like a dagger was just pushed into it. "Cheez Whiz on a sandwich—that's disgusting."

I laugh. "It kind of is, but it's the way I grew up. Probably why I don't really eat them. How do you order yours?"

"Provolone and caramelized onions."

I make a face of disgust. "You even order it like a preppy. Just say *wit' onions.*" He laughs, and I follow. "Shame we can't be friends anymore."

"Agreed. We're just gonna have to find something else to be to each other." The twinkle in his eye is undeniable, as is the subtle, flirtatious nature of his words.

I slap my hands together and dictate to him his next instructions. "Peanuts, butter, and salt."

Watching Sebastian cook is charming. I can see he is comfortable in a kitchen and is incredibly controlled with every action. When I tell him the candy must come to a golden-brown color, he analyzes it with purpose. For someone who behaves the same way in the kitchen, I find this level of focus to be a turn-on.

We work together through the next steps of the recipe. His fingers lightly swipe my arm when we add baking soda. My hip pushes against his when I add in some vanilla. Somehow, I wind up in front of him with his arms around mine when it's time to pour the brittle into the pan. When my back brushes up against his chest, I get a zing right through my body.

While it cools, we take Lady Featherington outside and play fetch with her in the alley.

"Do you get to play a lot with Duke?" I ask as Sebastian throws the ball to her again.

"That rascal has a ton of energy. He only gets walked three times a day though."

"She'll be the same once I get my own place."

He looks back at the door to my kitchen and grimaces. "I can't believe you live here."

"Pathetic?" I ask, not liking how I'll feel if he agrees.

"Shows gumption. I'd like to see you in a better place though. I know some people in real estate who can help you get a good rental. You can put that three grand to good use."

"Thanks, but I'll skip the fee and try looking by owner first. When my loan comes in, I have big plans for the money, and a high rental is not ideal."

"I'll let you know if I hear of anything."

I point a finger. "And no pro bono realtors. I'm onto you, Blake."

"Damn. That was definitely my plan."

I roll my eyes, and we go back inside, where I pour him a glass of wine. We spend the next half hour breaking brittle, stretching it thin, while laughing over jokes and tales of our grandmothers who each seem to have had their own unique ways of smothering us. Mine with hugs, pickles, weekly bingo nights, and paintings of clowns—I have seven. His with kisses, walking him to and from school—even in high school—and knitted afghans, of which he has twelve.

I grab takeout from the restaurant next door, and we eat while the brittle cools. I open another bottle of wine, and we talk about our favorite things to do in the city. I share my fascination with the rowing clubs along Schuylkill River. I can watch the crews come out of Boathouse Row and lose a whole afternoon, enjoying them go up and down the river.

Sebastian listens with keen interest to every word I say. I do the same as he talks about his role as Fiyero in a local production of *Wicked*.

"I'm amazed you find the time to do community theater," I say in surprise.

"Told you, I love to act."

"I thought that was the high school dream. Where do you perform?"

"At a playhouse in my neighborhood. The plays are in the fall. I'd love for you to come. They're doing *Moulin Rouge: The Musical*. It should be interesting."

"That's six months away. So sure we'll still know each other?"

"Positive. We're friends. Cheesesteak preferences aside." He winks.

I smile as I drink my wine and let the alcohol release the dopamine in my brain, making me feel relaxed and loose. At least, I'll pretend it's the wine and not the man I'm sitting with.

After dinner, we clean up and finish baking. As we melt the chocolate, I find us standing closer. His body sends a wave of heat my way, hotter than the stove.

When he sprinkles the sea salt, I tickle his ribs and force a salty mess on the ground.

As we eat it, he runs his thumb on my chin to clean a bit of chocolate.

Our evening is intimate, but that's as intense as it gets. I pack him up a tin of brittle to take home and a bag of my homemade treats for Duke, which Sebastian takes as his cue to leave. He places his wineglass in the sink and then grabs his bag that I prepared for him.

"This was a wonderful surprise. Thanks for teaching me your grandmother's recipe," he says as he grins my way.

"I had fun."

I open the door for him, and he stands for a beat before walking through. I follow him a step and watch as he turns around, leans down, and kisses my cheek.

"Good night, Amy."

Sebastian walks to his car, which is parked in the alley, looking out of place in the dingy space. He turns the car on and backs up to the main road.

"Sweet dreams, Sebastian." My words are said to no one as I close the door behind me and lock it. I turn the lights off in the kitchen and head into my room-slash-office.

As I curl into bed, Lady Featherington whimpers lightly from the floor.

I lean down and pick her up, tucking her beside me. Things might not be going my way one hundred percent, but I have my dog back, and because of that, I have everything I could ever want.

Well, almost everything.

CHAPTER THIRTEEN

"Five hundred."

I look over at Shawn with a raised brow, wondering what he's talking about.

"Five hundred truffle boxes for a corporate event," he clarifies as he hands me an order form, which is basically his scribble on a notepad. "The order came in while you were out, apartment-hunting."

I take it from him and stare at the request, blinking to make sure I'm reading it correctly. Five hundred chocolate truffle gift boxes at twenty dollars a box.

"Shawn, this is a ten-thousand-dollar order," I say, trying to keep my mouth from hitting the floor but having a really hard time doing so.

"I know, boss! Your largest to date." He slides across the room and snaps his fingers.

"Did you tell them we give a bulk order discount?"

"Nope." He smiles as he looks at me, proud of himself. "And there's a special request." He raises his eyebrows at me, like he's excited to tell me the rest.

"They want you to create a chocolate tasting station at the event as well. Don't worry; I already checked your calendar, and you're free. Just like every weekend for the next forever."

I give him a scowl and then look back at the notepad, which is difficult to read with his chicken scratch but I do my best. When I make out his words, I gasp at what they say and turn to him, placing my hand on the counter to brace myself. "You said the tasting table would be two thousand dollars?" I nearly yelp.

"Too little?" he asks, confused.

I walk over to the counter and put my bags down while staring at the paper. "I don't know. I've never priced out a tasting table." I squint at the paper and then point to it. "Does this say chocolate fondue?"

"You should call and confirm the details. I told the guy you'd call him back this afternoon. His name was Miles, just in case you can't read that last part." He moves to the boxing table, where he's been packing artisanal chocolates all morning.

The paper says Miles but no further information.

"Miles? You mean, Miles from Blake, Fields, and Moore? Sebastian's assistant?" I ask, still completely flabbergasted as to what's going on but getting a hunch it's not the dream order I've been hoping for.

"Yep, that's the guy." He snaps his fingers and then points at me.

My shoulders fall. "It's just another one of Sebastian's handouts. I'll call back and tell them we can't fulfill such a large order by next weekend."

Shawn nearly drops the carton he's holding while his eyes bug out. "Are you out of your mind, woman?"

"Are you talking back to your boss, man?" I give him sass back even though I'm not annoyed or mad.

Shawn means well. He merely is unaware of Sebastian Blake's desire to do things for me for free. At this point, I think he feels guilty for how our brief relationship ended. I don't need his charity or his pity.

"You're crazy, Amy. That's a huge order, and it could go a long way in growing this business."

Placing the paper down, I try not to think about how that kind of order could help me right now as I search in my bag and take out the spices I purchased to test out some new flavors.

"I already have a game plan on how to grow the business. My loan is approved, so the website is being revamped, and I'm going to try some new products. Also, I'm doing a mass mailing campaign to the local networks and magazines and then branching out to the nationals. I've reached out to dozens of food blogs for their addresses to send them samples. My goal is to spread the love of Amy Morgana Chocolatier without having to hire a publicist."

He grimaces while working, not looking up at me. "That sounds like you'll be sending out approximately a hundred or so boxes of chocolate. Pretty pricey endeavor for someone who hasn't gotten a check from the bank yet. Might be wise to take on a ten-thousand-dollar order to offset those costs," he muses loudly.

I roll my eyes and put my tote away.

The back door swings open, and Charity comes in with a huge smile and a cardboard tray with three coffee cups. "Happy Thursday, everyone!"

Tying my apron on, I address my best friend, "You're extra bouncy this morning."

"The sun is out, and the flowers are blooming." She hands me a coffee cup and then one to Shawn. "Thought I'd bring some java for my two favorite people."

Shawn looks at me, concerned. "Drugs?"

With a laugh, I shake my head. "My money is on a new man."

"For your information, I have a hot date this weekend with the barista at Love and Lavender." Charity sneaks a piece of chocolate from the tray that Shawn is packing from and grins. "Delish! Is that the whiskey and sea salt? So good." She tries to take another, but he swats her bangled hand away.

"Thanks. I'm working on lemon chiffon truffles for the summer. The website rebuild will have a section for showers and luncheons. Thought some citrus will work well for warm weather events, and I'll need a taste-tester."

She raises a hand. "I volunteer as tribute."

I give her a wink and get to work on my new recipe while Charity takes a seat at the island.

"How's apartment-hunting going?" Charity asks as I line up five bowls.

I'm going to make the recipe several times with varying amounts of lemon to see which is the best.

"It was decent, but with my limited budget, I'm not in love. Plus, I need a place that allows dogs."

"You can afford to splurge a little," she suggests, flipping her hair.

"I need to put as much money as possible into growing the orders, so I can move on to phase two, which is a storefront."

"And when is that expected to happen?" she asks as she eyes another piece that Shawn is packing up.

"It's a five-year plan," I answer easily.

"You'd get to your goal faster if you weren't so stubborn and turning down large deals from lover boy," Shawn chimes in. Charity's head swivels to him with raised brows, so he explains, "Sebastian placed a huge order, and Amy refuses to take it because it's"—he uses air quotes—" 'a handout.' "

"Oh, for the love of ..." She jumps off the stool and leans onto the counter. "Are you out of your mind?"

I scowl at Shawn and then look to Charity, who is drumming her fingers on the metal table, waiting for a proper reason why I'd turn down business.

"It's complicated," is the only response I can give.

"It's romantic. He's your knight in shining armor, who continues to show up to rescue you. The last time he was here, you had this magical night."

I laugh while keeping myself from rolling my eyes. "We talked about cheesesteaks and our dead grandmas. I'd hardly call it magical."

"The fact that you told Shawn and me about it the next day means it was way more than the drab evening you're pretending it was." She gives me a *don't lie to me* look that makes me turn away, getting back to my task.

She's right. I did tell her and Shawn about it. Sebastian and I hadn't kissed, and the conversation was basic, yet ... there was something special about the night. Having him here, in my home, in my business, with my dog, sharing a meal and wine and baking. We laughed and talked and enjoyed music.

Perhaps it was a bit magical.

I won't admit that out loud though.

Charity must sense this pause in conversation as an opening because she walks over, grabs my shoulders, and makes me face her.

"It was lovely. Are you happy now?" I give her a sarcastic grin.

She tilts her head to the side. "No. You're turning away business. This is not the Amy I know. My best friend would stop at nothing to drum up enough business and get her name out there whether it was one box of truffles or a hundred."

"Times that by five," Shawn chimes in, and Charity's jaw drops. "And some sort of tasting station."

Her eyes bug out.

Shawn takes the paper with the message for the order on it and hands it to her. She holds it up and squints as she tries to read it, her face making all kinds of crazy expressions as she does.

Charity walks over to me, placing her hands on my shoulders. "Amy Morgana, you listen to me. I don't care if you are secretly in lust for this man or if you hate his guts. There is nothing in the world you love more than this business. That is why you're going to put on your big-girl panties, fasten your chef's jacket, and get your ass to this event, where you are going to put on the best goddamn tasting ever. You'll hand out those boxes, and by the end of the night, the Philadelphia elite will know the name Amy Morgana Chocolatier."

"This doesn't seem like a handout to you?" I ask, scrunching my face and feeling unsure.

"You're living on a futon and taking showers in a nasty gym, where you have to wear flip-flops while trying to clean your booty. Swallow your pride for one night and get ahead in this world."

I smile at Charity's tone. She's gone all super-serious boss lady on me, and it's not like her at all. In fact, I like this authoritative stance on her.

"So, what you're saying is, this is a good idea?"

Shawn laughs, and Charity shoots him a glare.

"And you," she says to him, "clear your schedule. You're working the event too."

He points a finger at his chest. "Why me?"

"Because our head chef and face of the business needs to be talking to the people while you serve them. Amy Morgana Chocolatier is luxury artisanal chocolates. The creator of such luxury does not serve. Others must do it for her." Charity takes another chocolate, chews it, walks back to her seat, and sits down.

"Looks like we have an event to prepare for," I say, and she bolts out of her seat, clapping her hands in excitement.

Shawn, too, seems pleased I decided to do the event. The more I think about it, the more the idea of putting on a show of my chocolate sounds like quite the opportunity.

As I mix the ingredients, a small smile grows on my face, and Charity walks up, nudging me with her hip.

"You're envisioning it, aren't you? This is your opportunity. Don't let anyone take that away from you."

CHAPTER FOURTEEN

Glitz and glamour.

It's the perfect phrase to describe the event held at the rooftop atrium, where Blake, Fields, and Moore is hosting their annual gala.

Men are donned in suits as the women wear their most sophisticated cocktail attire. There's champagne, caviar, and crystal chandeliers. While guests nibble on canapes, they discuss business, and joke with raucous laughter as a band plays at the far end of the room.

Shawn and I are set up in a corner. The original request asked for a chocolate fondue fountain. To be honest, I'm not a fan of those things. The chocolate is always subpar, and to use my own recipe, it would have been astronomical. Instead, we have tiered rows of artisanal chocolates that we are using to pair with each guest's drink of choice this evening.

Since this is a mingling event, people are strutting about, working the room. No one is dancing, though I assume by the large dance floor, they will be later.

I adjust the collar of my chef's jacket and make sure the name on the coat is visible in its scripted font.

"You look great, boss." Shawn tries to calm my nerves as I watch people pass our table.

"Why aren't they coming over here?" I whisper to him through my smile.

"Probably because they just got here and they plan on diving into some of that steak on the other side of the room and getting a little hammered before dessert," he states. "Just smile, relax, and don't worry. You're getting paid whether or not they come over here."

I give him a half-smile even though I'm a ball of nerves inside.

Still, I stand here, as professional as possible, and smile as guests pass without sampling. I'm watching people flutter about in a sea of high-priced suits and diamond stud earrings when, suddenly, like parting waves of the Atlantic, the crowd moves, and in its wake is Sebastian.

There are hundreds of people in this room, yet none hold a candle to him. He's taller than most, leaner than most, and his laugh—although I can't hear it from here—is most definitely more vibrant than everyone combined. I'm halfway across the room, and I'm taken by the sheer charisma and confidence that ooze from him.

He's wearing a black suit with a matching tie. With his broad shoulders and tapered waist, the fine suit shows off his body, which is undeniably athletic. His golden hair is combed back, and his lips are pursed on a lowball glass filled with an amber liquid.

He's a stunning man. I've never been one for big or

brawny guys. My ex-boyfriends have all been lanky. The cool, low-key, unassuming kind of man. Everything Sebastian is not.

Sebastian is a mix of muscle and tone. He's sexy without being roguish. Built without the unneeded bulkiness. His features are soft and beautiful yet hard where it counts—like his jaw, his piercing gaze, and his lips.

My hand brushes against the other one at the memory of what his felt like on mine.

I place my hands on my hips, recalling how his felt as they gripped me tightly, never wanting to let go.

Shawn leans over and whispers, "Down, girl. You're practically foaming at the mouth."

I give him the side-eye, which I hope he reads as the equivalent of giving him the finger.

"I take it, that's the loyal lawyer over there?" He juts his chin toward Sebastian, who is making his way closer to us, still chatting away.

"That's him."

"You can try to act like you aren't into the guy, but your misty-eyed expression is a total giveaway."

"Not the conversation we should be having here," I whisper out the side of my mouth.

"Just saying. Dude is rich, and he really likes to help you out."

"Money isn't everything." I fidget with the tablecloth, making sure everything is straight.

"Trust me, I know or else I'd never get laid. He's a good-looking dude though. Probably could have any woman in this room."

I tilt my head at Shawn and scowl. "That's supposed to make me feel better?"

"No. Just stating a fact. He's a baller. Look at how he holds that woman's hand while she speaks. She's practically wetting her panties right now."

I glance over. Sebastian is talking with a woman who is significantly older than him. He has one of her hands wrapped in his. Not in a sexual way. It's a warm gesture that he must be coupling with a compliment because she's batting her eyes and leaning forward. A man at her side, presumably her husband, is beaming at her, agreeing with whatever it is Sebastian is saying. Sebastian releases her hand and then shakes the man's before moving on to the next couple.

"He's just working the room," I surmise.

Shawn nods. "Like I said, baller."

I roll my eyes with a grin as I continue to smile at the passing guests. The music being played is an old jazz standard that has me swaying a little.

Sebastian is getting closer, and soon enough, he makes his way over to our table. There are mountains of finely placed chocolates on the table, and instead of looking at any of them, his gaze penetrates me as I breathe deeper and smile brighter.

"Good evening, Amy."

My belly flutters, and it takes me a moment to speak. "Sebastian. Thank you so much for hiring us. It's absolutely beautiful. I've always wanted to attend an event up here."

His expression doesn't hide his surprise. "Is this your first time inside the atrium?"

I nod. "All work and no play, I suppose."

Sebastian shifts his head and then turns back to me. His brows lower, making the side of his eyes wrinkle as he stares at me, lost in thought. He smiles and then glances down for a moment, taking in the display. "This looks delectable. You're most definitely going to spoil our guests."

"Shawn here helps me create every piece," I say by way of introduction. "Sebastian Blake, this is my sous-chef, Shawn McCormack."

Shawn extends a hand. "Nice party. It would be nicer if we could get some guests over here to taste Amy's amazing products."

I turn to Shawn with a scowl. "This is not a vendor event. It's a party. If they come, they come. Please don't pressure Mr. Blake."

Sebastian interrupts my whispered scolding, "No, no. He's right. I wanted you here because we always do something extra for guests at these events. Last year, it was a photo booth, and the year before, we had Kareem Abdul Jabbar signing basketballs. This year, we're loading them up with chocolate. The guests should come over because this is their gift."

There's a group of people to the side, young twenty-somethings, who Sebastian walks over to. When he comes back, it's with an entourage of eight, who he introduces to me and Shawn. Then, he steps back as the people check out my offerings. A man takes the tongs placed on the table, examining each one, like he can't decide what he wants to choose.

"What are you drinking?" I ask him.

He looks back at me, confused. "Single malt scotch."

"Whiskey and chocolate are a perfect pairing since

157

their flavor profiles are so similar. It's best to enjoy both at room temperature." I lift my tongs and offer him a piece of sea salt dark chocolate to put on his plate. "Place this in your mouth for a few seconds before taking a sip. Scotch is naturally creamy with notes of citrus, so the chocolate will brighten up the scotch while the drink's subtle honey flavor showcases the bold salty note."

He does so and then chews, enjoying the piece before following with a sip of scotch.

His head nods in appreciation. "That's delicious."

"Do me!" A woman moves over enthusiastically. "What do you recommend for champagne?"

Shawn and I show our guests around the table, recommending chocolates to pair with whatever they're drinking—nutty flavors for bourbon, white chocolate for tequila, and extra-dark chocolate for merlot.

Once Sebastian walked over the first group, the floodgates opened, and the table is bustling with people tasting our product.

Not everyone wants their drinks paired. Some just come and sample without a word. Others are specific about allergies and dietary restrictions. Many just want something sweet after eating appetizers and visiting the carving or pasta stations.

Sebastian is back several times, always with someone he wants to introduce me to. Colleagues of his, affiliates of the business, and even a few people he's meeting tonight for the first time. He doesn't treat me or Shawn like hired help. He introduces us as his friends and raves about our products, even making suggestions on how they should use us for corporate gifts over the holidays.

While my cheeks are blushing and my heart is pounding, I retain my professionalism as I greet them and cater to their tasting needs. A few ask for my card, and I am happy to pass it on.

There's a moment where I wonder if I'm going to run out of chocolates since some people are coming back multiple times.

Two hours into the party, the attention to our table has simmered down, as most people are now dancing, drinking, and engrossed in conversation. I'd say a hundred or so people have already left, and there's still another hour of the event remaining.

I'm standing at the front of the table, where I'm making sure the tasting dishes are lined up in perfectly symmetrical form when a warm hand on my back has me looking up.

I know who it is before I see him.

Sebastian removes his hand and slides it into his pants pocket. I adjust a tendril of hair that's fallen in front of my face and breathe deeply.

"You have many new fans, Miss Morgana."

I smile as I shake my head and glance down at my shoes. "I've never done a large event like this. I've been to trade shows, but this was a new experience. I had to get my *cocktail-hour schmooze* hat on. It's a lot of work."

He grins that lopsided one that I miss. "You were brilliant. Just don't forget us little people when you're world famous."

I playfully slug him in the arm. It's a childish move that I instantly feel silly for doing. I might as well have given the man a noogie.

Still, he laughs because that's the kind of guy Sebastian is.

"May I have this dance?" he asks with an outstretched hand.

I blink at it a few times, wondering if I heard him wrong. I tilt my head with a raised brow.

"You can't tell me you don't like to dance because I know for a fact that you do."

I place my hand on my hip, and I use the other to showcase my attire of black pants and a mauve chef's jacket. "I'm not exactly dressed for dancing."

He pulls me toward him anyway. "I was unaware there was a dress code for dancing. Last I heard, you could do so in your underwear."

I give him a deadpan expression, which he refuses to acknowledge as he leads me to the dance floor. I quickly remove my jacket and throw it to Shawn, who waves as I'm taken away.

Sebastian guides me through the crowd, and the tempo changes from a Motown dance to a jazz standard. The opening chords to Norah Jones's "Come Away with Me" plays, and I relax to the familiar beats of the piano.

My shoulders fall as I look up at Sebastian in defeat. He grips my waist and pulls me flush against him. His other hand takes mine and holds it close to his chest.

I laugh to myself at how incorrigible this man is before I lay my free hand on his shoulder and let him lead me in a dance.

"I feel silly," I say, looking around at the beautifully dressed women on the floor. He doesn't say anything in response, so I lean up a little and see him more clearly. "You're dancing with the help."

"I quite like the help," he muses.

I give him my sternest eyes. "I'm serious."

He matches my expression with sarcasm. "So am I."

"People are staring."

"Let them. You're too beautiful for them not to."

My breath hitches at his words, and I have to look away. I turn my nose to his lapel and stare at it as we dance. His intoxicating scent is potent tonight. Citrus and woodsy and so very male. His large hand is splayed on my back; I can feel the heat of it as it warms my body up to my cheeks.

I swallow hard. "Do you have this large of an event every year?"

"We do. It's a thank-you to our clients, referral partners, and staff. My partners and I don't like doing anything this big around the holidays. Everyone's already so busy, and events are a dime a dozen. This is a good time to say thank you and give everyone a night out that they actually look forward to."

"That's a smart idea. Christmas in springtime."

"We have a holiday party that is not this formal. We rent out a pub for happy hour and let everyone get hammered. We also do a barbecue around Labor Day to end the summer."

Somewhere during our conversation, I moved from looking at his shoulder to staring up into his eyes. "The law firm that parties together stays together?"

"The job comes with a lot of stress. If you don't balance it out with friends, family, and a good work environment, it can burn you out."

He lifts our joined hands and points to the bar that's off the dance floor. His assistant is there with a group, laughing loudly at something someone said. His arm is around a girl, who is staring at him, beaming.

"Miles over there has been so consumed with work that his girlfriend almost left him last year."

"That's horrible. I assume they made it through. Let me guess ... you gave him the night off to go to some high-priced restaurant, dinner paid by you."

"That's absurd." He blanches, and I stare up at him with an inquisitive glare. "I gave them the keys to my beach house for the weekend and told him to take Monday off."

I laugh out loud. "Of course you did."

Sebastian spins me. It's not called for in the song, but it feels good to do it anyway. As he twirls me back in, I'm even closer, tighter, firmer ... *more* in every aspect.

It's so easy to fall under his spell. He's hypnotic in his words, spellbounding with his gaze, and I'm so bewitched that I might float right off this dance floor.

"You really take care of everyone, don't you?" I whisper.

"I try." His deep baritone vibrates in his chest as his attention becomes focused on my lips.

I let out a shaky breath and lift my chin. "Speaking of ... no more handouts."

"Is that what you think this is?"

"Isn't it?" I arch a brow.

"No," he states assuredly. "I wanted to showcase a phenomenal local business while offering a great favor to people who had contributed generously to our company."

"This isn't because you feel bad by how things were left?"

My question appears to have caught him off guard. It's a conversation we've been dancing around, both literally and figuratively.

"It does feel like unfinished business, you and me. I didn't want it to end the way it did," he says, and I nod. It did end, and him stating it seems so final. "There are many things I'd like to discuss with you—perhaps in a more private setting. But tonight, this was just me doing something good for you. I care for you, and I have a need to help those I care about."

The tender expression in his brown eyes is sincere.

"Who takes care of you?" I ask, breathy.

"I don't need anything."

"Everyone needs something."

"Well, there is one thing I want, but I don't think I'll be able to have it as my own."

My feet halt on the dance floor, as do his. He's staring at me—and not just at my eyes. He's looking so deeply that I swear he's gazing into my soul. Because in this moment, it feels like I'm the thing he wants.

My soul is screaming at him, begging him to take me.

Have me.

Love me.

Our hands release, and he places one on my cheek while mine finds his heart. It's thumping quickly, and I feel it racing against my palm.

His fingers glide down my temple and cup my jaw. I lean into his hand and stare into his gorgeous face. My lips part, and I take a heavy inhale.

His eyes fall to my mouth. His tongue dips out to lick his lower lip.

LOYAL LAWYER

I inhale deeply and lean in a touch. My body quivering.

He comes forward, and his eyes shift to the side. His brow drops, and I see it. The hesitation. There's something holding him back.

He looks back to my mouth, but I pull away, moving away from him, giving us much-needed space.

The song has now changed to a dance tune, and the people around us are moving in rapid beats while Sebastian and I stand here, staring at one another.

I take two more steps back and knock into someone. With an apology, I excuse myself from the dance floor and start to walk back to the tasting table.

Sebastian grabs my hand. I turn back to him but shake my head.

"I'm sorry. I got carried away," I start, but he stops me.

"Why did you just walk away like that?" he asks, dumbfounded.

Normally, I'd say it was nothing and leave. But there's something about his perplexed expression that has me saying, "You were about to kiss me, Sebastian. But you halted like there was something else that was more important for you to think about. Call me old-fashioned, but when a man is about to kiss me, I want to be the only thing on his mind." He goes to speak, but I halt him with my hands and my words. "Please, don't try to explain. You were right when you said we felt like unfinished business. But it ended. You have a beautiful life you need to focus on. Perhaps tonight was what we both needed to put this thing between us to bed. Figuratively, of course. Not literally."

"Amy, I—"

"Please. People are already staring, and I'd like to leave here with a reputation of being an exceptional artisanal chocolatier. Not a woman who got into it with the boss at the company party."

My words have him standing taller with a slight nod of his head, showing he understands my need for decorum. I take the opportunity to walk back to the table and stand with Shawn. He starts to speak, but I just give him my downturned eyes and silently ask him not to give his advice. I just want to work and move on.

As much as I secretly hoped there could be a world where Sebastian and I could coexist, it turns out, my heart is just not strong enough to be around the one thing in this world *I* want but cannot have.

CHAPTER FIFTEEN

It's been a long night. Shawn and I package up the remaining chocolate and pack everything into my car. I drop him off at his place, adamant that I can unload on my own. I need something to do to keep myself from overthinking about my night.

I bring the supplies inside myself and then take Lady Featherington for a long walk. When I return, I put everything away.

Now, it's just me and Lady Featherington lying on my bed and watching *Bridgerton* on Netflix. I might or might not have a tray of truffles next to me that I'm devouring at an unhealthy pace.

A ring at the alleyway door surprises me and has me checking my watch to see the time. When I look at my phone, I see Sebastian standing in my alley with his hands in his pockets as he rocks on his heels.

I rise from the futon and walk to the door, not caring that I'm wearing yoga pants and an oversize sweatshirt. My face is clean of makeup, and my hair is in a long braid. It's unsexy and plain, most definitely not a look I'd go for when seeing a man.

If he decides to show up, unannounced, then my dowdy appearance is what it is.

I open the door to see he's still wearing his suit from earlier, tie and all. His hair has been raked through, and his cheeks are flush.

If he thinks I look a mess, he doesn't say anything. Instead, he's staring at me like I'm a mirage in the desert.

"What are you doing here?" I cross my arms, not because I'm upset to see him, but because I just realized I'm not wearing a bra and the cold air might have an unwelcome effect in this exact moment.

"I came to say all the things I should have said earlier, but I didn't want to make a scene."

I let out an exasperated breath. "You don't have to apologize."

"I'm not here for forgiveness. I'm here to explain." His tone is louder, more fervent than I've heard from him before. He runs his hand through his hair and behind his neck, letting out a long, deep breath. "Can I come in?"

With my eyes closed, I briefly consider not allowing him in, but my manners get the best of me when I open them and see the clear distress in his face.

I nod for him to come inside as I step back. He walks through the threshold, and I close the door behind him.

The room is dark. There's no music or sweet smell of confections, like the last time he was here.

It's just me and Sebastian.

It's silent, except for the sound of my heart.

His back is to me with his head straight ahead,

staring at my painting. Its vibrant colors are subdued by the *vintage-book page* canvas it was created on. It's of a woman's face. Her bright green eyes bleed tears of the same color. Her lips are parted with words to say. She's a dreamer, a woman yearning as she looks forward for her desires.

I feel very much like her right now as I watch Sebastian's back rise and fall. His hands clench to the sides and release when he spins to me.

"You were right," he starts. "I wanted to kiss you tonight, but I hesitated."

His confession leaves me leaning to the side as I grip the counter. I let the cool metal surface ground me in reality, for fear his words will levitate and destroy me.

"I hesitated because I don't know if you want me as much as I want you. I'm crazy about you, Amy. Beyond crazy. I'm falling for you hard, and I can't seem to get up."

My entire chest ignites as my hopes lift. Tingles rise up and down my arms, and I have to catch my breath to keep up with the feelings inside my body.

"You can't say that. You're having a baby with another woman."

"I already love that child more than anything in this world, and he's not even here yet." He takes a step forward, his hands out in offering. "But I'm not in love with her. Our time ran out already, and this is a blessing that came out of a relationship that had run its course." He takes another step closer, his body just a whisper away. His voice just as low. "I know I come with baggage. This is more than any man should ask of a woman, but, Amy"—he grips my hands and holds them close to his heart—"if you'll give us a try, I swear I'll be the best man you'll ever know. I want to worship you, provide for you, protect you."

"I won't be responsible for breaking up a family if there's a chance you'll be together." My heart clenches at having to turn him away again.

"There's not a chance. She and I have had this conversation, and neither of us wants to be together. We want to co-parent. That's it. She knows I want you, and she wants us to work as much as I do. Did you hear me? I'm falling in love with you. So hard and so fast. I can't eat or sleep without you on my mind. A fool of a man would let you walk away without fighting like hell to give love another shot. I should have said this a long time ago instead of letting you walk out my door. I had numerous chances, but I hoped you'd come back to me on your own. You haven't, so this is me, fighting like hell for you."

A rogue tear falls from my eye. I didn't even know I wanted to cry, but his words are everything I've ever wanted to hear. He's vowing to worship, provide, and protect. They're such wonderful promises that have me shaking from his emotion.

Giving this man a chance means I could have my heart shattered. But I'm walking around with a bruised and battered one without him. It's crippling me.

"I don't need any of those things you mentioned," I say, and his face falls with worry. With my palm on his cheek, I bring his focus back to me. "I just want you. I've been a wreck these long weeks without you."

A huge smile ignites his face, and he holds my cheeks, making my arms fall to my sides in surprise.

"Then, what the fuck are we doing?"

I laugh at his reaction and shrug.

He moves a hand to my back and pulls me into him, caressing my hair and gripping me by the back of my head.

"Be with me, Amy," he breathes, inches from my lips. "Let me be yours."

It's the last thing he says before his lips crash down on mine, enveloping me in and sinfully taking what is his to take.

I grab him by the arms and kiss him back, parting my lips and rolling my tongue against his. His jacket is on the floor, and I'm fiddling with the buttons of his shirt in seconds. The sleeve gets caught on his wrist, so he has to break the kiss, cursing and ripping the thing off his body, making a button pop off the seam.

I take a moment to admire the man in front of me. Buff chest with a smattering of hair and a taut stomach with a tempting trail of hair leading down to his belt buckle.

With his lips back on mine, he grabs my ass and lifts me onto the counter. These are high counters, so our groins don't line up the way I'd like, but at this height, he has a great angle to my neck and jaw, where he nips and sucks his way down.

I rip off my sweatshirt and toss it onto the floor, watching Sebastian's eyes light up at the sight of my breasts, perky and ready for him.

"You're beautiful," he says, looking at my chest and then up to my eyes, holding the connection. "So beautiful."

His openmouthed kisses leave a trail of divine chills

on my jaw, clavicle, and shoulder as they move lower. With one pert nipple in his mouth, he sucks lightly while working the other with this thumb and forefinger. I gasp in gratification and bathe in the quivering sensations that run straight to my core.

I run my hands up the side of his torso. He's ripped and muscular. The dip in his shoulder blades alone are enough to send me into a whirlwind as I move my hands over his skin. We're naked on top, and I've never found pants to be such a nuisance.

I lift my hips for him to remove them, but he doesn't immediately, so I make a motion that's not so subtle, causing him to laugh into my neck.

"Oh, Amy, my Amy, my sweet girl. I want you so bad."

"Then, have me, Sebastian. You said you'd be with me. Then, do it." With a finger under his chin, I bring his face up to me. "Be. With. Me."

I take his mouth in mine, loving every swipe of his tongue and caress of his mouth. I undo his belt buckle and zipper while he lifts my hips. My pants come off first, and I flinch at the cold steel counter against the heat of my body.

While it might be chilly, I don't fight it as Sebastian lays a hand on my breastbone and slowly lowers my entire body down onto the slab, leaving me fully exposed before him—a meal on a table, ready to be devoured.

Where I don't like the height of these counters for kissing with friction, I do like how Sebastian has easy access to lower his face down to my core. He runs his tongue up the folds, making me buck slightly off the table.

"The most decadent things have been served in this kitchen," he says before running his tongue, flat and firm, against my most sensitive parts.

I moan and am rewarded with a kiss to my thigh.

"You are the most delicious thing"—he stops and does that tongue motion again, leaving me panting—"I have ever tasted"—he pauses a third time, and I grip the sides of the table—"in my life." He takes another long, sensuous swipe, and this time, he doesn't stop.

My hands are in his hair, pulling and rubbing as he feasts on my pussy. His strong tongue flicks my clit over and over and then runs long and hard all over my center. He laces his hand under my rear and lifts my hips, making me a virtual meal. I raise my head and watch him feast, reeling with ecstasy as my orgasm builds.

My ears burn, and my nipples are heavy and sensitive. Every nerve ending of my body is on fire.

I gyrate my hips along his face and get the added friction that nearly sends me over the edge. My body begins to spasm as waves of pleasure ripple up my core. I'm about to come when he moves his face and kisses up and down the inside of my thigh, calming my body before going back in for more.

I'm nearing complete orgasm when he abruptly stops, and I make an audible pout.

Sebastian hovers over me and kisses me slow.

As my hands grip his shoulders, he places his under me, lifting me off the steel and carrying me to the office. Lady Featherington comes rushing toward us as we walk in.

Instead of placing me on the bed, he seats me on my

desk. I'm naked, wanting, and needy as he walks to the futon and raises the bottom, pulling in one motion so it morphs from a couch to a bed.

He turns to me, a roguish smile on his face. "May I undress for you?"

I bite my lip and nod.

He slides his hand into his pocket and takes out his wallet, laying it on the desk. His large hands easily undo his belt, and his fingers flick the button of his pants. The zipper makes a humming sound as the teeth glide down, showcasing black boxer briefs.

There's an obvious bulge in his pants that becomes more evident as he steps out of his shoes and then pants. While he removes his socks, I glance down at his muscular thighs. Golden skin with the cuts and curves of an Adonis. While I could look at this man all night long, it's his thoughts that drive me wild. And from the way he's looking at me with intense eyes, he lets me know his thoughts are very naughty.

There's a chill in the air, yet my skin is quickly warmed when he lowers his briefs and stands before me, gloriously naked. His thick manhood is standing at attention, wide and proud. I quiver at the sight of it and find myself staring hard.

Sebastian places his hands on his hips and laughs. "Do you like what you see?"

I nod, my eyes still on his impressive length. "Very."

He takes a step forward, and his hand glides along my cheek, pulling my gaze up to his. "That's good. Because I am mesmerized by the woman before me."

His mouth is back on mine, and while I have so many places to touch on Sebastian, I choose his chest, laying my palm along his heart and feeling the beat against me. Our kisses keep in tune to the rhythm. It's rapid and fiery. Tempting and tantalizing.

Our hands become explorers, roaming over every peak.

His fingers caress my breasts, and I arch into his touch.

My palms graze his taut stomach, and he hisses.

His thumb sweeps over my core, and I gasp into his mouth.

My knuckles rub over the sensitive head of his erection, and he lets out a guttural groan.

"Fuck, baby. Your touch is magic," he drawls.

I grip the steel of his cock and pump, running my thumb over the swollen head and back down, letting him know just how magical my touch can be. He lifts his wallet and slides out a condom, handing it to me. Instead of taking it, I move closer and grip it with my teeth, tearing the edge of the plastic as he holds the bottom. The package opens, and I dip my fingers inside to take out the condom, slowly unraveling it onto his granite-like erection.

His eyes are hooded, sexy and salivating with lust. I like this expression on him because I'm the one causing it.

His hands slide under my hips and lift me to the bed. He is a man who will put my needs before his own, and while I love his touches, kisses, caresses, I happen to be a woman with no willpower when it comes to this guy. As soon as he takes a seat on the bed, I crawl on top of his thighs and straddle him, lifting my hips so the tip of his erection is dangerously close to my opening.

LOYAL LAWYER

The head of his cock glides along the outside of my folds, and I want nothing more than to slide down and bury him deep inside me.

Before I can take what I want, Sebastian rubs my clit with one hand and holds on to my ass with the other. With my hands on his shoulders, I lean back and reel in the pleasure as his mouth finds my breast again. He's all-consuming. A consummate lover who brings me to the brink of ecstasy. My gasps and moans can't be controlled.

"Sebastian," I chant out his name for lack of anything else coherent to say.

I desperately want to lower my hips, but his strength halts me from doing so.

With my every frustrated pout, he smiles as he gives faster swirls of his thumb and then sucks on my nipple. I'm gyrating, riding his hand and gripping his hair, pulling and tugging as the intensity of the orgasm he's been teasing me with builds again.

Higher and higher, I climb. My skin is a sheen of sweat. He's holding me close, his muscles tightening. My core clenching, my body quaking, and my gasps loud and quick as I come close to exploding.

Sebastian must sense it because just as I arch back and scream out in ecstasy, he lowers me onto him, his cock buried deep inside me as I pulse and come all over his shaft. He pumps inside me as I roll out my orgasm, stretching it out longer and further than any I've ever known.

I'm so wet, drenched to the core for this man, and shaking from the inside out.

His hips are moving with a force I've never felt, and

I meet his motions, feeling every bit of pleasure. He hits the spot deep inside me with the utmost precision that I cry out, unaware I could feel this powerful. His forehead rests against mine as we breathe each other in, gripping tightly and fucking. His eyes are midnight, and a deep line forms in his brow as he fights his own release.

With a swift motion, he flips me onto my back, the contact of our bodies never broken. He lifts my leg over his shoulder and goes in deeper, never stopping the barrage of pleasurable assault. His forehead is coated with sweat. His eyes are pierced dark with ecstasy, and his mouth is pursed, panting.

I lean up onto my elbows and look into his deep stare. "Come for me, Sebastian," I will him, my voice breathless.

He furrows his brow. "Are you sure?"

"I'm ready for you. I want to feel you lose control."

That's all the permission he needs. Like a man of the wild, a lion let loose, he unleashes his inner beast and chases his own pleasure. It's primal, and it feels incredible. It's also glorious to look at.

His skin is glazed, his eyes hooded, and those lips are pursed. I can feel his cock growing inside me, filling every inch of me, claiming me. Owning me.

He comes with a growl, and it's magnificent. He's beaming with pleasure as he calls out my name on his lips, over and over again, praising the woman who gave him this bout of nirvana.

My body shakes as a final wave of gratification swims through my veins.

As Sebastian lowers his body to me, it's not in spent energy. He rolls us to our sides, our legs entwined, our hands connected, and he kisses me, romantic and purposeful.

We kiss for hours.

We kiss for days.

We kiss like two people who have just realized they can kiss forever.

And we do. For now.

For now, it's just the two of us in our bubble with no obstacles of the future.

"After tonight, we're going to have to move our sleepovers to my place. Your bed is entirely too small."

I lean back and tilt my head to the side. "You're staying the night?"

He grins. "I'm not the kind of man who leaves in the middle of the night. Although I will be out very early to change before work and walk Duke. That is, if you'll have me?"

I run my teeth along my bottom lip and praise the stars for sending me this man. "I want you here. Always."

"*Always* sounds like an open invitation."

My heart flutters. "Then, I want you with me indefinitely."

He lifts my leg up over his hip and brings us closer. "Then, with you is where I'll be."

I curl into his arm and lie with him, basking in the afterglow. It's a bright and luminous moment. I've had feelings like this before. Ones that burn so hot that they scorch everything around it. I try to push those thoughts aside and hope this feeling is different. Maybe this time, the flames won't destroy me.

Maybe.

CHAPTER SIXTEEN

"Aren't you a sight for sore eyes?" Charity expresses cheekily with outstretched arms as I take my seat at Love and Lavender.

I wave off her dramatic greeting. "Nice to see you too."

She slides over a latte and a cardboard to-go box. "I ordered for us already. I'm starving."

As she takes a bite of her sandwich, I open my box and see she picked out the turkey and avocado club. "You're an angel. I only have thirty minutes before I have an appointment at the bank."

"Are you picking up the loan check?" she mumbles excitedly with a mouth full of sandwich. Her fingers sneak up to cover her messy chew.

I smile. "I sign the papers right after this. I'm crazy excited and yet absolutely paranoid. I've never taken a loan before. I never had college bills to pay off or a car payment. This is serious."

"Seriously huge! What's the first order of business?

A new kitchen, I presume?"

"No. I think the size works for now—until the orders become too much for the space. I'm revamping the website and looking into some advertising. Adding some new items to the menu. That's step one."

She nods in understanding. "If the orders take off, you'll need to hire Shawn full-time."

"Gladly so. He's the best employee ever. Even now, he's over there, putting boxes together. He could easily gripe that he's a chocolatier and not a box boy, yet he never complains."

"And he puts up with your jazz music. You know he plays loud-ass hip-hop when you're not around."

"Don't I know it? He loves to sing into the spatula. Gotten a great show more than once. The guy has no shame." I laugh as I take a sip of my latte. It's caramel and creamy, warming my chest. "I wouldn't have as much confidence with taking on new orders if it wasn't for Shawn. As soon as I can, I'll be giving him a raise, for sure."

Charity pauses before biting her sandwich again. "I think a full-time job is a good start."

I agree. I have so many plans for Amy Morgana Chocolatier, all mapped out in my vision journal. Taking chances on myself is what I do. I've just never done so with such a large price tag attached to it.

I look over at Charity and see she has a huge grin on her face. I close an eye and tilt my head, wondering what the heck she's thinking to be staring at me like the cat who caught the canary.

"You're making a face," I surmise.

She rolls her eyes. "Of course I am. We have yet

to discuss the big development. Not that you getting a small-business loan isn't huge. Congratulations yet again. But"—she rolls her tongue along her back teeth, as if waiting for me to dish, and when I don't, she practically bounces out of her seat—"Sebastian! Hello? You promised me details. It's been two weeks since you've decided to be a couple. Between my work schedule and you being busy, cooking or out with Sebastian, I haven't been able to get the juice."

I drop my shoulders and look to the side before smirking back at her. "You know you've gotten plenty of gossip from Shawn."

It's been one of those weeks where I've been running all over town and I miss my bestie when she stops by the kitchen.

"Yes, but he leaves out all the good details. You can't just disappear in a lust-filled haze without filling me in." She widens her eyes, like she's waiting for me to spill my guts.

I laugh out loud and set down my latte. "I guess it has been pretty amazing."

"Pretty amazing?" She drops her head back like she can't believe I just said that. "Girl, this latte is pretty amazing. My new shoes are pretty amazing. You hooking up with that Adonis of a man is way more than pretty amazing."

"Okay, fine." I feign ignorance and then allow the biggest smirk to grow on my face before I place my hands on the table and lean in. "It is mind-blowing, drop your head back, curl your toes, laugh in disbelief afterward because the sex is so good. Is that better?"

She eyes me suspiciously. "Seriously?"

"Cross my heart and vow to never lie about the love of a good man."

She sits back and sighs. "I've never been romanced that good."

"You will. I promise. When you find the right one, you will."

Charity sits back up and picks up her sandwich and asks, "Is that all you guys do then? Hump on every surface possible?" before she takes a bite.

"No one can have sex that much. But that's what I'm liking. It's not just about the naked times. I enjoy just being with him when I can. He works like a dog, which is great because it gives me time to focus on my business. I'm through with men who want me to drop everything for their needs."

"You do have a track record for picking losers," she states matter-of-factly.

I lower my gaze to her. "Watch it. Now, you're starting to sound like my siblings."

She makes a face like that was the biggest insult I could have ever given. "Well, clearly, you've redeemed yourself because you are with a true romantic hero now."

"He's just a normal guy, Charity," I explain. "He leaves his socks on the living room floor and squeezes the toothpaste from the top instead of the bottom, which is completely annoying."

"Yes, must be the worst," she drones sarcastically.

I giggle. "When he's slammed with work, I don't get to see him, but he always calls or texts. It's sweet. We've spent quite a few nights at his place because my futon is way too short for his six-foot-two frame. Lady Featherington and Duke get along great. I've even been leaving her there during the day, so the two can keep each other company."

"Even your dogs are getting along? This is too sickening."

I tilt my head with a sigh. "You'll find someone. Don't give up."

"You have to tell me something bad about him. There's got to be something. He's a lawyer. Is he a total control freak?"

I shrug. "Kind of. He's bossy, for sure. Sebastian likes to lead any situation whether it's at work or what we're watching on Netflix. He makes comments about my living choices, as he's not a fan of me showering in the gym. And he's brutally honest. The other day, I asked him if he liked this dress I'd just bought, and he told me it wasn't flattering. I almost died because, usually, guys just nod without even looking, but he eyed me up and down and suggested I change it for another color. He was right. Plus, he's over the top. Like, when we go out, it's always to the best restaurants, and he pays. A girl like me doesn't want to be taken care of."

"Again, not painting a bad picture here. A man who wants to take you to nice restaurants, cares for your safety, and actually tells you the truth is not a bad thing."

"I know, but I'm trying to find bad things for you because he's kind of perfect." I gnaw on my thumbnail and smile. "We hang out for a few hours after work. Have dinner and whatever else feels right at the time—"

"Sex."

I laugh. "Yes, but then we chill for a little while

before he grabs his laptop and gets some work done while I curl up next to him and read."

"You're like the cute, old married couple. I know I sound bitter, but I'm not. I'm truly happy for you."

"I know you are." I hear my phone ding with a text message from Sebastian that fills me with absolute joy. I turn back to Charity. "And I'm glad because he should be here any minute to join us. I told him where we'd be and to stop by if he had time. Looks like he has time." I hold up my phone to show her his text.

"If he's going to crash my date with you, he'd better be bringing me a friend of his as well."

I raise my eyebrows and tap my finger on my chin. "That's a good idea."

I take a bite of my sandwich and daydream about how great it would be to find a handsome attorney for Charity. Not that she needs a professional, but like me, she has gone through a few duds and is due for a nice, reliable man—someone who treats her good. He has to be funny though and up for spontaneity.

I swallow. "I'll have to ask if he knows of anyone at the firm who's single and can join us next time."

"Are you already trying to get me to bring another guy for Charity?" I hear the sexiest male voice say behind me—deep, rhythmic … mine. Sebastian leans in to kiss me before holding out his hand to Charity. "I don't think we've officially met, but I've heard all about you."

She meets his gesture as they shake. "Only the good things I hope."

He gives her a smoldering grin as he takes a seat beside me. "No, Amy has only revealed the deviant behaviors of her best friend, including a time you went streaking in front of the Liberty Bell."

She puts her palm to her face and feigns embarrassment. "I blame it on the booze. You know I can't handle a beer flight."

"A beer flight is a tasting. You had pints after that," I explain.

With a flick of her hand, she takes a faux bow. "No one can blame me for being boring."

"That's for sure," I say and then look over at Sebastian.

He's debonair in his gray suit and no tie. It's his style for days when he's not going to court, and it just happens to be when I find him the sexiest.

"I hope you don't mind me crashing," he says to Charity. "I only have a second, so I wanted to stop by to say hello."

I hold up my sandwich to him, and he takes a bite. When he pulls back, he's got a spot of mayo on his lip, and I rub it with my thumb before taking a bite myself.

"Mmm." He nods his head. "That is good."

I pick up the other half and hand it to him. "Here, take the second half."

He scoots closer to share the box with me as he takes a bite.

When I glance over to Charity, she's got hearts in her eyes as she takes in the ease between Sebastian and me. She's right. We're like an old married couple even though we've only officially been together for a few weeks. There's been this level of comfort between us since the day we met, and it's only getting better as each day passes.

We see each other when we can, and there aren't hard feelings when we can't. He opens doors and pays for dinner. He tries my chocolate recipes and listens to me drivel on about the new layout ideas for the website. I listen as he talks about past cases he's worked on, and I even indulged in a game of Pictionary with him because it's his favorite. He's theatrical and competitive, so I can see why. We walk our dogs and talk about music. It's by far the easiest relationship I've ever been in.

"So, you're wanting to meet someone?" Sebastian asks Charity, who snaps out of her dazed expression.

"Aren't we all?" She tries to blow it off with a wave and takes a sip from her drink. "Not everyone is as lucky as you two meeting via a wrong text. If you know of anyone who's not a total asshole or who doesn't have massive baggage, let me know."

My chest tightens at the baggage comment. While being with Sebastian has been easy, there is a very large elephant in the relationship that threatens to make it difficult.

Yes, I've come to terms with Sebastian being a father, but coming to terms and fully knowing what will happen in a few short months are two completely different things.

I know I'm living in blissful ignorance, but it's like the song "The Dance" by Garth Brooks. I guess I'll never know if the pain was worth it if I don't take the dance first. I just pray I don't fall too hard if he decides a relationship with me is too much in the juggle of his life.

When I turn back to Sebastian, I can tell the wheels in his mind are spinning as he stares off to the ceiling, like I've seen him do when he's trying to find the right words to say as he works on his closing arguments.

He slowly starts to nod his head. "I think I might know a guy. He's a lawyer too, and last I heard, he was single. Good guy, and he went into real estate law, so he doesn't work the long hours I do."

"Well, I'm game if you think he's worthy of all of this." She shimmies her hand down her body in an overdramatic way as she shakes slightly in her chair.

We both chuckle at her antics.

"Yeah, I think you two will do just fine," he says.

Charity's phone alarm goes off. "Time for me to run. I have to get to work." She takes a final bite of her sandwich and then packs up the remnants in the cardboard box.

Sebastian finds her endearing. "Do you have an alarm on your phone, telling you when you need to leave?"

"Hell yeah, I do. I tend to lose track of time pretty easily, especially when I get to hang out with my bestie here." She points at me and then stands, tossing her garbage in a nearby trash and recycling bin. "It's saved my ass plenty of times. It was great finally meeting you, Sebastian. Talk to your guy, and if he's down, we can go on a double date."

His chuckle fills the room. "I will. Great meeting you too."

Charity leaves with a wave, and I turn to Sebastian. "You're pretty wonderful, you know that?"

He turns to me and slides an arm on the back of my chair. "Is that only because I told her I'd hook her up with my friend?"

He leans in and kisses my neck and then the tender spot of my jaw, sending chills throughout my body that pool right where they shouldn't since we're sitting in the middle of a coffee shop and can't do anything about it.

I run my fingers up his thigh. "Not only that. You're wonderful because you're you."

"Well, you're pretty spectacular, so I guess that makes us a dynamic couple." He kisses my lips before pulling back with a smirk, knowing damn well how turned on he just got me.

I take a deep breath and then pick up my latte, needing to change my thought process, and then I remember I needed to ask him something. "Hey, do you have plans tonight? I have a meeting at the bank at four, but I was hoping we could toast in celebration of my new loan."

His smile falls as he shakes his head. "I'm sorry, but I do. Lauren has a sonogram tonight. I asked her to make it the last appointment of the day, so I could attend. It's a 3-D image, so I'll be able to see his face."

There's that gleam that ignites in his eyes when he talks about his son. It's hard for me to be annoyed with him when he is so genuinely happy.

"That sounds awesome. Have you thought of names yet?"

"I have. I'd like to name him Oliver, after my father, but I'm sure she has some very hip names planned, like Wyatt or Hudson. Perhaps she'll let me tug on her ear a bit at dinner tonight."

I sit up in my seat at this news. "Dinner?"

His stature tilts a bit as he sits back, looking at me to assess my reaction. "Yes. The plan was to go to dinner afterward. There are a few things I want to discuss with her. Are you okay with that?"

"Yes!" I say rather too convincingly. "You should take the mother of your child out for a meal."

I swallow down any bad feelings I have about this dinner—because I do have a few. I know how charismatic Sebastian can be. He is a natural flirt and can woo any woman, just with a greeting. I know he wouldn't cheat on me, but I can't deny that he wouldn't give Lauren false hope. I shake my head and rid myself of the dramatic thoughts. I'm getting way ahead of myself.

"What sort of things did you plan to discuss?"

"Her birth plan, for starters. I think we should take a few parenting classes, as neither of us has had small children in our families for quite some time. I'd also like to discuss our joint custody. Where our son will live and how often I'll get to see him."

I blink at the details. "That's a lot to discuss."

"It's a long relationship the two of us will have together. I've seen these things go south fast. If we do this with the mind-set that we're a family, I think the three of us can make it work."

"Three of us?" I perk up, feeling included.

"Yes. Me, Lauren, and Oliver. Well, assuming she lets me have my way." His grin showcases his positivity that he can convince her. He repeats the name of his future child a few times and continues to grin.

Meanwhile, I'm stuck on the word *family*.

The fact that he already sees them as one is his greatest virtue. It's the kind of thing that could make me fall in love with him. It's also the thing that scares me the most.

He grins and leans over to kiss me. I let his tongue will my mind away from all thoughts that bare the things out of my control as I melt into him. My eyes are hooded, and my lips are still puckered when he pulls back and rubs his thumb along my cheek.

"Sorry tonight won't work, but I have the entire weekend dedicated to you. Anything you want, I am at your beck and call."

I arch a brow at his grand proposal. "Really? So, if I told you I wanted to tie you to the bed and do wicked things to you all weekend long, you'd be game?"

"I'd love nothing more than to be buried in you all weekend," he breathes.

I laugh because he can be so sexy. "Good to know. I did have something else in mind though. Something a bit more PG-13."

He arches his brows in interest.

"My niece is having a birthday party. My sister is pregnant and due any day, so they're having a family-only get-together at my parents' house. It sounds small, but there's eighteen of us, and, well, I was hoping you'd come with me."

"I'd love to." He kisses my nose and then grabs his sandwich and takes a bite before looking at his phone that's going off. As he chews, he sighs, like he's sad he has to go. He swallows his bite and faces me. "It's Miles. He told me he'd call if my next appointment didn't have to cancel. So, I guess I should get going."

"That's okay. I have errands, and then I'm off to the bank. Wish me luck."

He takes the box and throws it in the trash. My latte is still full, so I take it with me and grab my bag.

"Just text me if they don't issue the check today," he says as we walk to the door, grabbing it and holding it open for me. "Actually, text me either way."

"Will do. And have a great appointment tonight."

We're standing on the sidewalk as he glances down at me with a glazed-over look in his eyes, and it's all from staring into mine. "I am the luckiest man alive, you know that?"

I sway my shoulders as I smile, not disagreeing with him.

He leans down and kisses me again. This kiss is full of longing and not wanting to let go. I feel his pout as he pulls away.

"Now, walk away quickly before I forget all my obligations for the day and stand here, kissing you like a fool until the cops come and arrest us for indecency."

I grin, biting my inner lip.

Sebastian is the quintessential gentleman. I'm a fool for worrying about his impending fatherhood.

Now, I get to worry about him meeting my father … and the whole Morgana clan.

CHAPTER SEVENTEEN

"This is the town you grew up in?" Sebastian asks as I drive through my hometown. Dogwood trees and wide sidewalks make it a beautiful suburb. Being from out of state, he almost seems impressed that such a lush area exists outside the city. "You must have had a great childhood here. Soccer teams and playing tag in the street?"

"I played basketball in elementary school but wasn't good enough for the high school team. I was more of a loner. Coming home to bake was the highlight of my day."

"Obsessed with chocolate even then?"

"Yes. And my parents have a big kitchen, so I could lay out all of my ingredients without getting in anyone's way."

He nods as he looks out the window, taking in the Tudor-style houses and large front yards. "This does seem like a great place to raise a family. And it's not too far a drive from Center City."

"Traffic can be a bitch though."

I'm driving Sebastian's car since he had to be on a conference call for most of the ride here. It's fascinating to listen to him work, using legal jargon and coming up with case law on the spot. Hell, it's even sexy.

We hit a touch of traffic on the way here but nothing like it can get during rush hour. He spoke on the phone while I sat in silence. It wasn't too bad since his car, with its soft leather cushions, is a glorious piece of German machinery that glides like a dream.

As we pull up to my parents' house, I get a twinge of nervous energy. I hope they won't say or do anything to embarrass me.

I park Sebastian's BMW behind my sister's Volvo and turn off the ignition with a grunt. Before I can exit, he grips my wrist, pulls me toward him, and places a simple kiss on my jaw.

"You shouldn't worry so much. Parents love me."

I watch as he keeps his cool demeanor while exiting the car, and follow suit with a shake of my head. I walk up to his outstretched hand and take it as we head to the front door, and I let us in.

The house is a bustle of activity. My three nephews are rushing around, playing laser tag. Only one stops to say hello before crashing against a wall and going into hiding from who I assume is his enemy brother, ready to shoot.

"That's Aiden, Caleb, and Connor," I point out to Sebastian as my niece comes strolling by, wearing a feather boa, hot-pink sunglasses, and Little Mermaid high heels while pushing a play baby stroller. "And this fancy little girl is Alice."

"Don't you look glamorous today?" Sebastian says to her, kneeling to his knees to get to her level.

Alice lowers her sunglasses to reveal a deep scowl as she places a finger to her lips and briskly says, "Shh. My baby is sleeping."

Sebastian puts his hands up in retreat and speaks in a whisper, "My apologies."

She puts her glasses back in place and continues her stroll, little heels wobbling as she walks.

"I like her." He watches her with wonderment.

"She's a spitfire all right. My sister says she's just like me. I don't see it."

Sebastian laughs. "I can definitely imagine her picking up a phone in a few years and bitching out a complete stranger over lost rent."

"Never gonna let that go, are you?"

"Never." He leans in to kiss my head.

His hand is on the small of my back as we walk to the backyard, where my family is scattered about the back deck. Matthew is cooking at the grill while Henry stands behind him with his arms crossed and foot tapping, looking like he's dying to take the spatula away from him.

"Those burgers have to be precisely at one hundred and sixty degrees Fahrenheit." Henry points to the patties as Matthew flips them haphazardly.

"Don't worry. I'll poke my finger in yours to make sure it's just right," Matthew says.

"It's called a thermometer." Henry grimaces and then sees Sebastian and me watching them. "Hey, Amy. Didn't see you sneak in here."

I smile. "Sebastian and I just got here."

My mother, who is over by the table, talking to Fiona and her husband, turns around, and the three of them come over, as does Matthew, who abandons his post at the grill.

Sebastian and I are now swarmed by four members of our family, who are all staring at him with mixed looks of skepticism or intrigue—depending on the family member.

"We've heard so much about you!" Mom is the first to greet Sebastian. She leans in for a hug, and he accepts it willingly. "Amy is so smitten. We weren't sure if you were actually coming."

I lower my brow. "I told you this morning I was bringing someone."

"Yeah, but your dates aren't that reliable," Fiona chimes in as she gives Sebastian the head to toe. "Or as handsome. You usually like them lanky and a little greasy. This one is super attractive."

"His name is Sebastian, and it's weird that you're talking about him like he can't hear you." I turn to Sebastian and excuse my sister. "Fiona is quite vain."

"Oh, please. You can totally judge a book by its cover. Your other boyfriends were lame. This one comes off like he can take care of things." Her hand pets his bicep, which I pull away from her trajectory.

Matthew seems to be assessing Sebastian as well, but where he couldn't care less about his pretty features, he is definitely sizing him up. My brother loves nothing more than the knowledge that he can beat up everyone else.

"Yo! What do you bench? Two? Two fifty?" Matthew asks, and I roll my eyes toward Mom, who just shrugs.

Sebastian doesn't seem fazed. "Two eighty to three hundred. I try to stay about a hundred pounds over my weight. I want to be strong but not bulky. I don't have the discipline to get to the gym as often as I'd like. I do mostly cardio and strength training with free weights at home. Lots of push-ups."

Matthew eyes him skeptically. "Like a hundred? How long does it take you? I can—"

"Make it stop," I beg my mother, who raises her hands as if she's helpless to the situation. Behind her is a barbeque grill. "Matt, your burgers are burning."

"Oh crap!" He rushes over to the grill that's now smoking.

Mom and Fiona follow him, waving away the plumes in the air.

Henry is looking down with an expression of complete annoyance, his fingers pinching the bridge of his nose. "Definitely not going to be a hundred and sixty degrees," he mumbles to himself before extending his hand to Sebastian. "Sorry about that. You'll have to excuse Matthew. He joined an old-school iron powerlifting gym a few years ago and has been infatuated with fitness ever since. I'm Henry. The maturer brother."

Sebastian shakes his hand, and the two men hold on a touch too long, both their grips firm. Where Matthew likes to test brute strength, Henry will judge a man based on his handshake.

"Amy speaks highly of you. I read your original article on the pragmatic and randomized trial of the phase two trial for the antibody in early Alzheimer's disease."

I lean back and stare up at Sebastian, surprised he

read one of Henry's articles. My brother also seems surprised but maybe more impressed than anything.

"The antibody that targets amyloid deposited in the brain showed a better result for cognitive ability compared to the placebo."

"The hallmark of Alzheimer's disease is the accumulation of amyloid-B peptide," Sebastian states.

"The antibody targets that. The baseline iADRS score at seventy-six weeks showed significant decrease in amyloid peptide. We were quite pleased." Henry has a smug expression. Meeting someone who not only finds interest in his work, but can also banter about it is greater than foreplay to him.

Before Henry has a chance to deep dive into Sebastian's brain and steal his afternoon away, I interject, "Mom is putting the food on the table. I think it's time we all take a seat."

I'm pulling Sebastian toward the table before Henry has a chance to utter another word. Luckily, his wife has now walked over to him and is turning his attention toward their children, who are now wrestling in the grass.

"That was impressive," I whisper to Sebastian. "I didn't know you'd read my brother's research paper."

"Actually, I didn't. I just did a bunch of research last night. If I've learned one thing, it's to never come to the courtroom unprepared."

I bat my eyes. "You're so smart. I knew I chose you for a reason."

We make our way to the outside tables that are already set up with tablecloths and pink princess decorations with party hats for all of us to wear.

Before we sit down, my father approaches Sebastian with his hand out in greeting. "Sebastian, I'm James. Welcome to our home." He has an apron on that says *Kiss the Cook*, which is just adorable and so fitting for my dad.

Sebastian gives him the same firm handshake he gave Henry. "Thank you for having me, especially on such a joyous occasion." He smiles down to my niece Kelsey, who is climbing up in her birthday-girl spot. "Sorry we're late. I had to finish up some things for work before we could leave."

"Attorney, right?" he asks, and Sebastian nods in affirmation. "No worries at all. I like a hardworking man for my Amy. Just glad you could make it."

I grin over to Sebastian, who seems cool as a cucumber while meeting my family. He helps me with my seat before taking his own. Heather takes a seat at the head of the table, which Dad happily gave up so she'd have room for her enormous belly. She looks so uncomfortable, as she's due any day now.

"So, Sebastian," Fiona asks from across the table, "tell me about your job. Amy says you practice personal injury law. Please tell me you're not an ambulance chaser, like those creepy commercials that are on every hour." She quirks her head to the side with a smug expression covering her normally pretty features, which I want to rip off right now.

"Fiona, that's rude," I growl.

Sebastian places his hand on my thigh with a laugh. "It's okay. I know there are some creepy lawyers out there, but there are some good ones too. I like to think

I'm on the good side of things. My office specializes in civil rights law as well."

"Any cases we might have heard of?" Henry asks as he fills his plate with chicken.

"Did you read about the Jeremy Carson case? He was wrongfully accused of a crime and spent seven years in prison. There was also the Hotel, where a worker fell off the roof," Sebastian explains.

Matthew whistles through his teeth. "I know both those cases. Multimillion-dollar payouts. You make a cut of that? Damn. If you're looking for a place to invest, I can help you out."

I roll my eyes at my day-trader brother trying to get a deal at his niece's birthday. "He actually also does a lot of pro bono work to give back to the community. One free client for every high-profile one he wins. All of that pales in comparison to what he and his company donate to city foundations, including the Children's Theater," I state matter-of-factly and notice Sebastian's grin as he turns to me. I might have stalked his company website pretty hard when we first met. "Fiona, I believe your company did the advertising campaign for the reopening of the theater. His company also contributed to the restoration of the landmark."

Fiona seems impressed. "Well, it's nice to see you with a professional. Perhaps he'll rub off on you, so you'll stop living the pipe dream of an Etsy seller. Not that your chocolates aren't delicious. They're just not going to generate a livable income."

"When I met Amy, I was impressed with her business plan, and the products are substantial," Sebastian states, instantly filling me with pride that he's standing up for me like this.

"She makes chocolate behind a gym, where she's also sleeping. That's not really a career," Fiona explains.

Sebastian turns to me with a grin. "You should have seen my first place when I moved to Philly. At least hers has air-conditioning and a real heater. Mine was a tiny hole in the wall with just a floor heater that barely worked. Everyone starts somewhere. It humbles you to have rough beginnings. Makes you work harder."

My cheeks are starting to hurt from smiling so big as I listen to him speak. "Exactly."

"Amy Morgana Chocolatier is really taking off. She just catered an event we had for the firm, and she's still the talk of the town. A lot of our corporate clients already said they're going to use her for their holiday gifts this year."

"Really?" I turn to him in shock.

"Yes, I told you they loved you." His grin is filled with joy.

"Are you going to be able to handle that much business?" Mom asks as she takes a seat right next to me.

I sit up, assuring them that I can. "My loan was approved, so I have everything lined up, and I'm planning on bringing Shawn on full-time. Good things are happening."

Mom places her hand over mine. "That's fantastic news."

"Does that mean you'll finally get a real place to live?" Heather asks.

I pause for a second and then look at Sebastian. It's

funny how I was searching for apartments, but when Sebastian and I reconnected, I haven't gone to see one. It just hasn't been a priority, I guess. Sebastian runs his hand up my thigh, and I smile in return.

"Once I have everything in line with the business, I'll find a place. Sebastian has been kind enough to let Lady Featherington stay at his house most days, so that's been a huge help. I just want to get the website up and have the revenue stream coming in to pay off the loan first. One thing at a time," I respond.

"How much of your business is online?" Henry asks. "I have a friend who does everything via Shopify. Is that what you use?"

"I actually have my own shopping cart system that works pretty well."

He seems annoyed. "Amy, why re-create the wheel? Shopify is where it's at. Their stock is through the roof right now. Stop making things harder on yourself than they have to be just because you want to be different or stubborn."

"I'm not using it to be stubborn. I just happen to like the system I use now. If it's not broke, don't fix it," I explain.

Henry points the spoon he's using to dish up the potato salad at me as he says, "Because that system is way better than anything else out there."

I let out a sigh, knowing there's no point in trying to argue with him as I grab my water glass that my mother filled with the pitcher she has on the table.

"Enough about work," Heather says, rubbing her lower back, and I appreciate the pivot in conversation. "Sebastian, tell us about how it is that a guy like you who's, what … early thirties … isn't snatched up yet? It's so refreshing to have Amy bring home someone who is gainfully employed, has a nice car, and has his own home. So much better than the last idiot she was gonna bring home. That guy was having a baby with another lady."

I choke on my drink and start a coughing fit.

"Amy, are you okay? That was oddly timed." Fiona sits up like she's about to get the dirt on some juicy gossip, which I wish weren't the case.

Sebastian pats my back as I look up to Heather.

"That would be me," Sebastian says with a smile, not afraid to admit it. "I'm the guy with the baby on the way."

"Oh my God, I didn't …" Heather waves her hand, but Sebastian laughs lightly and gives her his most charming of grins.

"It's okay. You only want the best for your sister, and you're right. I was an idiot. A man should be smarter with these things, but it's happening. I have a child on the way. A boy actually," he says with that crinkle in his eye that he gets every time he thinks of his son.

Everyone's face drops as Sebastian grins my way, acting unfazed by the bomb he just dropped and not ashamed one bit.

Fiona leans forward. "So, this is the guy you were talking about at Easter? How long have you been together?"

"Two weeks," I answer.

"A few months," Sebastian says at the same time.

I look at him in confusion, wondering what the heck he's talking about.

"What? Did you sleep with some chick and then go straight to my sister the next day?" Matthew fumes like the older protective brother he is.

"Absolutely not," Sebastian states firmly. "The mother is an ex who I dated for quite some time. We were long broken up when she told me. I met Amy only a few days before I found out."

"She kept it from you for that long?" Heather asks, rubbing her belly and then looking over at her husband seated next to her.

Sebastian shrugs. "She wanted to make the initial decision on her own. Though it's not ideal circumstances, I'm thrilled to become a father. I am one hundred percent devoted."

"As you should be," my father states, more pleased to hear Sebastian's stance on the matter than upset that it's happening to begin with.

"So, what? You'll see the kid on the weekends? How will that work?" Fiona asks, cutting up food for her boys.

"We're still figuring out the details," Sebastian says. "But we had a fantastic dinner recently, talking about our plans for co-parenting. I think we're on the right path to finding a manageable lifestyle."

"How far along is she?" Heather asks.

"Twenty-four weeks."

"Who wants to bet these two won't be together come Thanksgiving?" Matthew asks everyone around the table, pointing at us like we can't hear him.

"Matthew James Morgana, you might be a grown man, but I will whoop you with my wooden spoon,"

Mom chastises, to which Matthew leans over and kisses her on the cheek.

"I'll take that bet. Bottle of Macallan 18 says I'll be here for turkey and stuffing," Sebastian says, raising his eyebrows to me like his words are his promise to me rather than the bet.

"That's a three-hundred-fifty-dollar bottle," Henry states matter-of-factly.

"Would you rather it be a twenty-five-year?" Sebastian's mouth tilts up in a slight grin as he tilts his head to the side in the cocky way I've seen him do when talking on the phone while he's dealing with other attorneys and he knows he's got them right where he wants them.

"Make it a twelve, and you got a bet." Matthew holds out his hand to Sebastian.

"Ah, not so sure of yourself now, are you?" Sebastian taunts.

"Oh, I'm still sure. Just making sure the bet is in my price range since I have to save for my kids' college funds."

"I can respect that." They grip hands as I shake my head at the male testosterone that's flooding the table. "Maybe I'll pick your brain later about some college investment plans."

Fiona grumbles, "You just bought yourself a solid two-hour diatribe about portfolios."

"I don't mind. And after, you can give me some parenting advice. I'm a newbie to all things babies." Sebastian lifts his glass.

If there's one thing the Morgana family loves to do, it's give advice. I can already envision the smartphones coming out as soon as lunch is over with photos of their kids as newborns and conversations of the best cribs, *Consumer Reports'* advice on swings, which pediatrician to use, and even how to treat a rash. It's good he has them now to ask for help. I only know so much on the topic.

I clear my throat and stand. "Now that that's been settled, can we get back to the reason why we're all here?" I say as I put the birthday hat on Kelsey and then myself.

Sebastian takes his off his place setting and puts it on too. "That's my girl. Always putting family first."

He looks absolutely ridiculous in his cone-shaped hat with pink unicorns, which only makes me love him even more than I already am starting too.

Yes, it's new love and slowly simmering deep within my heart. I'm doing my best to keep it at bay, but when he puts his hand on the back of my chair and rubs his thumb on my shoulder as he listens to my siblings while simultaneously reiterating to everyone who will listen how amazing I am, it's hard to control it.

Man, I really, really hope he wins that bottle of Macallan.

CHAPTER EIGHTEEN

Summers in Philadelphia are the most enjoyable time of the year. Sure, the Christmas decorations in the historic city make for a wonderful winter, and the spring tulips and fall leaves are beautiful, but the summer months are filled with excitement.

With the windows open and the music blaring, Shawn and I are packing up the last of the day's orders, which are being shipped out for a bridal shower.

"I like these new boxes. The quality is swankier than your last," Shawn muses as he brings over the last tray of truffles.

"They are a high upgrade, which I'm hoping will gain presentation points and visually lift up the quality." I hold up one of the new chocolate boxes. They're still mauve, but the card stock quality is much thicker. "Just a few more, and you're done for the night."

"I can deliver these for you."

I grin as I turn his way. *How'd I get so lucky to have such a great employee?* "That's sweet of you. No hot plans tonight?"

"Nah. Raynne and I split, so I'm lying low for a few days."

I shake my head. "Why am I not surprised? Do you stay with anyone for more than a couple dates?"

He shrugs like it's no big deal. "I like the variety—shoot me. That chick was feisty, but damn, was she crazy, so that one wasn't my fault. Girl put a wireless Ring camera in my apartment without telling me."

"That's a bit excessive, but how did you not know a Ring was installed at your front door? Don't you walk by it every time you enter?"

He laughs as he turns to me with his eyes opened wide. "Because it was *inside* my house, not outside. Yesterday, my sister came over, and Raynne called immediately. 'Why do you have a girl in your apartment?' she asked. I was like, 'How in the hell do you know who I have here?' She said I was denying it and had proof because she was watching me! The camera was buried behind my books, like a little sneak. I told her, no way. It's over. I can't be with a woman who doesn't trust me."

"Wow. Well, you can't say we didn't try to warn you. It's the misspelled name; it's like a curse for you."

He sighs. "I need to find me a nice girl with a good head on her shoulders. I'm not getting any younger."

I laugh. "You're twenty-five. I think you have time until you have to settle down."

"I didn't say anything about settling down. I just want to be with a woman and not have to worry about her going through my drawers when I'm out or making a fake Snapchat to snoop."

"I would offer a suggestion, but I met my boyfriend by dialing the wrong number."

He purses his mouth and contemplates the idea. "I could try that. Maybe I can meet myself a sexy accountant or something. It'll be the hot new dating trend. I bet I can get it to trend on TikTok."

I nudge him hard with the side of my body since I can't use my hands. "You just stick to meeting people the old-fashioned way. Want me to see if Sebastian knows anyone? He's hooking Charity up."

Shawn glares out the side of his eye. "Your man is hooking Charity up with a hotshot attorney?"

"I'm not exactly sure with whom—someone he went to school with."

A grimace crosses his face as his brow furrows. A harrumph comes from his chest as he focuses more on the song playing. He's silent as he works with me to fill the boxes with truffles. The music helps us move quicker as the beat is more up-tempo than what usually plays while we work.

Where I excel at tempering chocolate—heating and cooling it to the desired shininess or snap of the chocolate—Shawn is excellent at molding. He has a design technique that makes the perfect mold for the presentation boxes. For someone who decided recently that he wanted to be a chocolatier, he has a gift.

He's bouncing to the music yet zoned out as he works, which happens often.

"What did you want to be when you were a kid?" I ask him, pulling him from whatever he was thinking.

"A ball player. An astronaut. A principal. Pretty much a different thing every day. That's why I never made it to a four-year college. I went to community college to get my feet wet, and then I could decide what I wanted to major in. Nothing stuck. I was miserable, so after I got my associate's, I went to work for a construction company. I hated that even more than college, so I took a bunch of odd jobs until, one day, it just hit me. I always liked to bake. That's not something that was thought of as a career in my family before."

"Was your family supportive?"

"Yeah." He grins. "Surprised the hell out of me. I hustled my way into the culinary academy, and the day I got in, they threw me a party. Honestly, I think they were all just relieved I'd picked a damn path. There's nothing worse than a man without a purpose in life. I found mine, and now, here I am."

He's so talented. I'm sure his family knew that all along. There are only a few weeks left in his training, so he'll be able to explore his options fully. I was planning on waiting a few more weeks, but why hold off the inevitable?

"The orders have certainly picked up, and the new advertising is drumming in online sales. I think it's time we made it official."

"Are we now going steady or something?" he teases.

I giggle. "Something like that. How would you like to work here full-time? Forty hours a week, set schedule, and I just applied for a small-business health insurance plan, so while I can't give you an hourly raise, I can get you medical. What do you say?"

With his eyes down, he grins a huge, wide smile and then looks up at me like I'm out of my mind. "Amy, in the two years I've been working here, I've seen you quadruple your business. The quality is amazing, and, sure, this place is a dump, but it's also the best place I have ever worked. You put your heart into everything here, and we have fun. What other job can you jive with your best friends like this at? I'd be crazy to say no, which is why I'm not. To be honest, I wasn't even looking to work anywhere else. I knew you were gonna pull through."

If I could hug him right now, I would, but my sanitation gloves are holding a box of truffles. Shawn lifts an elbow for a pound, so I lift mine and give him a nudge.

Just like that, I have my first full-time employee, and I'm not freaking out at all. Everything is falling into place.

Once we're finished, Shawn helps me clean up, and we make sure everything is ready for tomorrow. He won't start full-time for a few weeks, but once he has his degree, it'll be great to have him here every day.

While he takes out the trash, I head to my office-slash-bedroom and change into a pair of jeans and a tank top.

"See you early tomorrow, boss," he says when we lock up in the alleyway. "Unless you want me to come in late so you can sleep in," he says with a smirk on his face at the sight of my overnight bag.

I point to him. "Nice try. Just because I'm sleeping elsewhere doesn't mean you can come in late."

He laughs, which I'm sure is because he knows I'd never let anything get in the way of work. "Hey, can't blame me for wanting to sleep in." He motions to my bag. "Why don't you just move some of your stuff to his place, so you're not lugging a bag all the time?"

"We've only been together for a few months, and

we're still new to this relationship. I'm perfectly fine with leaving my things here, tidy in my place, where I can find them."

"Right. He can keep your dog but not your underwear."

"Plus, a toothbrush and some toiletries. I mean, a girl has to be prepared." I give him a cheeky grin and then wave him off as I walk to the bus stop and head to Sebastian's office.

As I enter the building, I wave to the front receptionist, who buzzes me in without a question. The first time she did it, I felt so special because I knew Sebastian had made the unique arrangement for me. He even made me a badge in case there's someone new at the desk who isn't familiar with me. Tonight, my Blake, Fields, and Moore card stays tucked in my bag as I saunter through the lobby and up the glass elevator.

When I get to Sebastian's wing of the office, Miles stands as soon as he sees me. Instead of the cool demeanor behind those black-framed glasses, tonight, he seems apprehensive.

"Is he in a meeting?" I ask, pointing to the closed office door.

Miles inhales. "Yes. Well, I mean … not exactly," he says slowly.

I narrow my eyes, unsure by what *not exactly* means. "Okay. I'll just hang here then."

Normally, I go straight to Sebastian's house after work, but since I was done earlier than usual, we decided I'd meet him here, and we'd go to his home together.

I'm standing against the wall, watching as Miles taps on his desk. I open my mouth to make small talk when

Sebastian's office door opens, and I stand straighter, waiting for him to come out.

Instead of my tall, handsome boyfriend, I see a pregnant woman walk out the door. She's very pretty with blonde hair and a button nose. Her boobs are huge, which I'm assuming is from the pregnancy, yet she carries herself like the added weight on her body is a fashion accessory to be flaunted in a fitted floral dress that hits above the knee.

I smile at her as she steps out.

Sebastian appears next, and when his eyes meet mine, there's hesitation on his face as he looks to the woman and then back to me. I glance over to Miles, who is staring at the three of us with raised brows and an uncomfortable smile. Sebastian slides his hands in his pockets and sets back on his heels, seemingly unsure of what to say.

She must sense there's an eerie silence because she spins around and checks out the three of us before settling on me with a curved brow.

This is all the reaction I need to know without a doubt that this woman is Lauren.

Sebastian swallows a lump in his throat.

I don't know what I'm more bothered by—the fact that I'm standing here with a woman who is carrying my boyfriend's child or the fact that this is the first time I've seen Sebastian not one hundred percent on his game.

I clear my throat, obviously needing someone to break the uneasy tension in the room.

He inhales and then gives one of his cavalier smiles.

Even if it is a little forced. "Lauren, I'd like for you to meet my girlfriend, Amy."

Well, this is awkward.

She holds out her hand to me. It's dainty and limp, making me wonder if she's expecting me to kiss it instead of shake it. "Hello. It's nice to meet you. Sebastian told me he'd found someone new."

Her tall stature and raised chin exude her confidence. If I were to nitpick, I'd say, I don't like the way she uses the term *someone new*—like I'm just a plaything he found and will dispose of, like I'm an old hat—or how she's eyeing up my flip-flops with an expression of disdain that is a far cry from the beige patent leather heels she's wearing despite the fact that she's nearing the end of her second trimester.

I let the negative thoughts rush out of my head and keep my cool. Just because she's very beautiful and bearing Sebastian's child doesn't mean she's sizing me up or putting me down.

Oh, who am I kidding? She is one hundred percent doing those things.

Now, it's my time to force a smile. "Yes, it's nice to finally meet you."

"I'm sure this little man is all he talks about. He's going to be the best daddy. Already has his schedule cleared. I'm gonna need him twenty-four/seven in the beginning." She nods slightly with a small grin. "Well, Sebastian, thank you again for your help with this." She holds up a file. "We're still on for nursery shopping, right?"

He nods his head and turns to Miles. "Yes, next

week. Please make sure you clear an hour for me on Thursday afternoon."

Miles starts clicking through the computer screen as Lauren walks over to him and adds, "Also, clear the third Saturday in next month." She turns to Sebastian, "My mother is throwing us a baby shower. My family is dying to meet the father, so you have to attend."

Sebastian nods again as his eyes blink rather profusely. "Of course."

"I'll need your mother's address and anyone from your side who you want to invite," she adds easily.

Instead of looking at Sebastian's reaction, I find myself staring at Miles, who seems to be mouthing the word, *Wow*, as he keeps his focus on his screen and away from her.

"I'll email you a list. Have a nice night," Sebastian says as he gives Miles a tilt of his head in the direction of the front door.

Miles stands and walks around his desk to usher Lauren toward the front of the office. "I'll walk you out."

When the two of them are gone, Sebastian faces me and leans in for a kiss. "Hey, you're early."

I hold up my watch. "Nope, right on time."

He looks at the dial and seems surprised. "Oh, wow. That took longer than I'd thought it would. We did our wills today."

"That's a bit morbid. You're both so young."

"God forbid something happens to one of us, but we wanted to make sure our families are present in our absence. It was her idea and a brilliant one. Her parents mean the world to her, and having them in the child's life is important to her, no matter what."

"Is she thinking you'd really keep their grandchild from them if that were to happen?" Even I know Sebastian would never be that kind of person.

He shrugs. "I kind of felt the same way, but I guess it's always better to have everything in writing, just in case. Believe it or not, if I'm not there to sign the birth certificate, my son will be considered illegitimate. Can you imagine such a thing? Bad enough her church won't baptize him because we're not married. Luckily, mine will without a question."

"You two have so many things to prepare. And you're shopping for a nursery?"

"Yes. She asked in passing, and I agreed. Figured I'd get the same one for my house. That way, when he's with me, everything is familiar."

"That's a great idea actually." I let out a ragged breath.

"Right. Well, let me grab my things, and we'll get going." He turns and enters his office.

When Miles returns, he's rubbing the back of his neck as he takes a seat at his desk.

Good to see I'm not the only one who found that entire exchange to be uncomfortable.

Now, if only I had the guts to tell Sebastian how I really felt.

Maybe first, I should be honest with myself.

I just don't know where to start.

CHAPTER NINETEEN

Sebastian and I leave his office and walk to the parking garage in his building before hopping in the car and heading to his home.

On the drive, all I can think about is the encounter with Lauren. I can't imagine being in her shoes. Being pregnant with a man's baby who is dating someone else has to be a horrible feeling. You should be basking in the planning, together as a couple, not having scheduled appointments. I wouldn't be surprised if she views me as an intrusion in her future plans. Perhaps she's waiting on Sebastian to have his fill of me and move on … or move back to her.

When we get to his house, Sebastian goes to change out of his suit. I go straight for Lady Featherington and Duke, who are pawing at my knees, ready to go out. I put their leashes on and grab a bag, taking them out for their walk.

Usually, Sebastian and I take them out together, but tonight, I want some fresh air for myself. I've been in the kitchen all day, so stretching my legs on a warm summer evening is exactly what I need to defog my brain.

The dogs are a great distraction. Duke is very protective of Lady Featherington. Every time she squats to pee, he stands at attention, as if he were blocking her from prying eyes. When she's done, she wipes her feet on the grass and then struts forward, taking the lead with Duke on her tail. If another dog comes near them, Duke rushes forward and snarls at them, keeping them away from his lady. When he becomes distracted by a passing car, she growls at him and sets him back on his walk.

I've caught the two snuggled together on the sofa more than once. She always lets him eat the Kibbles 'n Bits first, which I think is because she knows he likes to devour only the soft pieces. And when he gets lost in chasing his tail, which he does often, she barks at him until his attention is diverted to something else, like a chew toy or Sebastian's slipper, which is the only item of his that he likes to destroy.

Back at the house, I head straight to the kitchen, needing to continue keeping my mind busy and off of questioning everything, so I start heating up the dinner I prepared earlier today—the lobster bisque I planned to serve Sebastian months ago. I take it out of the Tupperware and pour it into a pot to simmer on low. I also packed two small containers of chocolate. One cocoa and one a very special blend.

When Sebastian enters the room, wearing the sexiest pair of gray sweats and a tight-fitted black shirt that shows off his ridiculously perfect physique, my insides melt at the sight of him.

I turn back to the soup and give it a final stir before shutting it off.

Sebastian comes up behind me, wrapping his arms around my waist and kissing my neck. "You sure are quiet tonight."

Before my mind can think, I blurt out, "Does Lauren ever ask about getting back together with you?"

He lets out a surprised huff as he holds me closer. "I knew that was what was wrong. Meeting Lauren freaked you out. That's my fault. I shouldn't have waited so long."

I let out a breath and drop the back of my head to his chest. "Yes. It would be nice to have a warning next time. I would have worn something better. Maybe added some lipstick."

"You're perfect."

"I came from a long day of work."

"You're gorgeous. No woman in the world holds a candle to you."

"She does in so many ways. And I can't imagine how she feels, being pregnant with your child, yet here you are … with me."

"Hey." He turns me around, so I'm facing him. His knuckle glides under my chin, bringing my gaze to his sincere expression. "Don't forget that she's the one who broke it off with me. Yeah, we started to drift and never truly clicked, but she's the one who finally put the stop to it. She doesn't want me, and I'm relieved. Don't ever feel like you're in the middle or that you're some kind of other woman. We're both very fine with this situation."

He pauses and smiles with a light laugh. "Actually, better than fine. It is what it is, and we're going to co-parent, but no, there has been zero discussion on possibly getting back together."

"But you didn't break it off with her. You …" I pause, feeling like this is all too ridiculous. My concerns sound so childish. I put a stop to them, close my mouth, and look away.

When I don't meet his eyes, he places his finger on the side of my face and tilts my head up.

"I don't like to see you like this. Please, tell me what's really on your mind. No holding back," he says with a tone of worry.

His voice makes my heart turn into goo on an ordinary day. When it's deep with a whisper of concern, I'm so weak to his trance that I give in.

"I just feel like I'm in the way. If I weren't here, would you two try to make a go of it? She sure seemed to stake her claim on that when we met. Don't you think when he's born, you two will try to give your child a life that's not illegitimate? One where you can shop for one crib instead of two or make a schedule of where the baby sleeps on what day and who gets to decide what pediatrician you use or where he goes to school? And her family wouldn't be surprised to meet the baby daddy because you'd be a regular fixture in their lives. Holidays, birthdays, Sunday dinners … everything would just be as it should. But here I am, a big roadblock. That's probably what your family will think when they meet me. Sebastian's other woman who is keeping him from his rightful family." I run my hand in my hair and groan. I'm so annoyed at myself for saying all that stuff, let alone actually feeling it.

His face falls as he pulls me into him. I fall into his chest as he wraps his arms around my back and head, enveloping me in a huge hug. I sink into him and feel so embarrassed.

"Hey now. That was a huge leap. I want to hear all your thoughts, even the bad ones."

"I don't sound crazy?" I ask, righting myself and looking up at him.

He caresses the side of my head and smiles. "Absolutely batshit."

I groan again, but he halts me from hiding into his chest and grips me by the arms. He bends down slightly, making sure his eyes are locked in with mine.

"Amy, you're right."

My eyes widen as I wonder which point in particular I'm right about. I said so many things, which means this could easily have me devastated.

"None of this is how it's supposed to happen. I hate having to pick out double of everything and relinquish some of my rights as a parent. I despise that my mother is uncomfortable with announcing to her friends that she's expecting a grandchild because she'll have to explain the situation. My mother is lovely, but she's old-fashioned in some ways. And what I wouldn't give to be able to lie in bed at night and feel my son kick. Lauren's always texting me that she's feeling them, but I've yet to, and it kills me." He narrows his brow and seems almost pained. "All that is what I want, but there is no denying that it won't happen with Lauren. I don't love her. It's as clear as that. I love you."

My heart drops in absolute surprise. "You do?"

"Painfully so. Yes."

I swallow, stunned and elated. My chest seems to remember how to beat again as tingles go up my spine and straight to my brain. "But we've haven't been together all that long. It seems so sudden."

He shakes his head. "You keep saying that. At your parents' house, they asked how long we were together, and you said just two weeks, but I disagreed. Amy, as far as I'm concerned, I've been yours since the moment you called me by mistake. I chose you with one hundred percent of my being then. You have been my every thought, breath, and prayer. I ache when you're not with me and smile the moment I see your face. I've been a damn fool, trying to win your heart, so here I am, pouring mine out to you. I am in love with you, body and soul. I know you've been burned by love before, and you are taking this huge leap by being with me, so I was holding back on telling you, but if there is any doubt in your head on where I stand, on where my feet have been cemented since that moment we met at Love and Lavender, then you need to hear this now. I'm yours."

My heart is exploding in my chest as I cry out in absolute joy. I grip his face and kiss him, taking his passion and desire, his proclamation of love, and drinking it in with every fiber of my being.

Our kiss is heady and desperate. My hands are in his hair, and his are around my back, gripping me and lifting me up until my legs are wrapped around his waist, pulling me into him, never letting me go.

"Take me to the bedroom," I say as I bite the lobe of his ear.

He moans and starts to move me away from the kitchen. Clearly, we were never meant to eat that damn bisque.

Before we're out of the kitchen fully, I divert him back and instruct him to grab the Tupperware with the special chocolate.

"Dessert for dinner?" he asks as he climbs the stairs.

"Something like that," I say when we reach the landing.

He kicks his bedroom door open and ushers me over to the bed. I take the container of chocolate and pop the lid. I grab a brick, rise to my knees, and offer it to him.

Sebastian arches a brow and complies. I place the morsel on his tongue, and his mouth captures my finger on the way out, sucking on it.

"I told you chocolate was an aphrodisiac. This is the original recipe used by the Mayans."

He grins. "Baby, I don't need any help with my libido when I'm with you."

"I have been told my chocolate is better than sex," I say coquettishly.

"Clearly, they're making love to the wrong man, but I'll make a concession." He lifts a brick from the container and rests the chocolate against my lips. "Sex is better *with* chocolate."

I part my lips and eat up the sweet and spicy delicacy, letting it melt on my tongue as his hand roams over my shirt. His fingers dance dangerously over my taut nipple, sending a wild sensation through my entire body.

He lifts my tank top, and I help him out of his T-shirt,

drifting my fingers over the muscles and then leaning forward to kiss and lick everywhere I just touched.

Sebastian removes his pants and boxers and then tugs my jeans off. I shimmy out of my panties and continue to kiss and lap up and down his body, loving the warmth of his silky skin under my tongue.

He motions for me to get on all fours. My face is level with his enormous erection, and I waste no time in taking it into my mouth and licking it from base to tip, letting the salty taste of his pre-cum mix with the sweet taste of the chocolate.

His moans echo in the room, sending me into an erotic haze. I swirl my tongue in circles around the sensitive head and then glide up the vein until Sebastian's deep voice is chanting my name. When I deep-throat him the way he loves, he nearly cries.

"Fuck, your mouth is magic."

Warm hands snake around my head. His fingers weave into my hair, guiding my head up. He's standing powerfully and filled with desire. I know that look. It means he's ready to go wild beast on me.

"I need to be inside you." His voice is hushed, his breathing hard, as he takes a condom from his end table and slides it on his thick-as-steel erection while I lie down on the bed. "I have never felt so connected to a woman before. Sometimes, I feel like I can't breathe until I'm buried deep inside you."

Warm, heated lips suck on the soft skin of my throat as he lies on top of me and holds my hands at our sides, squeezing them. I constrict when his mouth lowers to my breast, nipping and sucking on the tender peak, sending shivers down my body and into my very core.

Together, we raise our hands, so they're over our heads. As he looks down at me, serious and purposeful, he nudges my legs further apart with his hips as he settles in place.

With our gazes held, he enters me. As he moves, his groin rubs against me, giving friction to my very swollen clit, and I gasp out in pleasure. My back instantly bows and arches into him. With a roll of his hips, he hits every nerve ending inside my body.

"Kiss me, Sebastian," I plead.

He gives me what I want and kisses me hard as he fucks me, loves me, rattles me to the core.

I come with a violent scream that has the dogs barking from the bottom of the stairs.

Sebastian's own release comes with a growl.

As we come down from our high, he discreetly removes the condom and then pulls me into his front and curls his body around mine. The sex was amazing, but this is even better. Knowing he loves me and that every emotion I've experienced with him is true makes me feel so alive.

I place my hand on his arm and hold it tighter against my body. With a slight turn to my head so I'm facing him as much as I can while keeping our position, I say, "I love you too, Sebastian."

I feel his gasp against my back as he flips me over, so I'm on my back, and he's above me, staring into my eyes. The grin that covers his face is the absolute sexiest thing I've ever seen on him.

He doesn't say a word. He doesn't need to. We both smile at each other, at our realization that this is real, us. We're doing this, and I couldn't be happier.

LOYAL LAWYER

When his lips touch mine in a sensual kiss, I realize I was wrong. *This* is the best moment of my life so far.

CHAPTER TWENTY

"Thank you, Mom. It feels good to be thirty-two and still have your mother remind you of how long she pushed, giving birth to you while in labor." Sebastian's hearty chuckle as he speaks into the phone bounces through the halls of his townhouse as I walk down the stairs.

I'm dressed for the day in a short floral dress with gladiator sandals and a sparkly headband. With a quick glance in the mirror, I assess my long, dark hair that I curled to make me look like one of the Coachella girls. Not my usual look, but I thought it would be perfect for today.

"Amy is taking me to a concert—a festival actually. Should be fun. What was that? You're kidding," I hear Sebastian say.

I pad down the hall to his office, where the sound of his voice is coming from, and peek in.

He's seated at his desk, leaning back in his chair and smiling, as a man should be on his birthday. Luckily, it's a Saturday, so he has the day free to himself. Double lucky that it's not the weekend of the baby shower. That was last weekend, and it was fine. Sebastian's parents and an aunt came to town, so the women could attend. Sebastian and his father helped bring all the gifts back to Lauren's house. Afterward, his family came back to Sebastian's house, where they met me, and we went out for a lovely dinner.

No one addressed the unusualness of the situation, having gone to an event for his former lover and then sitting at a table with his new one. They are too dignified for that, whereas my family would have made it the conversation to last through New Year's Eve.

He sees me at the door and ushers me in. His brows rise with an appreciative glance at the sight of me in my outfit for today. I reach for his extended hand and take a seat on his lap as he continues his phone call.

"Baby's good. He's measuring perfectly. Uh-huh. I'll ask about that. It's a good question. I don't know. Well, Amy and I painted the nursery this week, and the furniture is arriving this Thursday. It's gonna look perfect."

That's the other thing that's happening. The nursery at Sebastian's place is being put together. Since Lauren chose a linen white for the room, we used the same color. It'll be handsome with the modern cherry furniture that's coming. Sebastian already has the glider, changing table, and diaper bag.

It's been interesting, nesting with him. On one hand, it's a part of him that I love the most. His devotion. His ability to never scare and to take matters into his own hands by being a strong family head—even when the family is unconventional.

It's also the part that scares me.

He's rubbing the side of my arm, and then he kisses my bicep. I look down at him and smile.

"Amy's right here. Let me ask," Sebastian says into the phone and then looks up at me. "My mother is asking if you want to see the Philadelphia Orchestra with us in October. She's staying with us for two weeks to spend time with the baby and do some touristy things around the city. She's getting the tickets now. You in?"

I swallow and nod. "I'd love that."

"Great!" He smiles and shares the news with his mom, laughing and talking about something his father did before he thanks her for calling on his birthday and ends the call with, "I love you."

When he hangs up, he places his phone on his desk and settles back into his seat, looking like a very content man, especially as his hand travels up the inside of my dress.

"You look beautiful," he drawls.

I nibble on his ear and inhale that delicious scent of him. "Happy birthday."

"You already wished me that in the bedroom and the shower. Are you telling me you want to show me again?"

I giggle and move away from him a little in protest. "As addictive as you might be to me, there is no way I am letting you destroy my hair and makeup."

"*Destroy* is a powerful word."

I lower my gaze to him. "You are a sensual man who goes into overdrive."

He laughs. "Is that true? Well, I'll have to make a point to turn it down a bit."

I playfully slap his arm. "Don't you dare. Just give a girl a reprieve, so she can look smashing for her man all day on his birthday. It took me a long time to curl my hair."

He leans up and kisses me. "Fair enough. I'll save the destroying for tonight."

I grin as I get up from his lap and walk around the desk. Sebastian rises as well and adjusts his shorts.

This is what it's like with him. Fun banter, sexy times, and lots of dates.

"There's a new brunch place I want to try tomorrow. I asked Miles and his girlfriend to join us," he says as we walk out of the room toward the kitchen.

I pout. "Shoot. I didn't pack anything nice for brunch. I just have shorts and a tank."

"That should be fine."

"No. I'll run back in the morning and get a sundress."

"You know, Amy, you wouldn't have to be running all over the city if you just kept your clothes here."

I lift a shoulder. "I don't mind keeping my things in one place. It's—"

"Tidy. I know, you've mentioned that before." He winks as he takes his mug and fills it with coffee. "You stay here every night now. Even when I'm working late. At some point, you're gonna have to own up to the fact that you live here too."

"You know, I could easily start sleeping at my place again," I say cheekily. "You'd be in that big king-size bed, all by your lonesome."

"Nope. I wouldn't allow it."

I lift up on my toes and kiss him. "Then, don't start making a big deal about where I keep my clothes."

He shakes his head, yet there's still a grin on his face.

Turning around, I saunter through the house and grab my bag, making sure I have everything for the day.

"Charity is meeting us at the entrance," I call over to him.

He walks into the living room. "Great. I told Jeremy to meet us there too. You don't think this is a bad first meet for a blind date?"

"They both said they wanted to go to the music festival, and there will be plenty of distractions if they don't hit it off, which I'm hoping they will, based on how highly you speak of the guy."

"He is a world-class guy. Attorney, Princeton graduate. And funny—I was told that was a prerequisite."

"Then, it should be a great day. Ready to hit the road, birthday boy?"

He slides his keys in his pocket. "Lead the way, my love."

As far as blind dates go, Charity and Jeremy's is a seven out of ten.

We met up at the entrance of the Firelight Festival, and the two exchanged pleasantries while looking each other up and down. They both seemed happy with what was in front of them, which was a good sign.

The four of us caught the show that was going on when we walked in—a local band who had a huge following, playing a mixture of punk rock and soul music. They were fun, and Charity and I jumped and danced to the music while the guys listened and talked.

After that, we got drinks and enjoyed the gorgeous ninety-degree day.

Sebastian and I usually go to fine dining, so it was a treat to eat from food trucks. We each chose Philly cheesesteaks made to order and shared a bite of each other's to see if we could be swayed to leave our preferred orders. News flash: we can't.

Four shows, a couple of IPAs, and lots of laughs later, I've learned a few new things about my boyfriend. He loves cotton candy and fruity water ice. He despises blonde ales and knows almost every word to every song. The guy knows how to catch on to a song's hook and can belt it out even if it's the first time he's ever heard the song. I've never seen one of his shows, but I'm getting an idea of the showmanship Sebastian brings outside of the courtroom.

Despite his attire of cargo shorts and Lacoste V-neck T-shirt, he stands out in the crowd. It could be his tall, strong manly stature in a sea of boys, or the way his tanned skin and chocolate eyes seem to catch the sunlight in every way, or even the bellow of his laugh and that deep vibrato that carries over the music. Most likely, it's because he has charisma. It's in his walk and the way he orders food. Hell, he even caught my eye when he stopped to tie his shoe.

He always finds a way to touch me. His hands are on my lower back when we move through a crowd and wrapped around me protectively when we dance, and he lazily drifts to my backside for no reason at all.

As for Charity and Jeremy, the day is going well but not great.

"Okay, don't look now, but this guy has the juiciest

ass in the world," Charity says a little too loudly to me, which makes Jeremy's eyes widen. She gives a bashful, "Whoops, sorry. Yours is super cute too."

Sebastian leans over and whispers into my ear, "I don't know if she knows this, but a man never wants the word *cute* attached to any part of his anatomy."

I giggle and then turn to Jeremy. "Do you go to a lot of concerts?"

"No, actually. I'm more of a sports guy. I have season tickets for the Eagles, Phillies, and the Flyers," he states and then lifts a finger. "Oh God, and the 76ers, of course. I must have lost my mind for a second."

"Must be all those sporting events you go to," Charity says in a cutesy, sarcastic way.

"Come on. It's not so bad. The games are filled with energy, the tailgating is a blast, and it's a great way to mix business with pleasure."

Charity nods. "Fair enough. And there are super-cute outfits to wear for every game. I'd get decked out from head to toe. Rhinestones and glitter everywhere."

"I have red face paint. I can give you a full face for the Phillies games," he says.

"That's funny." She blows him off.

"No. I'm totally serious. Half-white, half-red, and I even write on my body when my friends and I are together. We've been on camera a ton of times."

She looks at him with a side-eye. "Oh. Cool. Sounds like fun."

Jeremy's phone rings, so he steps away from us to answer. Sebastian offers to get us more drinks at a nearby tent and then kisses my temple before leaving.

"Jeremy is pretty great," I say, gauging her interest.

"Yeah," she says, almost as if she's trying to convince herself. "He's certainly a lot of fun. He's been game for every band, no matter the music, and he's going with the flow of the day."

"Absolutely. And he's really hot."

"Yeah. So cute."

"So sorry for that," Jeremy says when he returns with his phone still in his hand. It rings again, so he holds it to his ear to answer. "Oh, wait. I have to take this too. Hang on. Hello? Is that so? Tell me more."

He walks away again.

Sebastian returns with drinks for us, careful not to spill beer out of the top of the plastic cups. "This festival is awesome."

"Are you having a good birthday, babe?"

"The best. I never would have done this. For some reason, I thought it was more for young twenty-somethings," he states before taking a sip.

I swallow my own drink. "That's what's great about it. There are bands that span every genre, so you get a mix of all age groups."

Jeremy returns again and takes his drink from Sebastian. "Thanks, man."

"The only time I've been to a concert like this was in Miami. Jennifer Lopez put on a show on South Beach for a client of mine, and it was the best." Sebastian smiles.

"We saw U2 in Central Park a few years ago. It was amazing," Charity gushes, and I high-five her at the memory of our girls' weekend.

"Okay, I don't want to sound snobbish, but if you haven't been to see Andrea Bocelli in Lajatico, Tuscany, you haven't really lived life. Am I right?" Jeremy says, and I see Charity inwardly cringe.

"So, what are everyone's plans for the rest of the summer?" I ask.

Charity answers first, "Just work for me. The rooftop at the Garden Room is insane at night. The tips are fantastic, so I'm taking on as many hours as they'll offer me."

"I go to the Garden Room all the time. When we have clients from out of town, we take them there for after-dinner drinks. The waitresses are like eye candy, so the … shit. That was really dumb." Jeremy's posture rolls back as he realizes his mistake.

"It was," Charity agrees and takes a huge chug of her drink. But as she always does, she finds a way to level the situation. "We usually draw straws when we see the epic douchey professional guys come in with their clients. You never know if you're gonna get sexually harassed or tipped an extra hundred because they think they're going home with you at the end of the night—which, by the way, I never, ever do."

Jeremy gives her a cheers. "To epic douche bags who should keep their mouths shut."

"Cheers to you!" she chimes, and they end up launching into a conversation about the band that's up on the stage.

Sebastian snakes an arm around my waist and pulls me into him. His chin rests on my shoulder as he drawls into my ear, "That could have been a disaster."

"Looks like it won't be a match made in heaven."

"You never know. The night's still young."

"I don't know. It seems to be getting older by the minute."

My comment gets me a tickle on my side, and then he takes my hand and leads me away to a row of carnival games. He takes a selfie of us with the stage in the background and the massive crowd gathered behind us. There's a football toss game, sponsored by the local sports radio station. Sebastian hands me the ball, and I give it a toss, missing the bull's-eye, pathetically. It's a *one toss per person* game, but instead of taking his turn, he offers it up to me. This time, he gives me pointers on what to do.

"It's all about the fingers. Middle on the top laces, ring finger on the second and third. Pinkie on the back." Sebastian adjusts my hand and then wraps my thumb around the ball, whispering in my ear, "Raise it ear-level. Laces away. And throw."

I do. I miss again but not as bad as the first time. As a reward, he wraps his arm around my shoulders and kisses my temple.

There are a few rides at the back of the festival. Since it's his day, I let him pick the ride.

"That one." He points to a chair swing ride.

Where most seem to be a couple dozen feet off the ground, this is about a hundred and fifty feet high, and it bobs up and down as you ride. My stomach drops just as I look at it.

We stand in line and talk about the music that's playing, the great weather, and how crowded the place is getting as the day goes on. Before I know it, it's our turn, and Sebastian and I are taking side-by-side seats.

I double-check the lock on my seat belt, making

sure I'm firmly secure … and then I check again. Sebastian doesn't seem to be concerned at all. He has a cool confidence about him. A man who's untouchable.

We start to move, and the wind on my skin feels refreshing. The ride lifts, and I grip the chain of the handles. As we rise, the people below get smaller, and my heart feels like it's pounding hard in my chest. The clamminess from my hands makes them slide down the chains, which dig into my skin as I try to grip them. There's a tension in my back that's sharp from how tightly I'm holding my shoulders.

The swing is traveling fast, zipping around in circles and rising higher. And then it drops. That pounding heart is now making room for my stomach that has just launched itself up, threatening to make me sick.

A panic rushes over me, and I close my eyes, waiting for the ride to be over quickly. I try to calm myself by thinking of anything else. A pedicure, the stream of gooey chocolate as it's getting ladled out of a metal bowl, and even sex. Nothing works.

"Open your eyes," I hear Sebastian call over.

With a deep breath, I do, promising myself it's only for a moment.

"Look at me, Amy."

I roll my head to the side and see him. He's huge in the seat. A man of his stature is practically ridiculous, squeezing into this thing, yet he's smiling. I watch as his hands, which are resting on his thighs, rise up. He nods to me to do the same.

I shake my head.

Let go, he mouths.

I grip the chains harder as I look down, hoping for

the ride to be over soon, thinking if it is, I suppose I could take a chance. Glancing over at Sebastian again, I use him as my strength, my confidence to do as he asked.

Slowly, I release my hands from the chains and bend my arms at my sides, barely lifting them up. With a deep—very deep—and shaky breath, I lift them higher. I pull them back for a beat before fully committing and launching them above my head.

Eyes open, shoulders high, and mouth parted, I inhale the eastern summer air and stare out at the world around me.

To my surprise, I feel okay. No, I feel better than okay.

I spit-laugh as I let out a smile, looking out at the city that is passing by in a blue blur. I can see the bridge and the riverbanks that line the city, past the highways and roads, and into the green hills in the distance.

I lose control and give it up, relinquishing myself to whatever might be. The rise and fall of the ride now do nothing for my nervous heart. Instead, I search forward to the next movements because I know I can handle it.

It's freeing. It's addictive. It's magnificent.

The ride starts to lower, and we swing our way down to the ground. My legs are a little wobbly as we exit, but I do so with a laugh and a smile. As I trip slightly on the ramp, Sebastian takes my hand and weaves me back to the massive crowd that's gathered by the main stage.

I text Charity to let her know where we are. She says she's good with Jeremy and chooses a meetup spot in case we don't find each other by the end of the night.

The sun is starting to set, and off in the distance,

there's a vendor selling glow necklaces. Sebastian jogs over to purchase two, one for my neck and another as a crown, which he places on my head.

I run a finger over his cheekbone and down his freshly shaven jaw, rubbing my thumb over his lips. He kisses it and then my wrist, holding my hand as the music for the next band starts to play on the main stage.

The band is playing a Coldplay cover, and Sebastian's head swivels at the opening chords of the song. With a wide, beaming smile, he listens to one of his favorites, "A Sky Full of Stars."

"*You're such a heavenly view*," he sings along as he watches the lead singer.

Meanwhile, my full attention is on him.

The sunset is casting a pink and gold haze in the sky that makes him seem ethereal. From the curve of his brow to the straight line of his nose, each facet of his face is illuminated.

He's a beautiful man—that's for sure.

Yet it's not just his impossibly handsome face, that swagger, or the expensive things he treats me to, nor is it his career, high-priced clothes, or his townhome in the city.

No, what makes Sebastian the most beautiful man is his mind. It's brilliant and thoughtful, steadfast and dedicated to everything he does.

It's the Leo in him.

He's carefree and king of the party, yet he's focused and successful, always sticking to his goals. Loyal to his family, friends, his love. He's the fire that life needs.

He's what I need.

I've been successful. I've hung on to my ideals, and

I do everything on my own. Yet this feeling of Zen, of flying high in the sky with my hands up in the air and letting go of some of that control because I know I can handle whatever life throws at me, is completely freeing. No, I'm not talking about the carnival ride. It's life. Life is about taking leaps, yet knowing when your feet hit the ground, you'll have the wherewithal to handle wherever you land.

Sebastian taught me that.

I told him I loved him, and it was sweet, but—*fuck*—I didn't mean it like I do now.

In my entire life, I've never truly meant it when I said it to a man. People say it all the time because it feels like the right thing. It's a passionate response. It's powerful.

I know that because right here, right now, as I look at him in the middle of this dusty festival—smiling brightly, singing his songs, and holding my hand—I can say with one hundred percent certainty that I am in love with Sebastian Blake.

With a tug, I pull him close with my arms around his neck, soaking in his words as he sings and drowning them in a kiss. He wastes no time in seizing the moment, wrapping his strong arms around my waist and lifting me off the ground.

I kiss him with passion.

I kiss him with fire.

I kiss him with my entire being.

"I love you, Sebastian," I say with my eyes wide open.

He opens his and stares at me for a beat. His head tilts slightly as his eyes narrow a touch, looking at me, staring at me, searching me.

As if the answer to his unanswered question has been found, he lets out a breath, and his eyes crinkle. His lips brush mine again.

"Of all the things you could have given me for my birthday, that is the best one yet," he says with a big smile.

Now, it's my turn to tilt my head. "What's that?"

He grins. "More of you."

Leo

CHAPTER TWENTY

I hear my phone ring, and when I see Sebastian's sexy face filling up my screen, I swipe on the call with a huge grin on my face. "Hey, handsome."

"Her water broke," he says frantically as I hear him rustling around.

"What? Isn't it too early?"

"Yes." He pauses, and I hear more movement. He's most definitely talking into his AirPods and using his arms to search for something. "Shit, where are my keys?" he says more to himself than anyone around him.

"They're in your coat pocket," I hear Miles say in the background.

"You're a lifesaver. Thank you," Sebastian responds. "Cancel everything," he yells, and I can only assume it's because he's out the door and Miles is still standing in his office.

"Sebastian, what's going on?" I ask after I hear him breathe a few breaths into the phone.

"Oh God. Sorry," he responds like he forgot I was on the line.

Hearing him so frazzled has me standing from my desk, where I was doing paperwork, and wondering if I should meet him.

"Lauren's water broke. She's at the hospital—has been for a few hours. Why she didn't call me earlier, I have no clue. Now, I'm racing around like a maniac, trying to get there in time."

"Just breathe. You have plenty of time. Labor can take hours. My sisters were in the hospital for days it seemed like."

"She's already eight centimeters."

"Or not ..." I say in shock.

"She's only thirty-five weeks. This is too early. What if something happens to my son?" The panic dripping from his voice makes me grab my chest in pain.

"Don't think like that. If she's been in the hospital for a while, then everything is going smoothly. If there were problems occurring, she'd be in the operating room, getting a C-section, so don't worry about anything. Hundreds of women give birth every day. Things are going to be just fine."

I hear his engine start, and by the noise coming through the line, it sounds like he threw his AirPods down on the seat next to him, so I wait for the line to connect to his car.

After a few beats, I say, "Just be calm, okay? Don't get in an accident, trying to get there too fast."

He doesn't respond.

"Sebastian?"

"I'm here. Sorry. My mind is going in a million different directions."

"No reason to be sorry. Call me when you figure out what's going on."

"I will."

There's another pause as we both sit in silence—me thinking how our entire world is about to change and him, I'm sure, driving like a wild man through the streets of Philadelphia.

I consider just hanging up, but before I do, I say, "Hey, Sebastian?"

"Yeah?" His voice is even more distraught than before.

"You're about to be a dad. Don't forget that. Don't let your worry ruin it. Take a deep breath and enjoy it. I love you."

He doesn't say anything for a few seconds, but when he does, I hear the cracking in his voice. "Love you too. I'll call you soon."

He ends the call, and I plop down in my chair with so many thoughts and emotions running through me. I don't know whether to laugh, cry, jump for joy, or scream at the top of my lungs.

I know the waiting is going to kill me. I've tried to prepare myself for this moment, but now that it's here, my chest is tight, and my palms are clammy.

Sebastian's about to be a dad, and I'm sitting here, in a dump of an office, with a ton of work to do but not wanting to move a muscle, for fear that if I do, my fantasy, the life I've been living, will be over.

We discussed me going to the hospital, but I didn't think it was right. When I shared my concerns,

Sebastian agreed all too easily, which showed me he had my same thoughts. At the time, it stung a little, but I needed to remember that this was not about me. This was about his son being born, and whether he and I work out in the end, the memory of his birth needed to be about just him and the baby's mother.

So, now, I wait, dying to know what's going on but having no way of finding out until he calls me.

One thing's for sure: Sebastian had plenty of time to get to the hospital. It's been two hours and nothing. When Shawn arrived at work, he basically kicked me out of my own kitchen because I was a nervous wreck and he was afraid I was going to screw up the recipes and ruin entire batches.

He was probably right.

I went next door to the gym and got on the treadmill, hoping to run out my anxiety. I learned that it doesn't matter how much adrenaline you have running through you, if you don't normally exercise, that shit catches up to you real quick.

Not being able to breathe and having these crazy emotions running through me was not a good combination. I was afraid to shower because there wasn't a safe place to keep my phone in the gym's shower without risking it getting soaked, so now, I'm sitting here, a stinky, sweaty mess, scrolling through my emails that I have no intentions of actually answering, for fear I'll screw something up there too.

I let out a huff, and when my phone rings, I swear I jump out of my chair, making my heart pound out of control as I swipe through Sebastian's handsome face.

"Is everything okay?" I ask, sounding more like him two hours ago than I should.

"It's more than okay. Amy, I have a son. A beautiful, perfect little boy who weighs five pounds, seven ounces."

A weight that was crushing my chest is lifted, and I let out a gasp of relief. I cover my mouth as tears fall freely.

"You have to see him. He's …" His voice cracks. "He's so tiny, but the doctors say he's healthy and that there shouldn't be any repercussions from him coming early."

"Oh, Sebastian. That's wonderful. I'm so happy for you."

I really am. I had no idea how this moment would feel, but right now, that's all that's flowing through me—absolute joy for the man I love, who's thrilled out of his mind that his baby boy was just born.

"I'm going to text you some pictures. Then, I'm going to hang out for a while, but I'll see you later tonight. At my place? Don't wait on me for dinner. Go ahead and grab what you want. I'm sure I'll eat here."

"Yeah. Of course. You hang out there, and don't worry about me. I'll be there when you get home."

My phone vibrates in my hand, and I pull it down to see a text message from Sebastian. When I swipe it open, my eyes take in the handsomest man I've ever met with the biggest, cheesiest grin covering his face as he holds a baby boy in his hands.

"Sebastian," I say in disbelief as I bring the phone

back to my ear. "Oh my God," is all I can get out as more tears flow down my face.

Two more pictures come through. One of just Oliver—the name they chose, after Sebastian's father—and one of a tiny black-inked footprint on the inside of Sebastian's forearm. Both photos fill me with joy for the man I love.

Sebastian's a father …

His life from here on out will forever be changed.

Around eleven at night, I hear the lock turn and the door open. Instantly, I sit up from where I was lying on the couch and tuck my legs underneath me as Sebastian heads my direction.

"Hey, sweetie. Were you asleep?" He gives me a soft kiss before he plops down beside me, grabbing my feet and pulling them to cover his lap.

I lift the remote and put the TV on mute. "No, I was waiting for you. Tell me all about baby Oli."

His head drops back against the couch as a huge grin covers his face. When he lifts his head and faces me, I see the tears filling his eyes that he blinks away.

"He's amazing. Everything about him. His little toes are the tiniest things I've ever seen. I just wanted to hold them in my hands while he slept. Lauren held him for a while to breast-feed. He had trouble since he's so small, so we got a lactation specialist. Then, he had his hearing test and some other tests. When I finally got him, I just didn't want to let go. That's why I stayed so late. I didn't want to leave him."

"I'm sure you could have stayed. Don't most dads stay?"

He sighs. "Yeah, but Lauren's mom was there, and I could tell it was time for me to go."

I nod slightly, feeling the awkwardness of that situation radiate off of him. "So, you'll go back tomorrow? How long will they stay in the hospital?"

"If everything checks out, they'll go home the day after tomorrow."

I watch as he pauses and starts to chew on the inside of his lip. Something I've never seen him do.

I lower my head to catch his attention. "Everything okay?"

"Yeah." He rubs my leg absentmindedly. "It's just crazy, you know? I'm a dad, but it feels so weird, being here. And when he goes home, it will be there." He sighs. "I guess I didn't really take in how weird that would be."

I sit up, so I'm closer to him. "It seems like you and Lauren got it all figured out though. She said you can come there, right?"

He glances over to me, and I see the hurt in his eyes that he tries to hide. "Yeah. She did. I'm sure it will be fine." He leans over to grab his phone from his back pocket. "Check it out. I took a ton of pictures."

I curl up next to him with my head on his shoulder as he flips through probably a hundred pictures he took—no joke. Each one comes with a story about what was going on and how he felt at that exact moment.

I lift up and kiss his cheek.

"What was that for?" he asks.

"I'm just so happy for you. I love seeing how happy you are."

He lets out a pleased sigh. "I really am. I had no idea I could love someone so instantly and so much. The second he came out, I wanted to scream and holler and jump for joy, all at one time. It was this rush that I'd never experienced before. Watching someone being born truly makes you feel alive. It's still amazing to me that I made an actual human being. He's a part of me." He closes his eyes and shakes his head. "It's mind-blowing, is what it is."

I lean in even closer. "That's exactly why I love you."

He kisses the top of my head and then laughs a little. "It silly how all I can think about is what he'll be like and all the fun things I can't wait to do with him. Like throw a ball or take him to his first Phillies game."

"Hold on there, Dad. He was just born." I let out a laugh.

He turns suddenly to me, and I grin, not knowing why he jumped like that.

"What?" I ask.

"Dad." He chuckles to himself. "I'm a dad. Holy cow."

Elated emotion oozing off of him, and it's contagious, making me smile too.

"What did your parents say?"

"They're over the moon. I was so excited they were able to come to the hospital. And you were right. It was worth waiting to tell them the name until the day of. Seeing my dad's eyes fill with tears like that was definitely a moment I won't forget. They asked about you too. Said it was a shame you weren't there to celebrate with us."

I blow him off. "It's okay. I'll have plenty of time. How's Lauren?"

"She's a trooper. With him being so tiny, there weren't any complications or tearing or anything. She still screamed like hell though."

I playfully hit his arm. "Tiny or not, she pushed a human out of her vagina. Don't forget that."

"Never. I'll never forget the gift she gave me." He pauses and smiles from ear to ear. "That's exactly what he is. He's the gift that the world gave me. Something I hadn't even known I was missing but, damn, I wanted so much."

I lay against him as we both stare at the little boy who's filling his phone screen, the one who made the love of my life a dad.

CHAPTER TWENTY-ONE

It's been a whirlwind week, and I'm not even the one who had a baby. Just being there for Sebastian has been an absolute mixture of emotions. The hospital kept baby Oliver for an extra few days before he went home to Lauren's house, so I have yet to actually meet him.

Sebastian took a paternity leave and has been at Lauren's every waking moment. I love that he wants to be a part of these early days, so I'm sitting back while he's spending these precious moments of the first days of life with his son.

Every night, he comes home, exhausted but full of pictures and stories of how the day went. Hearing him talk about his son is the sweetest, sexiest thing I've ever heard from a man. I love listening to his day. I just wish I could be a part of them as well.

While he's living this dual life, I sit here, trying my hardest to be the supportive girlfriend in his current situation

I'm at my office, making a surprise gift for both him

and Lauren because, honestly, I don't know what else to do, and my orders are all set for the weekend. Of course, I stick to what I know and am in the process of making a huge chocolate bar that's engraved with his name—Oliver Deveraux Blake. Deveraux is Lauren's last name. Instead of hyphenating the baby's last name, Lauren agreed to have his middle name be her last name, and Sebastian was thrilled. Doesn't hurt that it sounds super regal.

Shawn is just about to head out after packaging the last of the supplies that came in today when he comes over to where I'm finishing off the mold.

"What are you working on?" He leans over the counter to see it better.

I shrug with a sigh. I know this should make me happy, but my emotions are all over the place today. "It's a surprise for Sebastian."

"Oh, is that the kid's full name?" He comes closer to read it. "His middle name is Deveraux?"

"Yeah, it's his mom's maiden name."

"No shit? I dated some crazy broad last year who had the same name. Man, she was a piece of work. Wait." He grabs the mold and yanks it toward him, where he reads Oliver's birth date, weight, and both Sebastian's and Lauren's name. "Sebastian's ex is named Lauren?"

His eyes meet mine, and I can see his wheels turning as he waits for my answer.

"Yeah," I say slowly, confused as to why he's asking.

"Lauren Deveraux?"

I nod more in question than agreement.

"Are you positive it's spelled that way?" he asks.

"Seriously? Yes, this is how you spell Lauren.

Spelling it L-O-R-E-N is mainly used when the name is for a guy. Lauren is not a name you spell some crazy way."

He purses his lips. "There is another way. Is she blonde, kind of pretentious, and has a great rack?"

I pause and turn to face him fully. "What are you saying, Shawn?"

"I'm saying, I think you should text Sebastian and ask him if she spells her name with a *Y* instead of an *E*. L-A-U-R-Y-N."

With a huff, I take out my phone and scan my text messages to Sebastian, looking for a time we've chatted about her to see how she spells her name. Oddly, I don't see it at all. We've definitely spoken about the woman numerous times, but turns out, she's never been the fodder for our text conversations. I shoot a text to Sebastian, asking which is the proper spelling. He shoots back a message, and I groan in annoyance.

"Ugh. You're right. It's spelled with a *Y*. I have to remake the mold." Sliding my phone into my pocket, I take the mold from Shawn's hands and assess it. "Unless I just forgo the parents' names. I got the baby's name right."

Shawn taps his finger to his lips, his brows deeply furrowed as he stares off in the distance.

"You okay over there?" I ask as I consider cutting the mold. *I mean, if her name is spelled wrong, will she really be that upset? It's an honest mistake.*

"Lauryn Deveraux. She's an advertising executive," he says almost too himself.

I nod absentmindedly. "I guess so. She's in corporate. Huh? I didn't know the spelling of her name or what she does for a living. Does that make me shallow? I guess I should know about the woman who bore my boyfriend's child." My words are falling on deaf ears as Shawn is lost in thought. "Are you thinking you dated Sebastian's son's mom?"

Shawn's face goes pale, like he just saw a ghost fly right in front of his face, saying it's here to take his life. He's frozen like a statue in both fright and shock.

I reach out to him. "Are you breathing?"

"When we hooked up, she said she was technically still with a guy, but things weren't really working out between them," he speaks barely above a whisper.

He reaches in his back pocket and pulls out his phone, swiping it in a hurry. His thumb roves over the screen.

"Shawn?" I lean down to catch his attention, but it's like I'm not here anymore, and he's in his own world. "Well, if you dated her, that's quite the coincidence, but it's nothing to get worked up about."

He pulls up his Calendar app and counts backward.

"It's nine months, right? I've always heard people talk about nine months later, a baby comes, but then my sister said it was ten months." He's blabbering to himself at this point while he does the math in his head, and that's when everything clicks in mine.

"Are you seeing when Sebastian's baby was conceived?" I ask in absolute confusion.

He doesn't move his head, but his eyes lift to meet mine, and my stomach drops. There's apprehension in those eyes.

"Maybe I'm the one who put that seed in her belly."

"You can't be serious." I'm shaking my head, looking

away because Shawn is acting like a drama king right now.

He closes the Calendar app and opens his Photos app. A few flicks of his thumb, and he holds it out to me. "Is this her?"

Staring back at me is the woman I met once at the law office that day. A woman I've seen in hundreds of photos every night when Sebastian tells me about his day. And there, right next to her name, is indeed Lauryn—with a *Y*—Deveraux, clad in a ski outfit and clinking beers with Shawn.

"Yes, that's her. Is she the one who filled your refrigerator with protein shakes because they were good for your stamina?"

"No. She's the one I met on that ski weekend in the Poconos in the martini-shaped hot tub."

"I forgot about that one," I say with a laugh, and then my face goes serious. That was last year, but it was late last year, around the holidays. I see where Shawn's misplaced concern is. It's in the timing. My face goes slack, and a feeling of dread courses through my veins. "There's no way." I take a step back, like even if it is true, I'm not willing to believe it.

He lets out a sharp hiss under his breath. "You tell me." He's back in the Calendar app, and I can see the frustration growing on his face. "How do you count pregnancy months? They're not the same as regular months or something, right?"

I blink slowly as I try to grasp what's going on. *There's no way this isn't Sebastian's baby. He has his eyes. I mean ... as much as a baby can have the eyes of an adult.* I stare at Shawn and don't see a lick of Oliver.

Shawn raises his eyebrows at me like I'm crazy.

"What?" I ask, confused.

"I asked you a question. Counting. Months. Help." He shows me his phone.

"Oh." I run my hands through my hair to rid my thoughts. "Count by weeks. It's forty weeks of pregnancy."

He starts back at today and counts backward.

"But wait, he was born at thirty-five weeks. Start at his birthday and then go backward."

He closes his eyes and takes a deep breath, dropping his phone to the countertop.

"What?" I step closer to him, wanting to shake him but knowing I can't—I'm his boss after all. "How long has it been?"

"I have to go." He grabs his phone and turns to leave.

I reach for his arm to stop him. "Shawn, you can't just leave."

"Yes, Amy. Yes, I can." A sharp jolt of his arm releases him from my grasp.

Wow. Not only has my stomach already dropped, but now, my throat is also dry, and I feel like there's a lump in my chest.

He's taking off his apron and grabbing his messenger bag.

"Shawn, wait. Are you sure? Do you really think you could be Oliver's father? Talk to me."

He stops and faces me so fast that I almost fall back on my ass. "No, Amy. Forget about it. There's nothing to talk about. Oliver is Sebastian's son. End of story."

"But if he's not, then you need to say something."

"I'm out. Kid's not mine. Forget I said anything."

"Shawn!" I yell as he slams the door behind him and walks out of the building.

I throw up my arms in disbelief as I spin around to talk about what just happened, but I realize quickly that I'm all alone.

My heart pounds as my stomach flips, so I wrap my arms around my waist, hugging myself to try to calm down.

What if he's the father?

My God, Sebastian would be devastated. He's been over-the-moon happy since Oliver arrived. He's said so many times how happy he is, being a father.

So, what do I do? Do I keep this possibility to myself? Because that's what this is. A possibility.

Memories of him not finding out for weeks flash in front of me.

Could she be lying?

I think about the difference between Shawn and Sebastian.

Sebastian's a very successful attorney who's got his life together and very much wants to be a father. Shawn, on the other hand, was working for minimum wage at the time while going to school. He doesn't even have a car, let alone have his life together.

If I were pregnant and there was a possibility between Sebastian and Shawn being the father, it wouldn't be a question on who I would *want* to be the father, but could I be that kind of woman?

Is she that kind of woman? Could she lie about something like this to fit the narrative she wants?

Visions of the way she was dressed with her high-end bag and the way she held her hand out to me like she was royalty make me run to the bathroom with dry heaves. She's a corporate woman, someone with a plan and an image. She was with Sebastian far longer than her weekly fling with Shawn. Odds are, it's Sebastian's, yet I can see why she wouldn't even entertain the idea of it being Shawn's. The outcome would be absolutely different.

It could also be why she waited fifteen weeks to tell him.

She had a lot to think about.

As I stare at my reflection in the mirror, I feel the tears start to prick my eyes.

How can I keep this from the man I love, but even more, how can I break his heart if it is true and Oliver isn't his?

I spend the next hour sitting with my hands in my hair as I lean my elbows on my knees in thought.

The battle between right and wrong or good versus evil is real, but right now, I don't even know what is right, what is wrong, and what is good or evil. I've come up with a thousand different reasons why I should stay in my lane and keep my mouth shut. But I've also come up with a thousand reasons why I can't let the man I love raise a child that possibly isn't his, especially if I want to be in this man's life.

And I really do.

I love Sebastian more than I thought I ever would, and seeing him with Oliver has just intensified those feelings. Yes, things are a little awkward, but those are my problems, and I know I'll be able to work through them eventually. But if I don't tell him, I'll always have the thought in the back of my mind.

What if it's true and we find out ten years from now that Oliver's not his? That would be a million times worse than finding out now, when he's a baby. Right?

I drop back in my chair and stare at the ceiling, hoping the building opens up and the answer falls down from the sky and slaps me across the face.

My phone dings with a text message.

Lauryn wants to get some rest, so I get to bring Oliver home! Are you at my place?

I stare at her name. I'm a huge believer of signs being everywhere, and the fact that he writes her name for the first time in all these months, right after I found out everything I did, is a huge sign.

I just wish I hadn't seen this particular sign.

I take a deep breath and respond.

I'm still at work, but I'll be there soon.

I turn off my phone, so I don't see his response. I don't want to be tempted to say anything. I haven't made up my mind yet if I should, so I take away all possibilities of making the wrong choice before I've thought it out.

The chocolate bar is still sitting here, waiting to be wrapped. I take my time with it before making my way to Sebastian's house.

When I arrive, he must hear me approaching because he swings the door open, looking like a little boy who's waiting for Santa to come with a new bike.

"I just put him in his crib." He blinks away tears.

It's the sweetest moment I've ever witnessed, and it's as simple as putting his child to bed.

He grabs my hand and rushes me to Oliver's room,

which he's made to look like a catalog nursery with no expense spared.

As I glance over the wall of the crib, I see the tiniest baby boy with a sleeper on that is just a little too big for his preemie size.

My foot kicks the end of the crib on accident, and Oliver jumps slightly, bringing his hands up to his face before slowly dropping them back down to the bed in a soft slumber.

Sebastian grabs my hand that's resting on the side of the crib and holds it tightly. I wrap my arm around his waist and lean into his chest. When he kisses the top of my head, I feel the love he has for me and the love he has for his son in spades.

My stomach hurts from the thoughts of today, but my heart soars to see this man, who I love so deeply with all my soul, so happy to have his son asleep in his home for the first time.

I still have no idea what I should do, but I know this is a moment I don't want to ruin for him, so I tilt my head up to see him face-to-face.

He leans down to kiss my lips. The gesture is so genuine, but all it does is truly tear me up inside.

CHAPTER TWENTY-TWO

Oliver only stayed until bedtime last night before Sebastian brought him back to Lauryn's house, so she could feed him. When Sebastian arrived back home, I questioned telling him about Shawn, but he was exhausted, so he crashed right away. Today, he was up early, catching up on work stuff before heading back to see the baby, so I decided to head down to the office even though it's Saturday. I don't have much going on but figured I would play with some new recipe ideas.

When I enter the office, I notice the alarm doesn't sound off from my entry, and when I check to see why, I jump at the sight of Shawn sitting at the long counter in the dark.

I grab my chest, hoping the weight of my hands might possibly keep my heart from jumping out of my body. "What are you doing here, sitting in the dark?" I ask as I try to calm my breathing and turn on the lights.

"I didn't know where else to go," he responds in a tone I've never heard from him.

His head is down, either too heavy to lift or the lights are too much for his eyes. I turn off half the lights. His head stays put.

I set my purse on the counter and then walk over to him, placing my hand on his shoulder. "What's going on?"

He tilts his head my way. I see just how horrible he looks—bloodshot eyes with dark circles underneath them—and it freaks me out. My easygoing employee looks like he's been through hell.

"Shawn, what happened?" I ask, my voice laced with concern.

"I went through the calendar some more and matched the dates with when I was hooking up with Lauryn."

My heart, which I thought was going to jump out of my chest earlier, now feels like it just stopped beating.

When I don't say anything, he lets out an audible sigh. "Yeah, my thoughts exactly."

"Do you honestly think Oliver is your son?" I ask barely above a whisper.

He nods his head vehemently, and that's when I smell the alcohol on his breath.

"Are you drunk?"

He lifts a bottle of Jameson from between his legs. "Bottoms up!"

I lean back and take a breath, not sure how I feel about this situation. On one hand, I walked in on my employee when he shouldn't have been here, and to make it worse, he's drunk. Yet at the same time, I feel sorry for him, and I guess I'm thankful that he felt this was a safe place for him to come and work through his problems.

I pull out a stool and sit next to him. "Tell me about the time frame."

I grab the bottle from him since he's had enough. Thankfully, he doesn't fight me.

He crosses his arms over the counter and lays his head down. "We met at the lodge at Camelback Mountain. It was the afternoon, and everyone got lit at the bar. She and I got to talking and never made it out to the slopes for the second ski run of the day. Instead, we went back to my hotel, where they had this awesome—"

"Martini-shaped hot tub. You mentioned it."

"She thought it was hysterical, and it's probably the only reason she went home with me. I was pissed when she said she was going back to the city to see her boyfriend. You know me—I do not get involved with girls in a relationship. Shit always goes south. I remember the boyfriend was a lawyer. Funny how you forget details until the moment you need them, and they suddenly come flooding back."

"I'm guessing your fling was around thirty-six weeks ago now."

He nods, and I close my eyes, wishing this weren't happening.

"What are you going to do about it?"

"Nothing," he mumbles.

I wrap my fingers around his elbow and give him a tug, so he sits up and faces me. "You can't do nothing."

He grits his teeth and stares up at the ceiling. "I know. That's why I'm here. Drunk. I came here because

I wanted to blame this place. If I didn't work here, I'd have had no clue this baby was even born."

"But you do know. So, now, you have to face it."

He snaps his face toward me. "I will not be a father to this kid."

I blink, shocked at his demeanor and praying it's more the alcohol talking rather than the real Shawn because this is definitely a side of him I've never seen.

"If it's yours, then you won't have a choice."

I jump back when he slams his fist on the counter. "I'm not ready to be a parent. I don't want this."

All I can think about is the difference between Shawn and Sebastian. Here's Shawn, acting like a fool over the thought of Oliver possibly being his, while Sebastian has embraced it with so much love and excitement that I don't know if he'll ever recover if he finds out the baby is not his.

My phone rings, and when I see Sebastian's face, my stomach drops.

"Don't you dare say anything." Shawn sits up, pointing at me.

I glare at him and swipe the call. I can understand the shock of maybe being a father, but his reaction is really starting to tick me off.

"Hello?" I answer, trying to act normal.

"Hey. I was going to grab lunch. Want me to bring you something too?" he asks.

I smile at how sweet this man is, especially compared to the guy sitting next to me right now.

I take in a breath and know I need to rip off the Band-Aid, or this will eat away at all of us. But it needs to come from Shawn.

"Sure, I'm at the shop. I'd love it if you could bring me something here."

Shawn grabs my arm with his eyes wide open, but I push him off of me. He needs to pull up his big-guy boxers—if there is such a thing—and face the music.

"Perfect. I'm actually right around the corner from you already. I'll be right there."

We say our good-byes, and Shawn grabs the bottle from me, takes a swig, and then drops his head to the counter again. Right now, I don't care what he does as long as it doesn't include running out that door.

The silence is deafening as we wait for Sebastian to arrive.

For twenty-four hours, I've contemplated talking to Sebastian. I've been a coward because it's too hard a conversation to have, especially without Shawn being one hundred percent certain that the timeline matches. Now that I know it does, that there's a real possibility that another man could be the father, I can't see how we don't have the conversation, no matter how difficult it will be.

"Are you going to tell him, or am I?" I ask after a few minutes.

"You," he grumbles.

I let out a breath, feeling uncomfortable about having to be the one. "I think it'd be better, coming from you."

"Yeah, well, I'd rather ignore the situation altogether, but somehow, my life is fucked up enough to have Karma bite me right in the ass. I knew I should have stopped playing the field. The game eventually catches up to you."

"You need to man up, Shawn."

"I thought I was. I finally got a full-time gig at my dream job, decent cash in my pocket, and I was gonna get an apartment."

I want to smile at his *dream job* comment, but I know that's not what I should be focusing on right now. "You're not losing your job, if that's what you're worried about. Mistakes happen. It's how you deal with them in the end that matters."

I run my hands through my hair and go over the thousand possible ways that I can break the news to Sebastian, and they all make me coil in a pool of nerves. My body starts to shake, and my hands turn clammy when I hear the back door open and watch as Sebastian walks through.

Shawn groans with his head still down while I say a silent prayer to myself, hoping this goes smoothly.

"Hey, beautiful," Sebastian says as he leans in to give me a kiss. For a man who has been going nonstop on little sleep, he looks immaculate in his blue V-neck T-shirt and khaki shorts.

He stops short when he notices Shawn still leaning over, basically laying on the table. "Everything okay?" He points to Shawn and then looks back at me.

I inhale a deep breath and then go for it. "You might want to have a seat."

Sebastian eyes the two of us while he pulls up a stool and moves the food he brought to the side, sensing this is not a casual conversation to have over a meal.

"I-I …" I stutter with a swallow. "I don't know how to say this."

He sits up tall, bracing himself. "Are you breaking

up with me?" His eyes narrow in confusion.

"Oh God. No." I grab his hands and give them a squeeze. "I'm so sorry to give you that impression. I love you very much." I pause as he smiles in relief while I rub my lips together. "I'm telling you this because I care about you."

His smile drops slightly, and his chest rises. "Does this have anything to do with Shawn being drunk and half-passed out in your kitchen?" he asks slowly.

I glance to Shawn, who's still lying here with his head down. I close my eyes and turn back to Sebastian. When I open them, I see the man I love, and I don't know if I can crush his soul like this. Maybe it is better if we just don't say anything. It's obvious who wants this child and who doesn't.

"Amy, you're freaking me out here. What's going on?" Sebastian asks.

"I just—"

"Is this your baby's mom?" Shawn holds out his phone to Sebastian, keeping his head down.

Sebastian looks at me and then at the phone with his eyebrows pinched in. "Yes," he says like he's not sure if that's a good answer or a bad answer.

Shawn brings the phone back to himself, swiping a few things before holding it back up to Sebastian to show the picture of Shawn and Lauryn at the ski resort the day they hooked up. "The date on this photo, is that around when you guys conceived your baby?"

Sebastian doesn't bother looking at the phone. He keeps his eyes glued to me. I watch as the wheels in his head turn, making his softened face harden into a tight-jawed bite of anger.

"What's going on here?" he asks through a tense jaw.

My breath staggers. "I was making you a surprise chocolate bar yesterday, and Shawn recognized the Deveraux name as a woman he hooked up with."

"When?" His tone grows defensive as his hands retreat from mine.

I sigh and shrug. "I'm so sorry, Sebastian, but the date lines up. There's a possibility Shawn is Oliver's father."

Sebastian stands so fast that the stool he was sitting on gets thrown back and falls on the ground, making a loud thud that startles me in the quietness surrounding us.

"Did you just shrug while standing here, telling me that this guy"—he points to Shawn but keeps his sight glued to me—"might be the father of Oliver instead of me?"

My mouth parts to speak, but I stammer. My eyes look down and up and all around, as I'm unsure of what to do or say. "This is an uncomfortable situation. I don't know what to do with my shoulders."

"Then, use your voice and spell it out."

I cross my arms and then drop them before lifting my chin and looking Sebastian in the eye. "Shawn slept with Lauryn at the time she conceived Oliver."

Sebastian places his hands on his hips and shakes his head. "You're unbelievable."

I raise my hands to put on his chest, but he pushes me off. I gasp in surprise.

"I'm not trying to upset you. It's just … if there's a chance Oliver is—"

"No!" Sebastian yells. "You are not going to assume

this baby isn't mine because your deadbeat employee can't do fucking math. Oliver is mine. I'm his father." He pounds on his chest.

"But don't you want to at least think about this? What if—"

"Don't you dare finish that sentence." He steps up closer to me. The man who is always cool and controlled has fire in his eyes. My larger-than-life Leo, my optimist, the commander, has a dark side. A place of scorn and stubbornness. "You never wanted Oliver. You said you were okay with it, but you never were."

"How dare you say that when I have done more than most women in this situation! I've sat idly by while you basked in this time. I've been supportive, devoted."

"Then, why are your clothes still here when I have an empty closet, just waiting for you to finally take the leap? There never was a world where you and Oliver slept under the same roof. You were always the first to say that you shouldn't be a part of the baby planning, shower, birth. You've excused yourself from everything, and it's never been for me. It's for you. You've always wished he never existed. I bet a piece of you is excited with the prospect that he could be Shawn's."

He paces a step and then looks back at me before continuing, "You never gave Oliver a chance, and you never gave me one. I never had a hundred percent of you. You always had one foot out the door, ready to run. I just could never figure out if it was me you were unsure of or Oliver. Now, I know it was both."

"Sebastian, that's not entirely true."

He closes his eyes and lets remorse cover his face.

LOYAL LAWYER

"The fact that part of that speech was true is enough to break my heart."

The tic in his jaw tics, his face as sharp as granite. With a hardened stare, he walks toward the door.

"Please, don't leave," I beg, but it's no use.

Sebastian storms out, leaving me breathless—and for the first time since I met him, not in a good way.

CHAPTER TWENTY-THREE

Sebastian

I leave Amy's place in a mad rush, my knuckles reddened with how fierce I'm gripping the steering wheel. I'm used to stressful situations, I thrive in intense environments, but hearing Amy suggest that I might not be the father of Oliver is too much for me to handle. It's like a knife to the stomach, only it's not just one, but a thousand pulling in and out, like they're trying to kill me all at once.

Red. I see it everywhere. I stormed out of there because if I hadn't, I would have lost myself to the fire burning inside me and raged—which is not something I do often. I like being calm, organized, and just. What happened in there was torture to my heart.

Amy's never been okay with me having a baby. The first night I told her about the pregnancy, I saw it on her face. The shock, the despair, the disappointment. It was understandable. We'd just started dating, and that was a huge ball for me to drop.

Still, I pursued her. I wasn't lying when I said I'd never felt for another woman the way I do about her. She's feisty and intelligent, funny and enchanting. Her beauty is immeasurable, and we're attracted to each other with a fierceness of animals pawing at one another in the dawn of heat. Damn, if I haven't spent many nights watching her naked form, asleep in my bed. Her dark hair splayed on my pillow and her long lashes fluttering as she dreams. The face of an angel, the heart of a saint, and the body of a vixen. She calls to me—mind, body, and soul—in ways that bring me to my knees.

Until tonight.

Shawn and his pathetic drunken state. He's no man, behaving like that. I'm sure he believes the story he's drinking his sorrows over, which is disgusting, to say the least. A man takes responsibility for his actions with a barreled chest and a strong gut. He doesn't cower in a bottle of cheap booze.

"Fuck!"

The way Amy jumped on the believability train has me cursing. I bet she never questioned his story, the timing, the details. Her heart wants this to be true, so she was more than eager. I thought I knew her, that I loved her, but how can I love someone who would try to hurt me this way?

"Ahh!" I roar into the cabin of my car as I careen down the highway.

Wrath at Shawn and his story. Resentment at Amy and her reaction. Fury at myself for still loving her despite the fact that she doesn't want the one thing I love as much as her.

Oliver.

My son.

MY.

SON.

He has to be mine.

My foot hits the gas pedal. I've never driven this fast. I don't know where I'm going, and if I keep this up, I'll crash, so I exit and pull over at the first opportunity and slam my fist against the steering wheel.

"Goddamn it!" I yell out.

A man walking by is startled by my outburst, but I pay him no attention as I drop my head back against the headrest.

After taking a few breaths, I start to lay out the details because I will prove to them that Oliver is mine.

He has to be.

Thinking back to the last times I was with Lauryn, I knew something was off, but I never would have thought she was cheating on me. I've always been very straightforward with my girlfriends. The one thing that I will never forgive is adultery. If you don't want to be with me, fine, end it. Just don't see other people behind my back.

That was how Lauryn and I ended. Quick, easy, and painless. We didn't play with emotions or string the other along in pure selfishness. At least, that's how I thought we'd ended. Infidelity was never on the radar. She would never. Well, I always thought she wouldn't.

The first woman I'd ever loved cheated on me, and it felt terrible. I was young, in college, and bawled for days. It wasn't my brightest moment, but my heart is fragile when it comes to love. I take what I want, care for it, love it. If you break it, I break too.

I thought that was painful to live through back then, but this is a totally different situation. There's a baby—*my baby*—who I've held since he was seconds old. I cut his umbilical cord and held him on my bare chest for skin-to-skin contact.

Shawn wasn't there. He's never been there.

Of course he hasn't.

Shawn obviously hasn't spoken to Lauryn in months because by his drunken state, he just figured this out, too, which means Lauryn can solve this very upsetting misunderstanding in seconds because she must have never reached out to him the way she did to me, saying I was the father.

I know Lauryn isn't perfect, but I don't see her being the kind of person who would lead someone astray like this when there's a possibility he's not the father.

I have to be the father.

I put the car in drive and peel out of my spot on the side of the road, needing to get to her.

At her building, I put the car in park, turn it off, and throw off the seat belt, slamming the door behind me. As I take two steps at a time inside her apartment building, going to the second floor, I still can't get there fast enough. I need this feeling inside me to go away. I need to hear her say what I know to be the truth deep in my soul.

When my knock is louder and harder than it should be, I close my eyes, trying to calm the rage boiling inside me. I hear her open the door, but fear grips at my chest, and I don't have the nerve to open my eyes until I ask the worst question I've ever had to ask in my life.

"Did you cheat on me?"

She doesn't respond, and I feel the bile creeping up in my stomach, burning like a fuse that's about to explode, as I repeat to myself, *It's not true. It's not true.*

I will myself to open my eyes, and when I do, I regret coming here at all. I've seen this expression on many people throughout my career. It reads *I'm guilty, but I'm going to use everything in my power to lie like my life depends on it.*

We stare at each other—me losing my mind inside but trying to stay calm because I won't give up hope. Not yet.

"Why are you asking that?" she asks, stunned.

"Shawn. Early twenties. A chocolatier. Goes to culinary school."

Her pale blue eyes widen as her already-alabaster skin goes pure white. "How do you know him?"

"Is there a chance I'm not Oliver's father?" I ask much louder than I should.

"Come inside," she says, her voice cracking.

"Answer me. Now!"

"Are you trying to disturb the whole building?" She peers out to the hallway and grabs my shoulder, bringing me into her apartment. She turns to face me with her hands on her hips. "I don't need my neighbors hearing our private conversation."

"This doesn't have to be private if I'm the father. If I am, you should be shouting it from the rooftops. Every single person should know without a doubt that I'm Oli's dad. The only reason you wouldn't want anyone to hear this conversation is if I'm not. So, tell me, Lauryn, am I or am I not the father?"

She closes her eyes, and instead of seeming annoyed by my question, as one would when falsely accused of something, I see hesitation. It's the type my clients give before they're about to lie. Or worse, when they're going to confess.

"I don't know."

I feel the air leave my body as my heart plummets down to my stomach. I run a hand through my hair as the other grips the wall. I bend forward, fighting off the sickness threatening to take over.

"You. Don't. Know?"

"I don't, all right? My period isn't regular, so it's hard to pinpoint the exact time I got pregnant. I was only with him once. Maybe twice. You and I were always together."

I lift my eyes back up to her. "Did you use protection?"

"Yes." Her gaze is tilted up toward the ceiling. She's lying.

"Tell me the truth."

"I don't remember. I was really drunk the first time. I would never have cheated if I wasn't completely under the influence. He's young. A fling. You and I were fizzling out."

"You fucking slut," I spit out, not regretting my words one bit. I know I'm not this type of person. I don't fight dirty, but this takes things too far.

I watch as my words hit right as they intended. Her eyes redden, and her mouth parts with a gasp. If she hurt me, I plan on hurting her right back.

"That's not fair," she says, holding back tears.

"Fair? You do realize that you've lied to me for the past five months, saying I'm the father, when there's a real possibility I'm not!"

She reaches out to touch me, but I push her off of me. When she recoils into herself, I feel slightly better … until I feel worse.

"Why would you not tell both of us that we could possibly be the father? Was it the money? Were you afraid of what the big bosses would say if they found out you'd gotten knocked up by a guy barely in his twenties, who made minimum wage? It sounds so much better to say your high-end lawyer ex-boyfriend is the father."

"Control your damn ego, Sebastian. Not everything is about how successful you are!"

"Then, explain why you ran to me and not him because trust me when I say, the kid I saw was in shock about what he'd figured out!"

Tears fall from her eyes, but it only fuels me more. She might not know, but I'm like a bull in a china shop if I need to be. I'll be the most loyal person you've ever met in your life, but screw me over, and my dark side comes out in full force. And believe me, you don't ever want to see the dark side.

"I swear it has nothing to do with money or what my colleagues might think. I wanted you to be the dad because of who you are on the inside. The man I know."

"You mean, the man you cheated on."

She lets out a sob and covers her mouth as she nods. "I know you're a good man. And I've seen that every day since I told you I was pregnant. I haven't wanted a thing from you. Not your money or your status. I just wanted you to be the dad, so my son would have an amazing man for a father. I barely know Shawn."

"Obviously," I spit out, and she takes a step back at my reaction.

"How did you find out about him? I don't even have his number. It was a fling. A horrible mistake."

"Trust me, I wish I didn't know him. And from his reaction to all this, you do not want him to be the father."

"I don't. Believe me, Sebastian, I know you love Oliver just as much as I do. I can feel deep down in my soul that you're his dad," she pleads.

I drop back against the door and tug at my hair, hoping the pain I feel from it will take away the pain in my heart. This isn't who I want to be. I don't want to make someone else cry. But I need to know.

"There is nothing in my life that I want more than to be his father." My voice cracks while I stop the tears threatening to escape. "But we have to know for sure. I can't go the rest of my life with this question in the back of my head. I will be in Oliver's life, no matter what. There's no way I can just walk away now. But we have to find out the truth."

She nods as she purses her lips, trying to hide the quiver of her bottom lip. "You're right."

Tears fall freely from my eyes, and I don't try to stop them. "I'm going to the nursery to hold him for a while. Please, don't join us."

She lets out a sob as I head back to his nursery, needing to hold his tiny body against mine.

When I walk into his room, I hear his movement as

he stares at the mobile above his crib. Seeing him breaks my heart even more.

I reach down to pick him up and head over to the rocking chair, where I take a seat and position Oliver where I can see him clearly. Well, as clearly as I can while my eyes keep filling with tears.

I reach for his finger, and he grips on to mine.

"Hey, baby boy." I choke on my words that I try to get out. "I want you to know that I'll always be here for you. Even if we find out I'm not your father. I will always look at you like my son. I know you don't understand me right now, but I promise you, I won't go anywhere. And if Shawn turns out to be your dad and doesn't step up like he should, then you don't need him. I'll proudly fill his shoes."

I pause to take a big inhale. One part of me feels like we shouldn't do the test. I want to be his father, and that's all that matters. But the other part of me feels like Shawn needs to know. Even if he's freaked out now, later, he'll want to know who his kid is, and Oliver deserves to know who his biological father is even if finding out in the process kills me inside.

I owe it to him.

For now though, I'll hold on to him as much as I can and enjoy these moments that I might never get back.

My contact at the hospital was able to get us an appointment for a paternity test. I brought Oliver and myself, and together, we had our blood drawn. I held him in my arms, steadying him as a nurse kept his arm restrained while another inserted the needle. It pained me to see his cries at the poke that he shouldn't have needed to receive. When it was over, I stood quickly, tucked him against my chest, and rocked him to a lullaby my mother had taught me as a child.

I only had a short window before I had to bring him back to his mother for his feeding, so we took a walk in his stroller as he went to sleep.

When I finally brought him home, I stayed well past when I had told myself I'd stay. Leaving him just wasn't something I was capable of.

Getting Shawn to the hospital hasn't been as easy. I only need my blood to prove my own paternity, but every man needs to take responsibility for his actions, and since there's a chance he could have fathered Oliver, he has to do his part.

I don't want to have to go to Amy's shop to track him down either. We haven't spoken since I walked out of her place. My behavior that night is something I'm growing more ashamed of every day. While her willingness to accept Oliver is still something I question, I now know her concern over Shawn's story was just. My heart and mind are at war with each other, but I can only deal with one thing at a time, and right now, Oliver has my full attention.

Shawn has refused my requests for a sample, but when I'm finally able to get ahold of him, I explain I can get a court order to do so. He caves, and thankfully, he's on his way to my office now because, apparently, hospitals *freak him the fuck out*.

When he arrives, Miles escorts him into the

conference room, where a phlebotomist is waiting for him. I stand on the outside of the door, watching to make sure it's done properly even though I know the company I hired is reputable and it's not necessary for me to oversee.

After the test is done, the woman administering it leaves, but Shawn stays in his seat, looking up at me.

I stare at him, waiting for him to say something.

When he finally scoots back in his chair and stands, he states, "A cheek swab would have been easier."

"If a newborn can do it, so can a grown man."

There's a sarcastic huff that comes out of his mouth. "I suppose I have been acting like an ass lately. This whole baby thing just got me freaked."

Folding my arms across my chest, I level my eyes with him as he shifts from side to side.

Shawn fidgets with his hand in his jeans pocket, and his other moves as he talks, "I didn't know Lauryn had a boyfriend when we hooked up. I found out after. There was no disrespect on my part, honest."

I let out a bemoaned sigh. "If you're worried about me kicking your ass, you have nothing to worry about. Unless Oliver turns out to be yours and you cross him, then I'll cock you in the jaw."

"Aren't lawyers *not* supposed to make threats?"

I balk at his nervous joke. "I'm not saying that as an attorney. I'm stating that as a man."

His mouth frowns as he nods, his eyes looking at the floor. He scratches his head. "I wouldn't know about any of that. My old man died when I was five. Car accident. It's been messing with my head ever since. Got into a lot of trouble over the years, taking my anger out on everything else. Now, here I am, doing exactly what he'd least be proud of. Panicking. Running. Being a damn baby."

In all my years as a defender, I've come across more cases that start and end with parental issues. Who we are as adults is greatly shaped by our parents, all in different ways. A man without a father is probably the greatest tragedy. I didn't know Shawn was without one. It doesn't excuse his actions, but it brings clarity.

"You're here now, so whatever the outcome, let this be a wake-up call. A man is not defined by his upbringing or his bank account. His greatest currency is his ability to love, to be loved, and to rise when the world is bringing him down."

He gives a half-smile. "That's good. Is it from some philosopher you learned about in college?"

I give my own half-smile. "Better than that. I learned it from my father."

There's a stillness in the room as Shawn nods and seems to take in the sentiment.

I turn to leave, but Shawn speaks, "Why aren't you talking to Amy?"

Out of all the questions running through my head right now, him asking that is the most trivial.

"I don't think that's any of your business," I state with my arms crossed.

"Look," he says as he steps toward me, but I don't move out of the exit, "none of this is her fault. You shouldn't be punishing her. I came to her when I found out. It's not like she was searching for something to ruin what you had going. She truly cares about you. I saw the way she was with Hardin. She thought she loved that guy, but she's never been as happy as she is with you."

"Thanks for your concern, but I don't need to justify anything to you. I just needed your DNA, so you can leave now." I step out of the way, allowing him to exit my conference room.

"She's miserable, man. Absolutely torn up. I've never seen her this shaken. She won't eat, I can tell she's not sleeping, and believe me when I say, she's ripped into me multiple times about how I'm behaving. She prays. I've walked in on her twice as she begs God that Oliver is yours. I feel the same way, too, and not just because I'm scared shitless to be a dad, but also because of how she talks about you. How great a man you are. How happy you are to have a son. You deserve for Oliver to be yours. You're going to be an amazing dad. I don't know if I have it in me. Not yet."

Thoughts of Amy in despair tug at my heart. I rub my chest and fight the stabbing pain that sits there as I think about her crying, not eating, praying.

I swallow those emotions down and square my shoulders. "Well, if Oliver is yours, then I'll do everything to make sure you're a part of his life. That boy deserves a father. He just might end up with two."

These past few days have been the longest ones of my life as I wait for the results of the paternity test.

I've tried to stay away, but here I am, knocking on Lauryn's door, wanting nothing more than to see my son. And that's how I'm looking at it. He is my son, and until someone tells me differently, I'm not going to stop feeling like he's mine.

When she opens the door with him in her arms, I instantly reach out, asking to hold him. She hands him over with a smile on her face. Tensions were high between us at first, but the love of this little boy has trumped our personal feelings for the moment.

I enter her apartment and head to the living room, where I can get more comfortable and enjoy my son to the fullest.

"Can I get you something to drink?" she asks, already walking to the kitchen and opening up the refrigerator.

"I'd love some water, thank you," I say, smiling down on baby Oli.

He's truly the handsomest baby I've ever seen. His eyes are starting to change from the blue they once were to a more hazel green. His tiny nose is so cute, and all I want to do is kiss it. When his little fingers grip around mine, my heart melts like it's the first time I'm seeing him all over again.

When Lauryn brings me my water, she sets it down on the table next to me and then takes a seat in the recliner off to the side.

"I love the way he looks up at you when you hold him," she says.

I don't know what to say in return, so I just grin and keep my attention on him. It's hard to not be here, but it's even harder to think that in just twenty-four hours, my life will change forever, and I'll know if he's truly Shawn's or mine.

"How's Amy? You know, if you want to bring her over with you, I'm okay with that. She's important to you, and therefore, she should be here with you," she says, making my head spring up in surprise that she would ask that.

I blame Amy for not wanting to be part of Oliver's life before he arrived, but I know Lauryn has always kept her at arm's length as well. I didn't fight it because her health and well-being during the pregnancy were important. Until the birth, I wasn't going to push it.

Perhaps Amy wasn't completely at fault for that one.

Lauryn's question also surprises me because she knows Shawn is her employee, and that's how we put things together. I assumed she hated Amy for changing the way she had her perfect life laid out. The father of her choice. Her indecency hidden in the shadows.

Her forehead creases as she looks at me. "What? Why are you staring at me like I just asked if we should move to Mars?"

I take a deep breath and grab one of Oliver's toes, loving how tiny it is in my fingers. "Amy and I haven't spoken."

"Why not?" she asks, exasperated.

"You know why. Let's not talk about it."

"You're not talking to her because of Shawn? How does that have anything to do with the two of you?"

"She's the one who wanted to tell me. It's obvious Shawn is freaked out and doesn't want to be a dad. Sometimes"—I clench my jaw, hating what I'm about to say—"I just wish she had let it be."

Her head lowers as she looks at me from under her brows. "You're joking, right?"

I glance up at her, confused. "Why would I be joking about something like this?"

"Because she didn't do anything." She pauses as she takes her feet that were tucked up on the chair and sets them on the ground, leaning forward to be more serious. "Look, I know what I did was wrong. I should have told you about Shawn when I was pregnant, but that's *my* mistake. Not hers. Why is she being punished, yet you're here with me? With us?"

I grit my teeth, still fuming at the thought of her cheating on me, but when I rub my hand over Oliver's smooth head, I take in a healing breath and feel myself calm down.

"Because of him. You gave me him. How can I hate you for that?"

"But what if—"

"Don't say it," I whisper out before I tilt my head up to face her. "Please don't say it. We'll know tomorrow. If this is the last day I get, thinking he's my biological son, I want to enjoy it."

"I agree. But I also think that you should be enjoying it with your girlfriend by your side. I know you have feelings for her."

I nod as I rub his head again. "I do. But … I just don't know. If I lose him because of her …" I don't finish that thought.

"Will you please get your head out of your ass, you egomaniac?" she says, and I let out a sharp laugh. Those are definitely not words she says often. "You won't lose him because of her. You'll lose him because of me. Tomorrow might be one of the best days of your life, or it might be one of the worst. I don't want you to go through that alone. I know I'm not the one who should be there for you. And have you even told anyone else besides Miles? Do your parents know what's going on?"

I shake my head. "No."

"Then, why are you pushing her away?"

I drop my head back, more in thought than anything. "I just get this feeling she wanted this to happen. She said she was on board, but something has been holding her back. We've been together for months, yet she would only bring over clothes for a few days at a time even though I cleaned out a spot in my closet for her. I even brought up her moving in once, but she said she wanted to wait until after Oliver was settled in. She needed us to have our time together before changing it."

"You think that's her way of not committing?"

"There's always an excuse. Always an escape plan."

Her hand flies to her head as she looks at me like I'm a child ready for a scolding. "You had a baby with another woman! Moments after you met, you sprang it on her that your ex was pregnant. That's a lot for a woman to take on."

"Trust me, I know. I had to woo her hard to get her to come back to me."

"Did you ever think that she told you about Shawn because she loves you and she wanted you to know the truth? How could she have kept something like that from you?"

"You did!" I spit out.

She closes her eyes for a brief moment. "Yes. And I'm sorry. But only because I wanted what was best for my son, but I wasn't taking your feelings into consideration. She was. Because she cares for you."

"And you didn't?"

"No. I didn't say that. It's just different, and you know that. We didn't click that way. Not the way you seem to have with Amy at least. You never looked at me the way you do at her. Just the mention of her name brightens your expression." Her hands rest on her knees. "Final question, and then I'll leave it alone. What would you have done if this information had come out five or ten years down the road and you found out she had known the entire time?"

There it is. The one line in every courtroom battle that makes you question the entire trial. As upset as I am with Amy's role in the current events, if she'd held on to it and never told me, lied to me, that would have destroyed us.

I laugh to myself because that's what is happening now. We're being destroyed by my reaction to her actions.

"It's complicated."

"Yeah, life is, with every aspect, but being with someone you care about shouldn't be." She gets up and comes to sit next to me. "Don't put your anger toward me on Amy. I told you a while ago that I was happy you met her, but I haven't been the most inviting to her, and that's my fault. That all ends now. Just like I want what is best for Oliver, I also want what is best for you."

"Oliver is what's best for me," I whisper while holding his tiny fingers.

She places her hand over mine, the three us joined together. "That will never change, but you need that partner by your side too."

"Then, what about you? Who's going to be by your side?"

"Someone will come along. I have no doubt that when the time is right, he'll be here." She looks me in the eyes. "The time is right for you, Sebastian. Amy is right. Don't let her slip away because of something I did. I won't be able to live with myself if I screwed up Oli's life and yours at the same time." She leans down to kiss his head.

"I'm not going anywhere. If Shawn doesn't step up, know that I'll always be here. And if he does, well, then I'll settle for Uncle Sebastian who takes him to Phillies games and teaches him how to throw a ball." I lean in and say jokingly, "Because I don't think Shawn's really a sports guy."

A laugh bubbles in her throat. "I don't think so either."

"Have you spoken to him?"

She shakes her head. "I'll wait until after the results are in. The fact that you discovered this is wild. I never planned on seeing him again, and I don't plan to unless I have to."

I stare down at Oliver, and though I'm still terrified to find out the truth for the first time, I don't feel like I'll die if he's not mine. I know I'll always be a part of his life, and if that test comes back negative, then I'm going to have to learn to be okay with that.

As much as I try to deny it, my feelings are exactly the same when it comes to Amy. I just wonder if she'll ever be mine again.

CHAPTER TWENTY-FOUR

Amy

You know that saying, *You never know what you truly had until it's gone*? Well, that's exactly how I feel right now. Of course, I knew Sebastian was amazing and the guy I'd been dreaming of all my life, but I never considered losing him this fast, and my God, the suddenness of him walking out of my life has felt worse than a dagger to the heart. It's been a samurai sword to my entire soul.

I'm curled up in my office, watching Netflix with Lady Featherington, when there's a knock on my back door. As I check my app, I see my dad standing there, waving at the camera. His dorkiness makes me smile, and I stand to go let him in.

"Hi, Daddy," I say as I open the door.

He comes in to give me a hug.

"What are you doing here so late?" I ask as I shut the door and we head back to my office.

"I wanted to check on my little girl."

I sigh. "Did Fiona open her big mouth?"

I knew I shouldn't have said anything to her. She called during a weak moment yesterday, and I needed someone to spill my guts to. I should have known my entire family would find out shortly.

He places his arm around me and pulls me in for a hug. "Only because she cares. Tell me what happened."

I fill him in on Shawn and how we're not sure who Oliver's father is. "The worst part is, Sebastian accused me of not wanting the baby and that I wasn't committed to him."

"Well, sweetie, why do you think he felt that way?"

I drop down on my futon and pull the blanket back over me once I tuck my feet underneath me. Lady Featherington takes her spot back right next to me, like I never got up.

"Because I wouldn't fully move in with him. He always made comments about how I lived there too. That it was my home."

He takes a seat on a chair I have next to my desk and looks around my office-slash-bedroom. "I thought you two *were* living together. At least, that's what Heather told me a few months ago."

I let out a breath, knowing deep down what he's saying is right but not for the reasons he thinks. "I practically was, but I left my clothes here and would just pack a bag."

"Not that I was all too excited about my youngest child living with yet another man out of wedlock, but I do have to say, I was surprisingly okay with the idea. Sebastian seemed like a respectable man, and you're not a baby anymore."

I roll my eyes with a laugh before sighing and settling back into my sullen emotions. "I wasn't sure if he'd still want me around once the baby was born. I felt like if there was a chance for them to be a family, I didn't want to stop them."

"Just because they were welcoming a baby into this world unconventionally doesn't mean you'd be in the way. Were there any signs that he wanted to reunite with this woman?"

"No." I shake my head but keep my eyes glued to the blanket. "I suppose I just couldn't let go of how I would feel if I were in her shoes. If Sebastian weren't mine anymore, I'd be devastated. If I were carrying his child as well, I'd be broken. I'd want to be a family because, for me, that's everything."

"You love this man. I can see that."

"With my whole heart," I respond with conviction.

He rubs his thigh and looks up, seemingly in thought. "Perhaps your mother and I put too much emphasis on what a traditional family was. You know as well as anyone that families come in all shapes and sizes. If you love this man, you have to love the child too. Being a stepmom is a big role to take on."

"I do. I only met Oliver for a moment, and he's a heaven-sent angel," I say without a second thought. "I'm so excited for Sebastian to be a dad and for me to be part of his experience."

"Part of his family."

I sigh. "If that's what he ultimately wants, then yes."

He stands and comes to sit next to me on the futon. His hands are folded on his lap, and he takes a deep breath and nods slightly before speaking, "Amy, do you want to know why you're my favorite child?" He leans in to whisper, "Don't tell your siblings I said that."

I laugh, and he continues, "You were our surprise baby. First, we were panicked. Another mouth to feed. We didn't have enough room, and Mom was going back to work. Our hands were full with your brothers and sisters. By the grace of God, you came anyway. Big, bright eyes and smiling since the moment you were born. We carted you around to every game, recital, lesson, and practice. Henry with his tutors, Matty and the sports, Heather had dance, and Fiona was in every art class imaginable. You just went with the flow.

"Where everyone else needed to be pushed, you barreled right along. Our kitchen became your theater, and you performed for us daily, whisking the most horrible concoctions together until, one day, you created the most heavenly chocolates. When it was your time to shine, there was no stopping the person you were going to become. I know we pushed the others to go to college or made sure they were choosing the right path for their careers, but with you, there was no pushing. You're the girl who paves her own path. But have no doubt that your mother and I have been by your side, rooting for you and waiting to help with anything you might need. We couldn't be prouder of what you've created in your kitchen, in your world, and in your heart."

He leans in to wrap an arm around me, and I rest my head on his shoulder.

"I suppose I have always marched to the beat of my own drum in this family," I surmise with a grin.

"You've never been a *follow the normal way things should be done* kind of person, so why would you think the man you fell for would be any different than you?"

I look up at him, silently asking him to go on.

"Yes, having a baby with an ex isn't orthodox, but it's not horrible either. People do it all the time. And if anyone is going to take on that role with Sebastian, I have no doubt that you're the right person to do so. Your adaptable spirit from growing up as the youngest of five children proves you can. And with your *not letting anyone stop you from getting what you want* side, you shouldn't allow yourself to get in your own way too. If you want to be with Sebastian and baby Oliver, then you should be. Don't let any insecurities stop you. Especially if he's telling you that you're who he wants to be with."

A light breeze comes through the open window and tickles my cheek. It's like the universe is giving me a hug and saying, *Listen to your father.* It's right because there is no one more understanding and profound as my dad. I suppose these men don't get enough credit for the roles they play in our lives.

"I don't know if I'll get the opportunity to show Sebastian that I want this. I haven't spoken to him in days."

"Well, that doesn't sound right. Didn't you meet Sebastian because you were standing up for yourself with Hardin and got the wrong number? I think it's time you pick up that phone again and stand up for what you want."

I bite the inside of my lip. "I really love him," I admit. "I guess I don't want him to shut me out again."

"If you truly want to be with this guy, then you make sure he knows, and you fight for what you want. Be the feisty little girl I know, who I could never say no to. I'm sure he'll come around."

"And if not?" I turn to see him better.

"If not, then things weren't meant to be. But at least you'll know you tried. Sometimes, that's all you can do. You just never want to look back at your life and ask *what if*."

I curl up against him. "Thanks, Daddy."

"Anything for my baby girl." He kisses the top of my head.

The next day, I drive to Sebastian's office, where Miles tells me he took the day off. So, I head to his house, and as I stand out front of his home, I've never been so nervous. My palms are sweaty, and my belly is in knots. My dad was right though. I've always fought for what I wanted out of life, and I want to be with Sebastian and Oliver. These last few days have just proven that even more.

I fell in love with Sebastian. It wasn't love at first sight, but within a few short months, my love for him grew profoundly and strong. His stories over drinks at an old bar in Philadelphia, the way he danced on a rooftop atrium, the feel of his arms as we held each other in a jazz club, and when he cooked brittle in my kitchen … these are all the times he inched his way into my heart and stretched out inside of me, filling my soul with love and adoration. With devotion. With loyalty.

Being with him made my entire world a better place. When I wasn't with him, I'd feel weird, not knowing what was right or wrong, but when I was with him and he shared every tiny detail of what made him the wonderful man I knew, he made me whole again.

Making love to him made me feel so unbelievably loved.

Remembering this feeling, I lift my hand and finally get the nerve to knock on his door and fight for what I want.

He opens it and stands there, seemingly shocked to see me. I watch as those caramel-chocolate eyes soften, filled with intense emotion that match my own simmering in my chest.

"You're right," I start, needing to get right to the speech I rehearsed numerous times on the way here. "Even though I was basically living at your house, my heart was too scared to fully commit. I was scared. Scared you'd leave me the way Hardin had. Scared I'd keep you from being the family with Lauryn that I would want you to be if I were in her shoes. I never want to come between those who want to be a family. But I need you to know that I love you, and that includes every piece of you, which means Oliver too. Whether he's your biological son or not—"

"He's mine," he says in almost disbelief.

I stop and blink a few times, wondering if I heard him correctly. My heart, on the other hand, is absolutely elated. "He is?"

I want to throw my arms around him and cheer from the top of my lungs, but I hold back. Instead, tears slip down my face that I can't stop. My smile is huge, and I don't want to contain it.

Sebastian is nodding, a smile tugging at his lips, his

eyes crinkling at the sides. I hear Oliver's bassinet music playing through the monitor Sebastian is holding, and I cover my mouth with my hand to stop the sob that follows.

"Lauryn just left," he says. "She said I could spend some quality time with him, so he's here."

"Oh, Sebastian. I'm so happy for you." I cross my arms over my body to stop myself from wrapping them around him.

He looks directly into my eyes. The way his stare is pouring loving emotion from it takes my breath away. "I was just about to call you."

My lip quivers as I ask, "You were?"

He nods. "I need to apologize. I was on my way to you yesterday, but then the results of the paternity test came in, so I've been a bit preoccupied, and I wanted to do this the right way." He takes a step forward, his body so close to mine that his heat barrels into me. "I was an asshole. I took my fears out on you, and that was wrong. I always vowed to protect my family, but I forgot the most important thing."

"What's that?" I breathe.

"You're my family, Amy. The moment I heard your voice, you became my world."

I can't take it anymore, and I rush to him, throwing my arms around him and holding him tightly. "I'm so sorry," I cry.

"You don't have anything to be sorry about," he says as he runs his hand down my hair, keeping me pressed against his chest. "It was my own insecurities."

"I want this, Sebastian. I want all of it. I want you. I want Oliver. I want to be in both of your lives."

"And we want you too. Fuck, I *need* you. You're who I want to be with. No one else. Oliver is my priority, my son, and my heart, but you're the love of my life. I can have both."

I tilt my head to see him better, and he leans down to kiss my lips.

"Please forgive me for accusing you of not wanting Oliver," he says as he stares into my eyes. "I was freaking out, and I took it out on you."

"And please forgive me for keeping one tiny toe out the door because that's all it was. I'm fully committed to you, Sebastian, and if you'll have me, I'll move everything in tomorrow."

He grips the sides of my cheeks and smiles. "Looks like you just got yourself a man with the cutest, most lovable baggage you'll ever see," he teases.

"Oliver will never be baggage. He's our son after all."

"God, I love the sound of that." He leans in, kissing me before pulling back and tugging on my hand. "Come on. Let's go get our baby boy."

EPILOGUE

THREE YEARS LATER

"I can't believe how good they were!" Charity is clapping with ravenous enthusiasm as the actors in the community theater take their bows.

It was a stunning production of *The Wizard of Oz*; some might say that it was absolutely brilliant.

And by some, I mean, me.

I loved it!

Charity and I are standing in a long row of adoring fans, including my entire family, Sebastian's parents, and one weepy-eyed Lauryn, who can't seem to control her pregnancy hormones now that she's expecting baby number two with her new husband, Mike.

"Gotta say, it was awesome," Shawn bellows from the other side of Charity.

The two are holding hands and hollering as the main actors are now coming out and taking their individual bows.

LOYAL LAWYER

While everyone is waiting for the girl who played Dorothy to come for her standing ovation, I'm excited for the man coming out right before her. The one who played the Scarecrow. The sexiest one, I might add!

Sebastian comes jogging out, his hands up in the air, and we all yelp with wild applause for a job well done. In the three years we've been together, I've marveled at his performances, each one better than the last. This one was perhaps the best because our boy had his first role as well.

As if on cue, Oliver leaves his place along the line of Munchkins and comes barreling over to his father. Dark hair and hazel eyes, Oli looks just like his daddy. Sebastian lifts Oliver in his arms, and they take an extra second to soak up the magic that comes from a room full of people cheering them on.

As the curtain closes, we grab our belongings and usher out to the back of the building to wait for our loved ones to exit from backstage.

It's a beautiful night. A warm fall evening in the heart of Philadelphia. It reminds me of the evening of my wedding to Sebastian, which was two years ago this month. We held it at the Philadelphia Museum of Art, the one with the iconic *Rocky* steps. It was a huge affair. With my family's and Sebastian's impressive roster of friends, colleagues, and associates, we needed a venue that could hold over three hundred people. We danced to a twelve-piece jazz orchestra, devoured a five-star meal, and feasted on chocolate until the sun set over the river and a fireworks show lit up the night sky—a surprise for me from my new husband.

Oliver was just a year old but made the handsomest

ring bearer ever. Sebastian walked down the aisle with him, as Oli had just learned to walk. Matthew held him for the duration of the ceremony as Sebastian and I said our vows.

It is still the best night of my life, and I've had some pretty spectacular ones since then, all surrounded by the people I love, most of them here with us tonight.

"Daddy and I have to take off. Please tell Sebastian and Oli that they were spectacular!" My mom gives me a hug and kiss, and then they say good-bye to my siblings and their families, who are also ready to leave.

"We'll see you at the house for Fiona's birthday?" Heather asks as she gives me a hug.

"Yes, we'll be there. It's Lauryn's weekend, but she said it's no problem." I wink over at Lauryn, who is bidding her adieu to my brothers.

Over the years, we've done well at co-parenting Oliver. Of course, that has come with a ton of hiccups. Holidays are usually the most stressful as we balance how much time Oli spends with both parents, both of whom want him on Christmas morning.

Vaccines, doctors, schools, and day care have made for quite the ride in navigating the world of parenting, but in the end, we seem to make it work.

I suppose it's good for laying the groundwork for what we're about to go through, as Sebastian and I are expecting another baby of our own.

Heather rubs my bump the way I have each of hers. "You really don't want to know the sex of the baby?"

I shake my head with a smile. "There are so few surprises in life. This is one I can make special."

Charity, who has overheard our conversation,

chimes in, "Seriously? You met your boyfriend by accidental dial, and then you found out he was having a kid with someone else. Oh, and then there was the bomb of a possible baby-daddy mix-up. I think you're good on surprises for the rest of your life."

Heather and I laugh as Shawn groans. While he's grown up a tremendous amount in the past few years, his behavior from back then still makes him uncomfortable. Charity wraps her arms around her now boyfriend and kisses him on the cheek.

I rub my belly and sigh. "Those were surprises, but this will be the best yet."

Sebastian and Oliver come out to join us and our family and friends, still standing here, clapping for them. Oliver runs to his mom, who is a fit of giggles and happy tears for her boy. Sebastian shakes his dad's hand and accepts his mother's praises, who gushes about him all the time.

When he's done greeting everyone else, he comes to my side and wraps me in his arms. Strong hands are quick to get on my stomach as he greets our baby as well. Since finding out we were expecting, he has held and touched my stomach often—something he missed out on with Oliver. Even in his sleep, his hand finds the place where the baby is resting, ready for the moment he'll feel that first swoosh against his hand.

"Mrs. Blake, are you gonna tell me what you thought of my performance?" His mouth moves to my lips and envelops me in a quick yet passionate kiss.

"I thought you were the most magnificent man without a brain. I never thought straw could be so sexy."

"Oh, really?" His brow quirks with a devilish gleam in his eye.

I swat him in the chest and then kneel down to Oliver to give him a hug. "You were wonderful! And you remembered all of the lyrics. I'm so proud of you, Oli!"

"I sang super loud, so you would hear me. Could you hear me sing?" he asks with an excited expression.

"I did. You were better than your dad!"

This makes Oliver laugh.

When I rise, I teeter a little, and Sebastian is at my side to make sure I don't fall. The action makes me laugh because I might be pregnant, but I'm only halfway along and not very large. I can't wait to see how he reacts when I'm the size of a house.

His hand rests on my stomach with his other on my back. "Let's get you in the car and safely to dinner."

I roll my eyes.

"Can I go with Daddy?" Oliver asks his mom, who, of course, gives her permission.

I take Oliver's hand, and I head out with my two men.

Leo ♌

"Tonight was fun," I say to Sebastian as I take off my shoes once we're back home.

After the show, we went for dinner, where we took up the back room because there were so many of us. We laughed and ate and had a merry time while Oliver sang songs for us.

Oli went back to Lauryn's house since it's a weekday. He stays with Sebastian every other weekend as well as two nights a week for dinner. He calls it their bro nights, and I find it absolutely adorable.

While Sebastian wants Oliver over all the time, he works too much and knows it's best for him to be with his mother. He makes the most of his time with his son by going to ball games, the zoo, museums, and he is at every school event he's invited to; although he doesn't see Oliver every day, he's a very hands-on dad.

Still, on the nights Oliver's not here, it's almost too quiet. I miss having him around. Maybe when his little brother or sister is here, Oliver will spend more time with just me and the baby even if Sebastian is working late. I want the siblings to bond and be just as close as I am with mine.

"Charity and Shawn seem to be holding strong," Sebastian states as he unbuttons his shirt.

I stop to admire his silky, smooth skin as he exposes his chest. Maybe it's the pregnancy hormones, but Sebastian still gets me in a frenzy when I look at him.

"It's been a year since they decided to give it a go. I think they're in it for the long haul now. It's officially the longest either of them has been in a relationship."

I slide off my dress and hang it in the closet. When I walk out, wearing just my bra and underwear, Sebastian is staring at me like he's hungry for anything but food.

"Damn, you're sexy, Mrs. Blake."

My hands roam over my stomach, which has grown significantly in the past four months.

Shirtless, in just a pair of dress pants, he takes a step

forward and removes my hands from my waist. "Don't cover up the miracle that is my child."

He raises my fingers to his lips and gives each a sultry kiss. I feel those kisses down to my toes.

"You're extra affectionate tonight," I muse as his hands roam over my breasts, which have also increased in weight.

"I'm just loving on every inch of my woman. Starting with here." His mouth lowers to my neck and places French kisses along the soft skin at the side. "Here." He moves to my clavicle and then down to the swell of my breasts, which are being freed from my bra by his skilled hands. His tongue swipes over my nipple, which has me moaning and groaning with an arched back, begging for more. "And most importantly, here."

Sebastian drops to his knees, lowers my panties down my legs, and places soft kisses on my inner thigh, lightly backing me up into the dresser and giving me leverage to lift my leg so he can further his promise of devotion on my very core.

This is my husband. A man who gives everything he has to show his admiration. He does so with his physical support, emotions, and now, his extreme heart, all being shown with every flick of his tongue, caress of his hands, and words that are like a sultry lullaby.

"My beautiful Amy. You have no idea how hot I burn for you. It's always like this with us. Every time. What a lucky bastard I am to have you as my wife."

I come on his tongue, calling out his name.

In no time, I'm undressing him as we dance over to the bed and fall into each other in heated passion.

LOYAL LAWYER

Our story started as unconventional as ever. A scorned woman and the loyal lawyer. Together, we weathered storms we hadn't been equipped to navigate, but we did it nonetheless.

And now, as our bodies roar in a sea of bliss, we unite as one.

And that's how we will be.

Forever.

BEFORE YOU GO...

Do you want more of the *Falling for the Stars* series from Jeannine and Lauren? Check out the other books that are out now!

Naughty Neighbor: Falling for a Libra
Charming Co-Worker: Falling for a Sagittarius
Rebel Roommate: Falling for an Aquarius
Arrogant Officer: Falling for an Aries
Bastard Bartender: Falling for a Gemini

ABOUT THE AUTHORS

Jeannine Colette

Jeannine Colette is the author of the Abandon Collection – a series of stand-alone novels featuring dynamic heroines who have to abandon their reality in order to discover themselves . . . and love along the way. Each book features a new couple, exciting new city and a rose of a different color.

A graduate of Wagner College and the New York Film Academy, Jeannine went on to become a Segment Producer for television shows on CBS and NBC. She left the television industry to focus on her children and pursue a full-time writing career. She lives in New York with her husband, the three tiny people she adores more than life itself, and a rescue pup named Wrigley.

Want to hear about new releases and get exciting emails from me? Sign up for my monthly newsletter!

https://bit.ly/JeannineColetteNewsletter

WWW.JEANNINECOLETTE.COM

Check out her books on Goodreads:
https://bit.ly/2r3Z9RJ

Follow her:
Facebook: www.facebook.com JeannineColetteBooks/
Twitter: www.twitter.com/JeannineColett
Instagram: www.instagram.com/jeanninecolette/
BookBub: www.bookbub.com/authors/jeannine-colette
BookandMain: www.bookandmainbites.com/ JeannineColette

Join her Facebook group: JCol's Army of Roses

Lauren Runow

Lauren Runow is the author of multiple Adult Contemporary Romance novels, some more dirty than others. When Lauren isn't writing, you'll find her listening to music, at her local CrossFit, reading, or at the baseball field with her boys. Her only vice is coffee, and she swears it makes her a better mom!

Lauren is a graduate from the Academy of Art in San Francisco and is the founder and co-owner of the community magazine she and her husband publish. She is a proud Rotarian, helps run a local non-profit kids science museum, and was awarded Woman of the Year from Congressman Garamendi. She lives in Northern California with her husband and two sons.

You can also stay in touch through the social media links below.

www.LaurenRunow.com

Sign up for her newsletter at http://bit.ly/2NEXgH1

Check out her books on Goodreads:
http://bit.ly/1Isw3Sv

Follow her on:
Facebook at www.facebook.com/laurenjrunow
Instagram at www.instagram.com/Lauren_Runow/
BookBub at www.bookbub.com/authors/lauren-runow
Twitter at www.twitter.com/LaurenRunow
BookandMain: www.bookandmainbites.com/
LaurenRunow

Join her reader group on Facebook: Lauren's Law Breakers